W9-AWG-821

Also by Mira Lyn Kelly

The Wedding Date

May the Best Man Win

The Wedding Date Bargain

Just This Once

Back to You

Hard Crush

Dirty Player

Hot Friction

decoy
date

MIRA LYN KELLY

sourcebooks
casablanca

Copyright © 2019 by Mira Lyn Kelly
Cover and internal design © 2019 by Sourcebooks, Inc.
Cover design by Dawn Adams/Sourcebooks, Inc.
Cover image © Shirley Green Photography

Sourcebooks and the colophon are registered trademarks of Sourcebooks,
Inc.

All rights reserved. No part of this book may be reproduced in any form
or by any electronic or mechanical means including information storage
and retrieval systems—except in the case of brief quotations embodied
in critical articles or reviews—without permission in writing from its
publisher, Sourcebooks, Inc.

The characters and events portrayed in this book are fictitious or are
used fictitiously. Any similarity to real persons, living or dead, is
purely coincidental and not intended by the author.

All brand names and product names used in this book are trademarks,
registered trademarks, or trade names of their respective holders.
Sourcebooks, Inc., is not associated with any product or vendor in this
book.

Published by Sourcebooks Casablanca, an imprint of Sourcebooks, Inc.
P.O. Box 4410, Naperville, Illinois 60567-4410
(630) 961-3900
Fax: (630) 961-2168
sourcebooks.com

Printed and bound in Canada.
MBP 10 9 8 7 6 5 4 3 2 1

Chapter 1

As a rule, Brody O'Donnel was an easygoing guy. He liked to laugh, he made fast friends, and he tended not to get too spun up about shit outside his control. He'd been told he had an old soul, a generous heart, and wisdom beyond his years. Nice stuff.

If you asked him, though, he'd tell you he was a perceptive guy with realistic expectations and an appreciation of the things that really mattered: good friends, warm crème anglaise, and landing an open spot in front of Belfast on a Saturday night.

His skin was thick, and not a lot got under it.

But *this*? He blew out a disgusted breath and slammed the car door. This was where he hit his limit.

Gwen Danes was already out of the passenger side when he rounded the front end of his SUV, a frilly little goody bag from Bret and Claudia's wedding shower dangling from her fingers, and her warm, whiskey eyes trained across the street to where a few other friends who'd been at the couple's shower were already on their way into the bar. A few friends and *Ted*, the object of Gwen's apparently unrelenting secret obsession and the pencil-neck dickweed currently throwing his A game at some out-of-town cousin just in for the weekend.

What did she see in that guy?

"Enough's enough, Gwen," Brody said, meeting her at the curb and tucking her under his arm as they waited for a break in the traffic. "If I have to watch you moon over that tool another month, I'm going to lose it."

Gwen elbowed him in the ribs. "I wasn't mooning over him."

Like hell. He'd give her this, she was subtle about it. Most of her friends didn't know about the crush she'd been harboring for at least a few years. But he'd known the score within minutes of meeting her.

There was a gap between cars and they jogged across, but Brody stopped her outside the bar's front entrance. "It's time for you to get over Ted."

Gwen crossed her arms, the light jacket she'd worn to the shower not enough protection against Chicago's biting November wind. "I'll get right on that. Now can we go inside?"

He opened the door for her and followed her in. When she looked like she was going to head over to their other friends, he caught her elbow and leaned close to her ear. "Hold up. Come with me, and I'll make you a drink first."

Her eyes lit with anticipation. Yeah, he had her number all right. She loved his drinks.

Leading her to the bar, he nodded to a few of the staff and regulars. There was an open seat at the end, and Brody directed her toward it before circling around to the back side and pulling out one bottle after another.

After missing most of the afternoon and evening for the shower, he ought to be tending to the crowd or checking on his crew. Maybe even catching up on the paperwork Jill kept reminding him was still on his desk in back. And he would. But after.

Working quickly, he mixed the cocktail and finished it with a pass of the small kitchen torch.

Planting his hands on the high-shine finish of the bar, he leaned in and waited, his focus locked on the lush swell of Gwen's burgundy-glossed lip cushioning his best martini glass. The dark-chocolate concoction he'd spent the night before perfecting tipped back, and he held his breath in almost painful anticipation. Just a sip for the first taste. But then, as he'd hoped, her mouth curved as she went back for a second, longer swallow before letting out the moan of appreciation that got him half hard every damn time he heard it—even though that's not how it was between them.

Carefully setting the glass on the polished bar in front of her, Gwen smoothed the thick spill of honeyed blond back from her face. She shook her head, giving him the awed expression that had had him creating a new drink for her every week for the last two months. "Brody," she sighed. "*That* was better than sex."

He barked out a laugh and shoved his fingers through his mess of curls, binding the hair back with the elastic he always had on hand. "The drink's good, but better than sex? Someone's been doing you a grave disservice, gorgeous."

Raising a brow, she conceded, "Maybe I just don't remember."

Which brought him back to the issue at hand. The pencil neck.

"I'm serious about Ted. You're wasting your life waiting on that guy." And worse, it wasn't as though she was holding out for him to realize he was madly in love with her. Brody had never actually seen them together that way, thank fuck, but he knew without question that at some point over the years, the friendship Gwen swore up and down was enough for her—and protected as fiercely as a lioness with her cub—had included indulging in a few benefits on the side. She said she wasn't waiting for more, but he knew better.

What really pissed him off was that Ted didn't care enough to set her straight. No way the guy was dumb enough not to recognize how Gwen felt about him. And if he knew, how the hell could he justify taking advantage of her that way? Playing like they were both on the same page, when anyone with eyes and enough sense to see past the epic-and-enduring friendship would know they weren't.

"Hey, I'm not waiting on anything," she said, looking around to make sure they hadn't been overheard. "I go out with guys."

"They don't even have a shot with you, Gwen."

"What?" And now she was giving him that indignant, fired-up look he shouldn't enjoy quite so much as he did. "Lies! I went out with Ben four times and Niles six."

"Yeah, yeah, I know how you are about giving things a fair chance."

"You don't say yes if you aren't willing to try."

Right. He'd heard it before.

The "fair chance" was Gwen's thing, and she took it pretty seriously.

"You might have meant to, but, Gwen, you were checked out on those guys before they ever showed up at your door. Thing is, you're not going to be able to give anyone a fair shot until you let Ted go."

She didn't want to agree, but she wasn't able to deny it. Her shoulders slumped, and the light in her eyes dimmed. "It's not like I haven't tried. I mean, sometimes I think I'm over him, but then…"

Brody got it. Getting over Ted would be a hell of a lot easier if he didn't make a habit of giving her false hope.

Wiping his hands on a towel, Brody cleared out of the business side of the bar and took the stool that had just opened beside her. When he had her attention, he leaned closer. "Ted's not the right man for you. I know it. But the only way you're going to believe it is if he shows you himself."

Her brows pushed together, and her nose screwed up. "Ted's a good guy, Brody. We've been friends forever. I don't know what you think he's going to show me that I haven't seen a hundred times before, but—"

"I think he's going to show you that once you *actually have him*, you won't want him."

"What are you talking about?" she asked, confusion in her tone.

"I mean I'm going to help you get Ted. Just so you can get him out of your system and get on with your life."

Gwen sat back on her stool. "You can't be serious."

But the look Brody was giving her said that's exactly what he was.

And he was telling her he thought he could *get* Ted for her.

Ted, who'd been playing with a few strands of Janna Houseman's hair while he gave her the crooked half smile Gwen had seen too many times and remembered all too well having directed toward her. That smile wasn't about friendship. It was about *closing*.

"Maybe I'm misunderstanding. What exactly do you mean by helping me get Ted?"

"I mean that if you agree to what I'm suggesting, Ted is going to be the one waiting for you at the end of the night. And it will be for more than a shady hookup he's going to pretend didn't happen the next day—"

"Hey, that's not how it was."

"Please, I'm begging you not to give me the details on how it actually was. I can barely stomach the idea of you guys being friends."

She gasped, but his reaction wasn't a surprise. Brody had taken an instant and intense dislike to Ted, one she still didn't understand.

"Then why are you offering to help me with him?"

"Look, I don't like Ted. But I do like you, and I want you to be able to move on from this. Because this thing between you two isn't love, Gwen. It's a persistent crush that should have been kicked eons ago. You don't think straight about him because you're so caught up in this suspended state of want. Once he's yours, letting his Tic Tacs click against his teeth while you watch Netflix every night, leaving the toilet seat up, and barking like a damn seal in your ear all the time, the spell will be broken. He's going to be just another meh boyfriend, and you'll be able to let him go."

Gwen blinked, shifting back in her seat. "You've put some thought into this."

He shook his head. "It's obvious. You just can't see it yet."

She disagreed. Brody was the one who couldn't see

it. She knew everything there was to know about Ted. If by some twist of fate he realized he was in love with her, she'd never give him up.

But Ted suddenly declaring his undying love for her wasn't going to happen. After all these years, she'd mostly accepted it. And sometimes she even thought she'd moved on. This, apparently, wasn't one of those times.

Gwen drummed her fingers across the bar. "So what exactly is your plan?"

Brody laughed and cocked his head. "Shake him up some. Ted already knows you're into him."

When she blanched, he leaned an elbow on the bar and angled his body so they were facing. "Gwen, come on. He has to know. That little eye contact at the end of the night? The way you're always close at hand…waiting."

She could feel the heat pushing into her cheeks. "Is that what I look like?"

He waved her off. "Not to anyone who hasn't slept with you."

"You haven't slept with me."

"Yeah, but I'm an unusually perceptive guy. Believe me, if anyone else had seen it, they'd be talking about it. And if people were talking about it, I would have heard. I haven't. But Ted? He knows. He likes it. Your attraction, your affection, he's had it for…what, a couple years now?"

"Yeah, years," she replied, shifting uncomfortably on her stool. More years than she was willing to admit to Brody or anyone else.

"Right. So your affection is like a warm blanket

for this guy. Something he keeps on hand in case he gets cold or lonely. I've seen it. The way he pulls you back in when another guy starts talking to you. How he suddenly needs to touch your arm, your hair. Something. But then as soon as you refocus on him, he's back with the buddy-buddy friends business."

Gwen was shaking her head. Perceptive or not, Brody was reading that wrong.

"What we need to do is take the blanket away. Ted needs to believe he's about to lose it for real, for good."

"A blanket?" She thought about the threadbare, lumpy quilt Ted kept at the end of his bed. It was beige and had a few suspect stains she'd never wanted to ask about. There had to be a better metaphor. "I don't want to be a blanket."

Brody's jaw shifted to the side, his deep-green eyes locking with hers. "So don't."

That wasn't what she meant, but whatever. The guy was big on making points. And dead wrong about Ted, who she was beginning to feel a little protective about. Until she glanced across the bar to where Janna bit her lip and peered up into Ted's eyes. That girl was definitely going home with him tonight. And knowing Gwen's luck, she'd probably end up running into Janna in the stairwell when she was coming back from the gym tomorrow. She'd have to smile and stop to chat as if there wasn't a reason in the world not to. And Gwen would do it too, because Ted meant the world to her, and she would do anything to protect their friendship. Even if she was dying just a little inside.

She turned back to Brody and took another long swallow of the decadent creation he'd mixed for her.

"So, what are you suggesting? I play hard to get for a while? Make myself less available?"

It wouldn't work. She'd tried it before, but in the end, their friendship had won out, and they'd been back to morning coffee and being each other's default dinner partner whenever they went out.

"Nah." Brody shrugged, then seeming to refocus on her, he leaned closer, lowering his voice as he spoke directly into her ear. "We're going to make him think *I took his blanket*…and I'm using it *so good*, it's wrapped around me *so tight* every single night, that he'll never get it back."

When Brody leaned back, Gwen could barely look at him. Her cheeks were on fire, and she felt a nervous fluster she hadn't experienced in what seemed like forever.

She cleared her throat and, hazarding a glance at the heavy-lidded green eyes dancing across from her, shook her head. "That was so dirty-sounding. And so completely wrong. I'm not kidding. I don't want to be the dirty blanket. Draw another comparison."

He laughed that warm, rumbling laugh of his. "Get over Ted, and you can be anything you want, Gwen." Then more seriously, he asked, "So what do you think?"

Truth time. "I think if you could make Ted want me, I'd never let him go."

She didn't know why, but that quiet admission in the middle of the bar took something out of her. It left her feeling hollow and more alone than she'd ever let herself feel.

Brody peered up at the ceiling and ran his big hand over his mouth. "Fair enough. Either way, you win, right? So what do you think?"

Tipping her glass back, she downed the rest of her drink. "What's this one called?" she asked, licking a bit of toasted marshmallow from her lip.

"Gwen's Campfire Kiss," Brody replied with a wink, crossing his thick arms over his chest so the seams of his dress shirt strained around the bulk of his arms.

"I think maybe I'd better have another. I'm about to do something crazy."

Chapter 2

TWO CAMPFIRE KISSES LATER, GWEN WAS FEELING WARM and loose but still not completely sold on Brody's plan.

"How is anyone going to buy this, Brody? You're a relentless flirt, and we've been hanging out for months as friends. I even told Ted there wasn't anything between us, so he's not going to buy some sudden change of heart."

Brody took a long swallow of his Guinness, nodding as he set it aside. "Allow me to address your concerns point by point. First, I may be an unrepentant flirt in general, but take my word that what's about to happen with you is going to be significantly different." He leaned closer. "*You're going to like it.*"

Before she could protest, Brody went on. "Second, there won't be anything sudden about what happens between us. We'll lay the groundwork and build slowly. Anything less, and Ted's going to think I'm just borrowing his blanket for the night. And I'm sorry, Gwen, but he's not going to try to stop me."

Her mouth opened like a goldfish, but as much as she'd like to throw evidence to the contrary in his face, she knew it was true.

"And third…" Brody ducked his head before looking up at her through the thickest, longest lashes she'd ever seen on a man. His already deep voice went even lower, dropping to a conspiratorial whisper as he reached up and brushed the corner of her mouth with his thumb. "Baby, you were talking about me?"

Her breath caught. That barely there bit of contact surprised her, all the more so because of the way he watched her as he did it.

She was a hugger by nature, and Brody was the touchy type, always throwing an arm around her, clapping friends on the back, and bumping fists. But that? What he'd just done was *different*.

Brody's grin went wide as satisfaction lit his eyes. "Surprised you, huh? That's good. It tells anyone watching that something just changed between us."

Anyone watching?

"Ah, ah, ah, Miss Danes. Eyes on me."

Her heart skipped a beat. "Why? Did Ted see?"

Brody shook his head, leaning that much closer. "No. But your friends did. And I'm betting they noticed that we've been here two hours and still haven't made it over to sit with them."

"Like maybe we just want to be alone?" she whispered, and Brody grinned.

"Or like we got caught up in whatever we were talking about and didn't even realize the time had passed."

She nodded. "I like that one. It's true. And you know how I don't like to lie."

"I know," he assured her. "It's one of my favorite things about you." Then straightening, he added, "As for Ted... This is going to be hard for you, but you've got to stop tracking him every time you guys are out together. For this to work, you can't always be checking where he is, what he's doing, if he's looking at you, or whether he's into the girl he was talking to earlier. Every time he catches you looking at him, it tells him *you're his blanket*…if he wants it, when he wants it, how he wants it."

Rather than let Brody see how close to home he'd hit with that summary, Gwen took another sip of her drink, letting the decadent chocolate and toasted marshmallow sweeten her tongue and warm her insides before she met his eyes again. And when she did, she blinked. Because there was something different about the way Brody was looking at her. Something a little less casual. Not quite as easy. Something just the *other* side of friendly.

"Wow." She swallowed. "Are you doing that on purpose?"

The corner of his mouth quirked up, and then he was reaching across the bar to catch a bit of her hair between his thick fingers. "What? Acting like a guy who's been thinking about how soft this silk would be for months and finally decided to find out?"

Heat pushed into her cheeks. "So this is what all the girls were talking about."

Brody had skills.

Rocking forward on his elbows in a motion that widened those crazy broad shoulders even more, he ducked his head, then peered up at her with a smile that made her blush. "What girls?"

A giggle she didn't have a chance against slipped past her lips, because seriously, that look! She had butter-flies, and she knew exactly what game he was playing. She knew that sexy man-smolder was pure fiction, but—*cripes*—it worked.

"That's great, by the way," he added with one of those guy nods that really weren't anything but somehow seemed so sexy.

"What?" she asked, sounding a little breathless.

"The way you're looking at me. With that perfect blend of confusion and nerves." He leaned closer and tucked a length of hair behind her ear, his touch setting loose a wave of goose bumps. "A little *curious*."

Well, yeah. After that look, how could she not be?

A shoulder bumped into her from the back, and she turned to find Tina bouncing behind her. "Time for shots, *chica*. We've got a round of slippery nipples back at the table. Let's go." Then looking across to Brody, she added, "Come on, you do one too."

"Tempting," he murmured, and Gwen could have sworn his voice dropped another octave as their eyes met and held. He pushed off the bar, nodding toward the back hall where he kept his office. "But I've got some work to do. You girls enjoy."

She turned from the bar to join her friends but stopped when he added, "Have a good night, gorgeous."

"Oh my God! Who left their freaking oatmeal bowl in the sink again without rinsing it?"

The clatter of dishes and muttering of expletives sounded from beyond Gwen's bedroom door. She pulled her pillow over her head and burrowed deeper into the covers. Sunday mornings could be rough. She loved her roommates. Really, she did, and she knew how lucky she'd been when Ted hooked her up with Gail and Sadie in the apartment one floor below his, but one day, it would be nice to wake up like a normal person. Slowly. Nicely. Maybe even not alone.

Her thoughts drifted back to the night before. To

Brody's outrageous proposal that they could make Ted jealous enough to come around. It was crazy. But still, the corners of her mouth curved as she imagined waking up in Ted's arms. Soft kisses trailing over her shoulder as he pulled her into his warmth and held her tight.

They'd been together a handful of times over the years, but the one time they'd fallen asleep together, she'd woken up stiff as a plank at the farthest edge of the bed, the space of a full human's width between them and Ted cocooned in twelve layers of blankets while she had a corner of the sheet.

It would be different if they were together. Really together.

Peeking out from under her pillow, she checked her phone next to the bed. It was after nine, so if Janna had spent the night, she was probably gone. There was something very wrong about knowing Ted's habits so thoroughly, especially as they related to other women. But Gwen couldn't help that she noticed things, remembered them. And after all the years they'd been friends, it would be nearly impossible not to.

She flopped on her back and shoved her hair from her face. Maybe Brody was right, and her feelings for Ted were holding her back. Too bad she didn't think he was right about being able to bring Ted around.

With a heavy sigh, she sat up in bed, rubbed her eyes, and crossed her small room to the vanity overflowing with styling and beauty products. A look in the mirror confirmed that her hair was, in fact, every bit as wild as she'd suspected. Even more so after a night of tossing and turning, wondering if Ted had taken Janna home. Wondering what they were doing. Wondering too many things she knew better than to wonder about. After taking a brush to the chaos, she staggered out to the kitchen where Gail was just finishing at the sink, the offending oatmeal bowl now drying on the rack.

Sadie shuffled into the kitchen next, her brown curls caught in a bun atop her head. "Coffee?"

"Almost," Gail answered, leaning a hip to the sink as she watched it brew.

By the time the pot was half full, they'd woken up enough to figure out whose turn it was to clean the bathroom and renegotiate the distribution of chores around the apartment. And when the pot gave its last sigh, indicating it was done, Gwen retrieved four mugs from the cabinet while Sadie got the fat-free half-and-half and Stevia. Like clockwork, the front door swung open, and Ted walked in. His blond hair was flat against the side of his head with a few rogue spikes sticking up on the other side. He looked pleasant and exhausted. A combination that set off a low churn of unease in Gwen's stomach.

"Morning, girls, Gwennie," he greeted, all smiles as Sadie handed him the fourth mug.

"Morning," Gwen replied, feeling a pinch of guilt as her oldest friend smiled warmly at her. What was she thinking, planning to manipulate—

"Have fun with Janna last night?" Gail asked, dropping into the creaky papasan when they got to the living room.

And that other pinch? It was something else. Something of a greener shade.

Ted shrugged, an obvious smile on his face. "A gentleman never tells."

Whatever bit of hope Gwen had been holding on to died on the spot.

"You're such a slut, Ted," Sadie accused with a laugh as he reached for the TV remote.

Gail stretched back, arms overhead, mug tilting at a precarious angle as she pointed her big toe at Gwen. "How about you? What was up with Brody last night? Things seemed sort of different with you guys."

Gwen's heart stopped, her coffee threatening to come back up on a cough. This was it. What Brody had said would happen. Her friends had noticed, and now they were talking about it.

Her every sense honed in on the man beside her, waiting for the reaction to come.

He turned his head to her, one brow raised, a crooked smile on his face. "Oh yeah? Gwennie getting some action?" he asked with an amused laugh, turning back to the TV before she'd even answered. "Good for you."

So much for not wanting to share his blanket.

The bar door swung open, and Brody looked up from the paperwork he'd put off the night before. Gwen stormed into the empty bar, dressed in a fitted black warm-up suit with her hair bound up in a loose knot. No makeup. And a small bag thrown over one shoulder.

"Back from the gym?" he asked, wondering if that pretty color in her cheeks was from working out or being worked up.

"The plan is a fail," Gwen huffed, arms crossed tightly over her chest.

"Not possible. It's too early to fail," he assured her,

gathering the documents into a pile he set at the edge of the table. "Kitchen's not open for another hour, but I could make you something myself. Something to drink?"

Those stiff arms unraveled, and Gwen dropped her bag into the seat across from his. "The girls asked me about you this morning, and when Ted thought we'd hooked up, he said, 'Good for you.'"

What a douche. How was she hung up on this guy? How had she ever been interested in him at all?

"He doesn't think he's got anything to worry about. Which is what you want for right now."

"*Good for you* is what I want?"

Hell, no one would want that. But for their purposes, it worked.

"We want him to realize what's happening gradually. Let it sneak up on him. So when he figures it out, he panics some. Worries about how far it's gone. We want him to look back and see that the signs were all there. We want him to wonder whether he's going to be able to get you back. We want him to *work* for it. And all of that starts with Ted being overconfident and thinking he doesn't have one damn thing to worry about."

There was a small furrow between her brows. Brody wanted to lean across the table and smooth it with his thumb, but instead, he sat back, folding his arms over his chest to mimic her posture.

Gwen hummed in response, her fingers drumming over her forearm as she looked around the empty bar. "So overconfident is good. Okay."

"Come on, I'll make you something to eat."

By the time they'd finished, the tables around them were full, a few already having turned over.

Gwen was relaxed, her arms folded in front of her, her eyes bright as she sighed in that contented way that warmed the center of his chest.

"Feeling better?"

"I do. Thanks, Brody."

She stood and started to slide the bag over her shoulder as Brody reached for it.

"I'll carry it for you. Let's go." At her questioning look, he leaned closer. "I'm into you, remember? And being the resourceful guy that I am, I'm taking advantage of any opportunity I can find to spend more time with you."

This time when he tugged on the bag, she handed it over, a smile curving her lips.

"Well, since it's about you being *into me*, by all means. And that's very sweet. You've got the makings of a quality boyfriend, Brody. If you were into anyone for real."

He caught Jill on his way out and let her know he'd be back in about an hour. It was a courtesy. She'd been with Belfast since the bar opened almost five years before and could probably run the place without him for a month. Longer. But he liked his people to know where he was.

Outside, the air was cool and crisp. The trees were bare of their leaves, but it was still beautiful. The snow would arrive soon enough, bringing with it the icy sidewalks and slushy streets that accompanied every Chicago winter. He knew it was coming, which made these last days before it did all the more brilliant.

They passed a few storefronts, and then Gwen looked over at him. Her teeth sinking into the full swell of her bottom lip. Man, she had a spectacular mouth.

"What?" he asked as they turned the corner, heading toward the residential neighborhood behind the shops and bars.

"Are you going to put your arm around me or something?" she asked, her brows high.

He laughed, loving that she was getting into it.

"Not yet. I'm playing it cool. Still feeling things out."

She raised a brow at him, looking delighted. "Oh, are you?"

This was going to be fun. He looked to the sky and shrugged.

"That's what I'm telling myself anyway. Pretty sure I'm already in deeper than I'm willing to admit. For now, I'm taking it slow so I don't scare you off."

"I don't know, Brody. Listening to you narrate a fictional interest is pretty scary. You're alarmingly good."

Brody barked out a laugh. They kept talking and walking until they were on North Kenmore, about a half block down from her place.

"What if no one sees us?" she asked. "Will you come up to the apartment?"

"Don't need to. Someone's probably seen us already. Looking out a window, driving by. But even if no one did, just hanging out like this is a start."

Brody turned around, walking in reverse so that he could look at her. "It's you and me getting comfortable around each other. Talking. Laughing."

Her brow rose. "I thought we were already pretty comfortable around each other."

They were, but he liked hearing her say it just the same. "The closer we get, the easier it'll be to sell this. People will notice the way you light up when they mention my name."

She coughed, her eyes going wide. "Ego much?"

"It can get a bit unruly. But that's just because everyone keeps feeding the thing. You especially." The way she was smiling, what did she think was going to happen?

Her steps came to a halt, her mouth falling open into an astonishingly pretty gape. Brody could see she was ready to demand an explanation, one he'd be glad to give her, but in the end, she just crossed her arms and shook her head. Her smile returned.

"Look, all I mean is we have fun. We laugh. And the more we hang out, the better friends we become, and the easier it is for me to get away with things like that stunt you still can't believe I pulled on our walk home...just to get you to laugh."

She stopped walking, as he'd known she would.

"What—" she started to ask, as he answered, "This."

He moved fast, tossing her over his shoulder so she draped down his back.

"Brody!" she shrieked, laughing as she tried to wriggle free. So not happening.

And then her small fists were beating against his back as she begged him to put her down. He would, but not just yet.

"Hey, you find a job yet?" he asked, one arm banded over the backs of her thighs as he strode down the sidewalk. Her long-term subbing contract was coming to an end after winter break, and while he knew she was hopeful they'd offer her a full-time position in the school district next fall, she needed work to fill the gap.

Her fists stopped, and she craned around, pushing herself up off his belt. "Nothing yet. It's tricky since I've got to keep subbing too."

"Think I've got a solution for you. One of the girls is moving to Colorado with her boyfriend next month, and if you want the job, you've got it."

Her breath caught, and he swung her around, setting her on her feet. Crazy, but he almost missed that slight weight of her on his shoulder.

"Brody, I don't have any table-waiting experience. Are you sure?"

He knew she was smart, reliable, and someone he could trust. "Jill can train you. And someone's always trying to pick up extra shifts, so if you're booked to work on a day they call you to sub, we'll be able to cover for you."

She launched herself at him, throwing her arms around his neck. His arm closed around her back, holding her against him as she pressed a firm kiss to his jaw, thanking him about a dozen times in the span of thirty seconds.

That smile beaming up at him was something else. So genuine and wide. Damn, she was gorgeous. Ted was such an idiot.

"Here I am planning to take things slow," he said teasingly, "and somehow I've managed to get you in my arms twice in the last five minutes."

Pinching her lips between her teeth, she ducked her head. A sure sign he ought to let her go.

Clearing his throat, he set her back and shoved his

hands in his pockets. "Here's the thing, Gwen. No one is going to know that the reason you smile when they mention my name is because you can't stop laughing at what an unrepentant ass I was that day in front of your place. They're just going to see you smile, and it's going to get them thinking…and if we're lucky, talking."

"And what if I roll my eyes when your name comes up?" she challenged.

"Hell, that might even work better. We'll have to see how it goes."

"I guess we will," she said, stopping in front of the building he knew was hers. "Thanks for walking me home."

He looked up at the windows, then back down the street before taking a single step closer, breaching her space by the smallest degree. Enough so she noticed that even with the way he'd been manhandling her down the block, this was different.

"This is where I stand just a little too close and tell you how much I liked walking you home, how much I always like talking with you."

Her head tipped back so she could look up at him, and damn if he didn't like it, even if he knew it was just for show.

"It is?" she asked quietly.

"Yeah. And then because I'm not ready to say goodbye," he said, tucking a few flyaway strands of hair behind her ear, "I'll ask you about your plans for the holiday this week. Find out if maybe I'll get to see you again. Because I want to see you again."

She licked her lips and gave him another smile, this one almost shy and maybe the most potent of all of them.

"I'm going home. Ted's giving me a ride Thursday morning. But Wednesday night we'll be at Belfast. How about you? Big family plans with the Ps?"

"There's just my mom, but no," he answered, looking down her street to where a couple of kids were playing on the sidewalk. "We aren't big on holidays together."

Her lips formed a small O, and he could see that she wanted to ask more. Maybe another time he'd let her. For right then, he gave her a wink, promising, "See you Wednesday, gorgeous."

Chapter 3

BRODY SENT THE DART SAILING THROUGH THE AIR AND watched with satisfaction as it landed dead center in the board. "Bull's-eye. And I believe that's the game, ladies." Cracking his knuckles, he turned, giving a gloating smile to Jase Foster, Max Brandt, and Sean Wyse, then laughing at the round of middle fingers, deep scowls, and air jacks that met him in return.

He was a lucky guy with a lot of friends, but these were the ones he went back the furthest with, all the way to freshman year of college when they'd shared a quad together. They'd all come from different backgrounds, had different histories, but for whatever reason, they'd become the first real family he'd ever been able to keep.

He loved these guys.

"Who's up for another game?" he asked.

Max shook his head. "Don't even bother, man. Wyse here can't keep his eyes off his wife long enough to aim for the board."

"She's your sister, man. And she's five months pregnant. How the hell am I supposed to concentrate on darts when she won't get out from behind the bar, even though I'm pretty sure her last day at Belfast was two months ago."

All eyes at the table turned toward the bar, where Molly Wyse was pouring a draft, a wide grin on her face as she chatted with one of the customers.

Yeah, it had been months since she'd worked for him, but Brody had never had much success in telling Molly what to do. And for whatever reason, this evening, she felt like pretending she still worked at the bar. Sean was just lucky she hadn't gotten it in her head to work the tables.

"Don't look at me," Max said, shaking his head. "If Molly had ever listened to a damn thing I said, she would've left your ass alone, Wyse."

"Yeah, I know." Sean straightened his tie, a sure sign of how out of control he felt. Then throwing a look at Jase, he said, "Dude, you're the only one who hasn't talked to her yet. Why don't you get her to come sit down? Or better yet, call Emily and have her do it."

Jase just shook his head, a sappy smile on his face. "No way. Em and Sarah went shopping at the outlets. I'm under strict instructions not to call unless there's an emergency." He shrugged. "This doesn't constitute."

Which left the three of them staring at the mama-to-be tending bar, with no idea how to get her to stop. Brody didn't want to be the one to have to say it, but he was pretty sure Molly was fine. She was pregnant, not made of glass.

But Sean had become the worrying type.

"I keep telling her she needs to rest, put her feet up," Sean said helplessly. "But it's like every time I mention it, she gets more indignant."

Brody wrapped his hand around his buddy's shoulder. "She's probably going a little stir-crazy with how protective you've been. I mean, she's not really that far along, and she's healthy and…"

The look Sean was giving him said he was wasting his breath. But Max wasn't ready to give up yet.

"Yeah, besides, you know she always liked to stay out late. That's why she had this job in the first place. She's a night owl."

"How about we grab another round of beers," Brody offered, putting his hands up before Sean could comment. "And I'll pour them, promise."

When he got to the bar, Molly was loading a tray of longnecks.

"Any chance you'll take a break, Moll?" he asked, nodding toward the table where the guys still sat. "Just so your husband can stop hyperventilating."

Molly shook her head, setting the next bottle down harder than she should. Her breath came out in a series of low curses as her hands fisted on her hips. "He's driving me insane."

Brody laughed, covering his mouth with his hand while Molly glared at him.

"Yeah, I know, he's the one I wanted forever. The love of my life. My walking, talking, ray of sunshine, freaking happily ever after. But he's also got me ready to lose my mind. You know he's working half days, right? Sean… is working…half days…when I still have four months to go." Blowing out a slow breath, she glared across the bar at her husband, who sank back into the seat he'd only the second before stood up from. He'd probably wanted to check on her, poor sap. "Seriously, what's he going to do for four months? Help me pull a Kleenex from the box in case I need to sneeze?" she grumbled, closing her eyes.

Brody pulled her in to his side, rubbing a hand over the shoulders where she liked to carry everything. "He loves you. Granted, it's to the point of insanity, but that still counts for something."

She nodded. "I love him too. So much. But suddenly, he's *everywhere*. All the time. And I—"

"You need a break from being treated as though you need a break every five minutes."

She blinked a few times and then turned her face into his shirt. He was pretty sure she was wiping her eyes and nose on his sleeve.

"Sorry."

He let out a gruff laugh. "That's what friends are for."

At that, she stepped back and gave him a shrewd look. "Hey, what's this Janet tells me about you getting all moony over some girl from the bar?"

Brody grinned and rubbed his hand over his chest. The rumors were starting already. And Molly wanted the dish. Thing was, Molly was as much family as her husband and the guys, and there was no way he couldn't be straight with her about what was going on.

"Come on back to my office, and we'll talk."

Her eyes narrowed, her mouth setting into a scary frown. "If this is some play to get me to take a break, so help me—"

His hands came up between them as he started backing away. "It's not, I swear. I'll even let you clean out my file cabinet, if you want. This thing"—he leaned closer, keeping his voice low—"it's private."

Now he had her attention.

Thirty seconds later, he was closing his office door behind him as Molly lowered herself to sit on the couch. "Private, like you ran off and eloped? Is she pregnant too? Brody, our kids can totally get married!"

"It's Gwen Danes. Bridesmaid in Bret and Claudia's wedding next month. Definitely not pregnant. And

I'm not sure how I feel about committing to the first arranged marriage on offer. I'd like to keep my options open for a few more years, you know."

Molly rolled her eyes, but then she was back on task. "Gwen... Blond with the *va-va-voom*?" she asked, making an hourglass figure in the air with her hands.

Crossing his arms, he gave her a hard look. "Kindergarten teacher," he clarified, because while Molly was more than right—Gwen was built like a fifties pinup model—no way was he encouraging that identifier.

"Right, right. I've met her a few times. Sweet girl. And isn't she the one from—"

He cut her off. "That's not how it is with us."

The laughter said it all. "Umm, you sure? From what I hear, you went all burly caveman on her, carrying her down the street. If that's not how it is, you need to knock that business off, and pronto. Girls get a little loopy when you toss them around as if they don't weigh a thing. It's all the muscles on top of muscles." She waved her hand at him. "And the hair. The ladies love the hair. Brody, we've had this talk before. You really have to be more careful about what signals you're sending. Girls have feelings."

She was too much.

"Trust me, Gwen knows the score. But I'm helping her out with something, which involves acting like we're together. Like there's something serious going on between us."

"But there isn't?" She blew a short breath out of her nose. "So much for our babies getting married."

"Sorry, Moll. So you know what's going on, we're

just friends. But if you hear anything about us being more than that, do me a favor and go with it."

The office door cracked open, and Sean peeked in. "Everything okay in here?"

Molly might be frustrated at how overprotective the guy had gotten, but there was no mistaking the love in her eyes when she looked at her husband.

It was hard to believe how effectively she'd hidden her feelings for so many years. And how hard Sean had worked not to see them.

If that's how things were between Gwen and Ted, Brody wouldn't be working so hard to convince her to let him go. But it wasn't. Ted knew Gwen had feelings for him. He had to. But still, the guy didn't have enough respect for his *friend* to keep his hands off her when he had no interest in anything more than a hookup here or there.

Molly tried to push herself up from the sofa, and Sean was by her side in a flash. But instead of letting him pull her up, she caught hold of his tie and tugged him down to her. Sean made one of those happy-guy low-throat noises, and yeah, that was Brody's cue to leave.

"You guys hang back here as long as you like. I'm going up front."

"Thanks, man," Sean answered, a look on his face that warned it might be a while.

Twenty minutes later, Brody was standing at the bar when Gwen stepped up beside him, giving him a bump with her shoulder. She was wearing a dark-chocolate fitted sweater with a scooped turtleneck, and her hair was woven into a loose braid that wound down over one shoulder and left a few golden tendrils of hair free around her face. *Damn.*

"Was wondering if I'd see you."

She nodded behind her to where everyone was gathered around one of the pool tables. "Stayed late at school, switching the classroom decor from Thanksgiving to the winter holidays for when we get back on Monday. Putting a few lesson plans together. You know."

He grinned. "A kindergarten teacher's work is never done."

"Not if she wants to give her district a good reason to offer her a full-time position in the fall," she acknowledged with a laugh. "But now I'm all set for next week, and tomorrow I can just enjoy being home. It's been too long since I was back, and I miss my mom and dad."

"You a daddy's girl?" He'd bet she was.

She laughed, giving him a shrug. "Maybe a little. We're pretty close, but probably more of a mama's girl at heart. We're a lot alike, and… I don't know, she gets me."

"That's great." He loved that she felt that way. Couldn't exactly wrap his head around it, considering the rare instances he actually saw his mother face-to-face, he inevitably wished he'd waited longer. And if there was one thing he could wish for, it was that they'd be nothing alike. But for Gwen, being a mama's girl fit with that big heart of hers.

"It is, and want to know what's also great?" She scanned the space around them, signaling that he should move closer. "I can't believe it, but you were totally right."

"Of course I was," he teased before asking, "About what?"

Rolling her eyes, she let out one of those gusty breaths that always got a smile out of him.

"People talking. Six different people have asked me about you since Sunday. And even when they aren't, all it takes is your name coming up, and suddenly everyone's singing your praises." She leaned closer, her whisper becoming more conspiratorial. "Did you pay someone?"

Brody coughed, stepping back to meet her eyes. She looked almost serious. "What?"

"Okay, for real, I've never had anyone bring you up to me before, and now it's like all your superfans are crawling out of the woodwork, clamoring to sing your praises."

"Gwen," he started, making sure he had her full attention. Something he was enjoying immensely. "I'm a good guy. People like me."

She waved a hand between them, pulling that face that indicated all kinds of backpedaling. "Of course, I know. I know."

Right. "I'm not so sure you do. Which isn't much of a surprise, considering the way your attention's been monopolized by Ted…and before you try to deny it, *don't.* But here's the thing. If you want anyone to believe you're considering Team Brody, you can't look too surprised when you hear people say good things about me."

"I didn't. I swear." Blowing a strand of hair from her eyes, she glanced around. "We've been friends for months. I know you're a good guy."

He cocked his head and crossed his arms as he gave her his best grin. "Prove it."

"Excuse me?" she asked, looking adorably taken aback.

"You heard me. Tell me about my finer qualities. And keeping in mind the holiday weekend and your preexisting plans tomorrow, let's limit the list to five. Pretend a friend wants to know what you like about me. What are you going to tell them—*so they believe you're interested*?"

Her mouth opened and closed like a goldfish, her eyes shifting from side to side. *Jesus*. If he asked her about Ted, she'd probably talk for two days straight before taking a breath. This was going to take some work.

Catching her chin in the crook of his finger, he suggested, "How about this? Think on it a few. You can tell me what you came up with after I check in with the kitchen."

———

Gwen sat at the table with her friends, half laughing at Nat's story about the Cheerios stuffed up one of her patient's noses. But the other half of her attention was fixed on Brody.

Five things.

It wasn't a lot to ask, and she certainly wouldn't have any difficulty coming up with them. But truth be told, he was right. She really hadn't thought much about him. At least not in terms of cataloging his finer attributes.

But as she watched him now, the most obvious things came to mind. He was handsome. Really beyond handsome, now that she thought about it. The man was built like a powerhouse. At least six feet, he was tall and broad and packed with the kind of muscles that made him look as though you could find him throwing a log over his shoulder as easily as a woman.

God, she still couldn't believe he'd done that. Couldn't stop laughing that he had.

He was solid and strong. And as far as the story that

poor, straining white Henley was telling, without an ounce of fat on him.

Yeah, he was impressive.

And now he was headed back her way, a pint of Guinness in hand.

His eyes locked with hers, holding as he closed in on the table. And then at the last minute, the eye contact broke, and he greeted each of the girls in turn. He complimented Gail on her hair and asked Sadie about her sister who'd recently had a baby. He wagged a finger at Nat as if she was trouble. And all of them were eating it up.

How had she never noticed before? Her friends seemed to be smiling at cheek-cramping proportions as they answered him and asked questions of their own, trying to draw him into the conversation. These girls *loved* him.

And not only that, they couldn't seem to stop touching him either. Gwen tried not to laugh as she watched Nat admire the thick leather band his oversize watch was mounted to before moving on to the few other leather ties and bands on his wrist. And now that she was looking, Gwen wanted to run her fingers over that assortment too. Not all guys could pull off that look, but on Brody, it was undeniably hot. Masculine to the extreme.

"You got a minute, Gwen?" he asked, his smile warm and inviting, confident and contagious. His focus intense and…appealing.

The chatter around them stopped, and Gwen felt the rush of heat to her cheeks as all eyes landed on her. She smiled in return and nodded, hopping off her chair. "Sure, you bet."

Brody's smile went wide, like she'd just told him he won the Lotto.

Man, the guy was good.

As they turned away from the table, his hand settled at the small of her back to guide her through the bar.

"Where we going?" she asked.

"Not back to my office, that's for sure." At her raised brow, he added, "Couple of my friends went back for some privacy to talk, and now the door's locked. Kind of afraid of what I'm going to find when I get in there. How about the Back Room?"

She nodded, following him through the open doorway with the neon script above.

Belfast's Back Room was an open space where people could dance when the bar had live bands on the weekend. A few small tables were set up around the periphery, but there wasn't any bar service, so it remained relatively quiet on weeknights. Brody led her to a table by the stage, holding her chair before taking his own.

"Let's have it. What have you got for me?" he asked, resting his forearms on the small circular table and taking up most of it in the process. The posture was casual but emphasized the breadth of his shoulders and arms in a way that was a little overwhelming. Had she really missed how impressively Brody was built?

Not anymore.

This list of five appealing attributes was going to be cake.

Gwen reached for her drink and took a long, dawdling sip. Then after an even breath, she straightened in her seat. Holding up one finger, she began.

"First, you're very nice." She closed her eyes and nodded for emphasis. "And second, incredibly funny."

She paused. Brody's chin had pulled back, his smile slipping from his lips.

"Nice and funny?" he asked, sounding like she had just issued two insults instead of the compliments her comments were meant to be.

"Yes, those are good things." Important things. Things that mattered to her.

"When you're shopping for a new best girlfriend, maybe." Bringing his pint of Guinness to his mouth, he took a deep swallow. Shook his head, and set it back on the table. "Gwen, you have to do better than this. No one, least of all Ted, is going to believe for one second that I'm getting under your skin if all they've got to work with are 'nice' and 'funny.'"

Fair enough. But she had other points as well. "Well, I haven't gotten to the whole body business."

And there was the overconfident smile and gleam in his eyes that she'd come to expect from this man. He sat forward, the corner of his mouth pulling up. "Now we're talking. This 'whole body business'… Explain."

"Explain?" she asked on a laugh. He was priceless. "Are you that desperate to feed your ego? Because I can't believe you don't know exactly what I mean."

"I'm going to take it on faith that pretty blush means you don't think I'm hideous. But remember what we're doing here. We're selling a growing interest. Which means that you need to be able to tell someone what you like about me. And that 'whole body business' doesn't really do it. Especially on the heels of 'nice' and 'funny.' But this one is important, because my body is very different from Ted's. He's lean, naturally skinny, but not super athletic. While I'm built more like a—"

"Lumberjack," she supplied, waving her hand in his direction. "You know, with how big you are all over."

The words were out of her mouth before she thought about them. About how they might sound to the inner fifteen-year-old most guys carried around with them until they were fifty. It was too much to hope that Brody wouldn't notice.

One red-brown brow rose in question as his jaw shifted to the side, giving him a crooked smile to match the gleam in his eyes.

"Some places even more so than others, but Gwen, I'm surprised you noticed."

And now she was fairly certain the pretty pink blush he'd mentioned was more like a blazing red burning across her face.

"You know what I mean," she chided once she was able to meet his eyes again. "You're so tall and broad and muscly." Especially the way he was sitting. When he leaned forward on his forearms like that, his shoulders and arms were massive. "And it's not just for show. I mean, I know firsthand how strong you are, and I've got to say, it's pretty hot how easily you can carry a woman with as many curves as I've got. We should move that to number one."

If her eyes weren't deceiving her, it was Brody with the pretty blush now. And she got the appeal. Because that was something she could see herself working for again.

Brody shook his head before looking up at her. "Glad to hear you think so. Because you're the one who needs to sound impressed. In fact, if it'll help, I'd be happy to offer a repeat demonstration."

For an instant, she let her eyes roam over his shoulders and arms, remembering the ease with which he'd handled her.

She shook her head to clear the thoughts.

"Very generous, but I'm good." Then it was back to business. "Okay, four, your cocktails are unparalleled. And five, you're very handsome. There. Five selling points for Brody O'Donnel. Satisfied?"

His expression was lukewarm at best.

Crossing her arms, she sat back in her seat. "Seriously? What's wrong with my list?"

She'd thought it was pretty good.

"Let me show you how it's done."

She couldn't wait.

"One, *that laugh*." He closed his eyes, giving his head a slow shake as he rubbed a hand over the center of his chest, the motion drawing her attention to both. "There's nothing like the sound of it. And damn, it gets me right here, every time."

His eyes opened, one brow raised in what she could only assume was some kind of I-told-you-so fashion. And yeah, that was definitely different from what she'd given him.

"Two"—he leaned in even closer—"her *mouth*. When she smiles, fuck, it's like the whole room lights up or something. And her lips…she wears this light berry gloss that keeps me up nights wondering if she'd taste as sweet as she looks."

The lips in question parted on a breath, and she blinked.

"Three, her eyes are like whiskey. This warm

brown… And I swear, when I look in them too long, I get a little drunk. Four, she's a teacher. A kindergarten teacher. And every time she talks about the kids in her class, you can hear how much she cares about them. How much she loves her job. You know, those are the luckiest little kids in the world. Except for maybe the boys, which brings me to number five. Because the curves on this girl…" He raised his hand to his mouth and bit his knuckle before letting out a short laugh. "I'd bet Belfast that fifty percent of that class is already in love with her and will be through time eternal."

For a moment, Gwen just sat there, staring at the man across from her. Too stunned by his list to move. But when she did, she had to concede, "That was amazing. Quality lines, and very convincing." She took another sip of her drink and then licked her lips, tasting the lingering berry sweet of her gloss mingling with her cocktail.

Maybe a little too convincing.

Her eyes narrowed. "Are you some kind of player?"

Brody slid off his stool, straightening to his full height and stretching out his shoulders for a moment before stepping over to her chair and helping her up.

"No, I'm observant. And for the record, I noticed all that before."

Gwen stumbled, her eyes cutting quick to his. "When?"

Throwing his big arm around her shoulders, he drew her in, ducking his head so he was speaking quietly into her ear. "Before I figured out you were hung up on that pencil-neck Ted."

Chapter 4

THURSDAY MORNING, TED HONKED FROM THE STREET BELOW at ten. Grabbing her overnight bag, Gwen stopped by the mirror across from the front door and checked her hair and makeup. Her eyes lingered on her glossy lips, and she wondered whether Ted ever thought about what her mouth tasted like, if he thought about their last kiss, if he—

Another honk, and she was fairly confident the only thing he was thinking was that she needed to hurry up.

Gwen locked the door behind her and skipped down the stairs outside to where Ted was waiting behind the wheel. Leaning over the passenger seat, he waved to hurry.

She laughed, climbing in and closing the door behind her as he took her bag and tossed it into the back seat beside his.

"Take it easy, Ted." She buckled up and sat back. "There's plenty of pie."

"There's no such thing as plenty of pie. Especially not the way your dad goes after it."

The Normandys had been joining the Danes family for Thanksgiving since before Gwen was born. It started the year the two couples had moved into neighboring houses around the same time. Neither was close enough to visit their own parents, so Gwen's mother had decided to do the big meal at her house and invite the neighbors. She'd always joked that fateful invitation had been all about the side dishes. She wouldn't have been able to justify making the full spread with just the two of them, but with another couple there, she'd been able to cook to her heart's content. And as the years went on, the tradition continued. Gwen's family always hosted Thanksgiving, and Ted's hosted Christmas Eve. And since Gwen and Ted both lived in Chicago and she didn't own a car, he always drove them back to Dobson for the holidays.

After navigating through the city, they started working their way southwest, exchanging one highway for another, bickering over the radio, and chatting the way only friends who had been as close as they were for as long as they had been could chat. It was easy with Ted. Comfortable. Almost perfect.

They arrived at her parents' house just after noon, and Ted didn't even bother taking his bag into his own house before running up the stairs to hers. She laughed, watching him wrap his arms around her mother as he begged her to tell him how many pies she'd made.

The man was obsessed.

Her mom really did make good pie, so Gwen got it. But as she watched his face light up, a part of her—the most ridiculous, pathetic part—wondered what it would take for him to be that enthusiastic about her. If she could ever be something he would run to.

Once all the greetings had been made, the hugs exchanged, and the first glasses of wine poured, she headed into the kitchen with the moms. They wanted to know about everything. Whether she'd been to any museums or shows lately. How the crime was in her neighborhood, because they'd read something in the paper and hoped she didn't have to worry about that sort of thing where she lived. They asked about her roommates and Claudia's wedding coming up on New Year's Eve and, of course, whether she was seeing anyone. These two women were so much a part of her life, both of them mothers to her over the years, both of them privy to more secrets than she'd shared with anyone else. But there was one thing they knew nothing about. Her feelings for Ted.

She'd never told them about the kiss down by the lake when she was sixteen. Or what happened in the car that last summer before college, or the handful of other moments she and Ted had had between them. She'd always justified the omissions because she and Ted were just friends, and she wouldn't want their parents to think there was more going on. She wouldn't want them to get their hopes up.

But as she stood in her childhood kitchen preparing to make yet another pie, just in case, Gwen had to wonder if part of the reason wasn't more about her. If maybe she'd been afraid to get her own hopes up. Like maybe if she'd allowed herself to voice what had happened or what she wanted, it might hurt all the worse when she didn't get it.

Ted's warm laugh rang out from the living room, as familiar as any noise in her house.

She hadn't gotten what she'd been wishing for all those years, but it didn't hurt. Sure, there was the occasional pang that still caught her by surprise, like when she'd noticed his attention on Janna after the shower. But *mostly* she was all right with the way things were.

When she looked up, Ted was walking through the doorway, her favorite crooked grin on his lips. "Oh, Gwennie, are you making another pie for me?"

She rolled her eyes. "You know I am." Closing the distance between them, he wrapped his arms around her from behind, slowly pulling her in to his chest, making her head spin and her belly somersault. "Marry me."

Emphasis on the *mostly*.

She'd heard it before and knew not to put any stock in that throwaway proposal. But still, the words made her smile, reminding her of too many daydreams to count.

But whether this cockamamy plan of Brody's panned out or not—and she wasn't holding her breath—she knew how lucky she was to have Ted as her friend.

By eight o'clock, the meal was done, the dishes had been washed, and everyone had found a spot around the living room while they played Trivial Pursuit without a board. It was part of the tradition, along with the movie in the background and the pumpkin spice candles her mom always lit for the holiday. As was the case every year, the game started out strong but became less intense as the hours went on. Eventually, it was limited to someone breaking the silence now and then when they found a question they wanted to ask.

The fire was going, and Ted was beside her, his arm stretched out along the back of the sofa. It was as comfortable as an old shoe.

Or blanket?

Gwen chuckled to herself, wondering where that had come from. Where else but Brody.

"What's funny?" Ted asked, bumping her head as he reached for the bowl of mixed nuts.

"Something Brody said. One of those things you had

to be there for." When he didn't say anything, she stood up. "More wine?"

She was met with a chorus of yeses, and Ted got up to help her collect glasses, each with someone's name scribbled on it using the metallic glassware pens Gwen had sent her mom for her birthday the year before.

Back in the kitchen, Gwen dropped the freshly drained wine bottle into the recycling and was about to take the overflowing bin out when her phone rang.

Ted looked over at her from the counter where he was opening another bottle of white. "Sales call?" he asked, looking annoyed on her behalf.

She grinned, shaking her head.

"Brody O'Donnel," she clarified, bringing the phone to her ear. "Hey, happy Thanksgiving."

"To you too, gorgeous. Is it late enough? Are you guys through with your meal?" he asked, his voice a low rumble against her ear. A nice one.

"We finished a while ago. How about you?"

"Hours ago. Spent the afternoon with the friends I do most of the holidays with, but now I'm back at Belfast."

"You're working?" she asked, surprised that he would be back at the bar on Thanksgiving.

"It's a slow night, so the only staff here are the ones who want the extra check. And I stay so another manager doesn't have to."

"That's sweet of you. Are you always so accommodating, or are you just trying to impress me?"

Ted's head came up, and he gave her a curious look. She shrugged and smiled.

From the other end of the line, Brody laughed, and she couldn't help but notice what a good laugh it was. If he asked her for five more things to like about him, that laugh would be one of them.

"So, Gwen, are you surrounded by family and friends right now?" he asked, ignoring her question.

"Just Ted. We're on wine duty."

"You have a few minutes? Promise I won't keep you too long, but you'll need to give me at least ten."

"Hmm, you with the rules. Now you've got me curious."

"Excellent. How about you give me a little giggle just to keep Ted guessing and then sneak me into your bedroom."

She giggled, then waved a hand toward Ted, signaling with a jut of her thumb she was going upstairs. The deepening furrow between his brows suggested he hadn't translated, but he'd figure it out. Grabbing her glass, she headed upstairs where she purred into the line, "There, I'm all yours."

Another rich laugh from across the miles.

"So what's with ten minutes?" she asked when she'd closed the door to her bedroom.

An approving hum sounded. "I'm glad you ask. The idea is to make sure Ted knows that I'm calling for something more than a simple question. This isn't about whether the jacket left behind at the bar was yours or if you've got someone else's number. It's about me calling to hear that pretty voice. And ten minutes seems like the right amount of time for a short chat, without monopolizing the time you should be spending with your family."

"Nice. Very thoughtful. You've got a real knack for this stuff." She swirled her wine. "Or maybe this isn't your first rodeo."

She didn't love the idea of Brody pulling out some playbook he'd perfected with another woman. Though, really, it shouldn't matter... But that twist in her gut told her it did.

"Believe it or not, this *is* my first time building a fake relationship with a woman, just so she can go out with another man, figure out he isn't what she wants once and for all, and move on with her sorely lacking love life."

She snickered, stretching out against her ruffled pillows. Reaching above her head, she ran a finger around her favorite cast-iron flower on the bed frame. "So I'll be your first," she teased.

Another one of those deep, satisfying laughs, and she thought she might be getting spoiled from them. "And I'll always remember you for it. Just be gentle with me."

This time, she was the one laughing, closing her eyes and shaking her head as she told him how ridiculous he was. Then, "So what's ten minutes of conversation get me? What's this supposed to look like, you know, if it's real?"

Was it possible to actually hear someone smile through the phone?

"If this were real, I'd be calling because I couldn't not call. Because I'd know I wasn't going to see you for a few days, and not talking to you would be eating at me, driving me a little more crazy every hour. I'd be calling to hear your voice and to hear how you were." His voice dropped lower, each word plucking at her senses. "To find out what your bedroom looked like so I could imagine you in it as we talked."

This guy was good.

Either that or she'd had too much wine.

Or maybe not enough.

"So sort of a PG version of asking me what I'm wearing?"

"Exactly. Because even though I'd desperately want to know what you were wearing—and even more, what you were wearing under that—we aren't there yet. So I'll settle for details about your bedroom. The walls are pink, aren't they? And tell me you've got a boy-band poster above your bed."

"Nick Jonas," she admitted, earning more of what was rapidly becoming her favorite sound.

He made her laugh and grin and giggle, with all his *if I were* nonsense, and because it was just so easy to get caught up in the conversation with that man, the call lasted closer to twenty minutes than ten.

Gwen topped off her wine before returning to the living room. Sitting down, she took a sip and wondered whether Brody was a wine guy. She knew he liked the hard stuff. And of course he drank Guinness. But if she had him over for dinner some night, maybe as a thank-you, or maybe *just because*… She bet he was one of those robust-red guys.

"So Brody, huh. What's that about?" Ted asked around the handful of nuts he'd tossed in his mouth when she sat down.

It took everything she had not to laugh. Because that was *exactly* what Brody had told her would happen. So she replied exactly as he'd instructed.

With a small shake of her head and the barest hint of a smile, she shrugged. "I'm not really sure."

Chapter 5

"THIS IS A PLEASANT SURPRISE," BRODY SAID IN GREETING Tuesday afternoon, wiping his hands on a dish towel as he followed Jill out of the Belfast kitchen. His hair was bound in an elastic, and he was dressed down in faded jeans and a gray Belfast T-shirt that fit so perfectly, Gwen was having a little trouble keeping her eyes above his neck. *Wow*.

"What brings you in, gorgeous?"

Good question.

She'd been thinking about him all day. Heck, she'd been thinking about him all weekend when she'd been home, and then again when she'd been out with some girlfriends for dinner the night before…and when she got off the train, she'd just found herself heading this way.

"Doing my part to perpetuate the facade."

Or maybe she'd wanted him to make her laugh before she went home.

"I'm about to make myself a sandwich," he said, flipping the towel over his shoulder and nodding toward the kitchen. "Come on back, and I'll make one for you too."

There were a couple of guys in the gleaming kitchen doing prep for the night, but at shortly after four, Belfast was running on a skeleton crew, and they mostly had the place to themselves.

"How's grilled chicken with jalapeño chutney on

brioche sound?" he asked, stacking jars and bins from the walk-in cooler.

"Like I'm suddenly starved."

There was that smug smile again. The one that told her he was pleased to get the answer he'd expected.

"Where'd you end up going for dinner last night?" he asked, laying a couple of chicken breasts across the grill before organizing the rest of his ingredients.

"The new place on North you told me about. It was fantastic. The girls send their thanks for the recommendation." She leaned in to the counter opposite where Brody was working, watching as his chef's knife blurred against the herbs he was mincing.

His skill and efficiency in the kitchen were mesmerizing. "We were talking about you."

"That explains the burning ears." The red onion was next, each translucent slice folding onto the counter as if it were taking a bow.

"Word on the street is you're a guy who likes to keep things casual."

"Word on the street?" he asked, brushing something spicy and fragrant over the chicken that made her mouth water.

"Okay, so I was asking about you," she confessed with a huff of breath. Then playing Brody's game, she added, "I mean *I'm into you*, so I'm trying to find out what you're like. If you're as good a guy as you seem. You know how it works."

"Is that right?" he asked, looking supremely satisfied. "And the word is that I'm *casual*?"

"Actually, there were a lot of words. Girls can't stop talking about you once they start."

"We've been over this. I'm a good guy."

That's what they'd said, pretty much across the board.

"But casual?" He wagged his head, considering, before leaning back in to the counter. "I wouldn't say that."

Maybe this was why she'd come to the bar instead of going home, because she was taking a step closer, her focus sharpening. "No? What would you say?"

"I'd say that I'm not a guy who tries to hold on to something when it's time to let go. But I've had plenty of relationships I wouldn't categorize as casual. Hell, just because something wasn't meant to go the distance doesn't mean it doesn't count."

"You've been in love?" she asked, more curious than she should be.

When he didn't answer right away, she stepped closer again. "Is that a no?"

He cut her a sidelong look. "I thought I might be in love a couple times when I was younger. Never actually got to the point where I said it, but I'd been testing the words in my head. In retrospect, I'm not sure what I was feeling really measures up to the hype. You know what I mean?" Crossing his arms over his big chest, he frowned down at her. "And before you ask if I'm one of those guys who doesn't believe in it…I believe. I've seen the real thing with my friends, up close and personal. I've just never had it for myself."

Still curious, she asked, "So what was your longest relationship?"

"Why do you care?" he teased, bracing one hand on her right side and his other on her left, effectively boxing her in with his big body. It brought her focus dead center on the width of his powerful chest and the T-shirt that wasn't leaving a whole lot to the imagination. To see his face, she had to drag her focus up, up, up to where she finally met the sea-green of his eyes. She swallowed, her thoughts scrambling a little because of his proximity.

He smelled really good. How had she missed that before?

God help the girl Brody was actually serious about… because even playing around, the man had serious pull.

"Maybe I'm just thinking about what I'll say if anyone asks me about you. I should be prepared, right?"

He shook his head, the corner of his mouth hitching higher. She could see his tongue pressed inside the full swell of his bottom lip.

"I don't think so, gorgeous. You girls are a bunch of romantics. Anybody who's pumping you for information about me is all about the lingering looks and heavy pauses. They want the butterflies-in-the-stomach stories, not the statistics on my previous relationships. Try again."

Jabbing her index finger into the center of his chest, she pushed. Being boxed in was too distracting.

"Fine, maybe I'm curious. We're friends. You know how nosy *we girls* can be with our friends."

She was met with a bark of laughter, and then Brody retreated to the counter across from hers. His hands were planted behind him, his long legs crossed casually at the ankle.

"Fine, you win. Longest relationship was just shy of a year, because I remember her talking about our anniversary coming up and that making me think about where we were going and how things had been."

"A year's a pretty good while. Was it hard to end it?"

"Not really. I mean, I could tell she was disappointed and hurt, and that feels like shit no matter what. But I think we'd hit our natural breaking point, so it was a lot easier than it might've been if we'd tried to *make* it work."

Now she was really interested. Because this was a side of Brody she didn't have any experience with. People were always talking about what great advice he gave and what a down-to-earth perspective he brought, but… "You say that like you think working on a relationship is a bad thing."

And that didn't really fit with what she knew about the man.

"I don't know, Gwen. I guess I just think when a relationship is right, you shouldn't have to force it. If it starts to feel like work, it's time to let it go."

What he was saying made sense to a point, but she'd always believed anything she cared about was worth fighting for. Brody must have seen her skepticism, because then he was pushing off the counter and heading back to the walk-in. "Give me a sec."

When he returned, he was holding a couple of stalks of asparagus.

"I know this is going to sound nuts, and I'm probably never going to hear the end of it, but here's the deal. I view relationships a lot like these."

Gwen's brows rose. "You're serious?"

"Yeah, yeah, I see that look on your face. But hear me out." He took a stalk by either end. "Asparagus has a natural breaking point. And when you bow it like this and let it happen, you end up with a perfect break. And what you have is going to be tender and good all the way to the end. But if you try to force things…get every little bit of green you can, chances are, when you cut your stalk, what you'll be left with is something tough that you'll want to spit out or have to choke down to swallow. And then instead of finishing your asparagus and thinking it was wonderful, you'll look back on the experience with bitterness and resentment."

"That asparagus betrayed you," she whispered, fighting against the laugh bubbling up in her chest.

Brody nodded sagely. "We could have parted as friends. But now, next time I see asparagus, I'm going to be rehashing that bitter end in my head. It's going to be ugly."

Throwing her head back, she laughed. "You're completely crazy."

He turned to the grill and pulled off the chicken, adding it to the brioche rolls already stacked with arugula and heaped with the jalapeño chutney and onions. "Maybe, but I'm also on exceptionally good terms with all my old girlfriends…so maybe not so crazy."

When he slid her plate in front of her and she took her first bite, she moaned her appreciation.

"That good?" he asked, watching her, his sandwich still untouched.

She swallowed, nodding. "So good."

Then after another bite, she licked her thumb. "I think you're only on such good terms with those girls because they don't know you're comparing them to asparagus."

―◈―

It had only been two days since he'd seen her and probably less than two hours since he'd talked to her, but when Gwen slid onto the stool across the bar from him, that cheeky grin in place and her eyes bright, it felt like it had been forever. It felt like maybe he needed to remind himself of exactly what they were doing together.

Or he could leave it to Gwen, who was doing a bang-up job on her own.

"It's totally working," she whispered, leaning forward and coming close enough that he caught a hint of her perfume. "Okay, I already told you how Ted kept teasing me about you on the car ride back on Sunday. But then today, he texted to make sure I'd be here tonight."

A part of Brody wanted to reach across the bar, take her by the shoulders, and give her a shake. Ask why she looked so delighted about the attention of a guy who needed to be manipulated into giving it. But that's not what this was about. It was about Gwen getting the chance to see for herself that once she had him, Ted wasn't the guy she really wanted. That it was time to let him go and let herself move on. Find a guy who would appreciate her from look one. Which meant giving the girl on the other side of the bar a solid thumbs-up over her news.

Getting started on the drink he'd come up with for her the night before, he shot her a stern look. "So now that Ted's starting to pay attention, you're going to have to be strong. I know your gut instinct is to go with it and return whatever interest he shows. But you can't."

She sat back an inch, tapping her index finger on the bar. "No?"

"Definitely no. If you give him what he's looking for now, you're showing him you're the blanket. That you'll always be there, and he has nothing to worry about. That all it takes is a text, and whatever else you might have going on gets thrown by the wayside. That's not what you want Ted to think." Brody threw up a staying hand, half disgusted that he needed to put the qualifier on there, and added, "Even though I know he would never consciously think that, because he's such a decent guy and all. But subconsciously? We don't want to go there."

Lips pursed, Gwen scanned the crowd and nodded. "That makes sense. So what's next?" Her brows arched, and her smile brightened. "Are you going to ask me on a date?"

"Not yet. We want to establish the attraction and pull between us before I ask you out, so no one gets the idea this is just you thinking what a nice guy I am and deciding to give me a chance. Ted needs something to worry about."

"How are we going to do that?" she asked, her eyes going wide as he slid her drink in front of her.

"We're going to turn up the heat."

Oh yeah. He definitely had her interest now.

"And by that you mean?"

She lifted the cocktail to her lips, taking a sip of the pink concoction with the peppermint-crusted rim.

Braced on his forearm, Brody rocked forward and caught a bit of Gwen's hair. He'd always thought it looked like pure temptation, so he was enjoying the freedom to touch this ruse offered. Lowering his gaze to the honeyed shine, he rubbed it between finger and thumb briefly before looking up to meet her eyes again. "I'm going to kiss you."

Her lips parted on a satisfying breath, and his focus honed in on the stray fleck of candy cane caught on her bottom lip. Ignoring his better judgment, he swiped his thumb across that soft swell, catching the bit of peppermint and bringing it to his mouth. Her eyes were locked on his thumb as he sucked the sweetness away. And perfect timing too. In the next second, Ted wedged himself into the space between Gwen and the person on the stool beside her.

Ted's eyes locked on Brody, an unsettled look in them. The guy wasn't sure what to make of what he'd clearly witnessed. Made sense. Gwen had probably been his blanket for as far back as he could remember.

This guy didn't deserve her attention. But despite the clawing need to tell Ted to go take a hike, Brody did the right thing and asked, "What can I get you, man?"

Seeing Gwen startled to find Ted beside her was damn satisfying. Especially considering the way she'd had that guy on her radar pretty much nonstop since the minute Brody met her.

She laughed, straightened on her stool, and gave Ted a wide smile. But this time when her attention slid away from the man beside her, it landed back on Brody. Twice.

Chew on that, Ted.

The pencil neck pushed an awkward hand back through his neatly trimmed dishwater-blond hair and cleared his throat. "Sounds like they're playing our song. What do you say, Gwen? Feel like a dance?"

The surprise was evident in her expression. She glanced down at her barely touched drink and then back to Brody, as if she wasn't sure what to say.

And yeah, no small part of him would've liked that look to be about something other than taking instruction on how to get Ted, but he knew better. And he'd be wise not to forget.

Still, for their purposes, that look couldn't have been more perfect, because he wasn't the only one who noticed. Now Ted's eyes were shifting back and forth between the two of them, the grim slash of his mouth suggesting he didn't care for what he saw.

"Go ahead and dance, Gwen. Have some fun. I've got a few things to do in back. I'll get you another drink whenever you're ready." Then flashing a smile at Ted before turning back to her, Brody softened his voice to add, "Just come and find me when you're ready."

Gwen's smile went as wide as Ted's went flat. But then she was sliding off her stool, and Ted was backing up, resting his hand at the small of her back.

It shouldn't have bothered him, but Brody bristled at seeing that touch. He told himself it was only about Ted being so unworthy, but part of him knew it wasn't true. Halfway to the Back Room, where everyone was dancing, Gwen cast a quick smile back at him.

She was getting to him. All those things he'd listed for her and about a hundred more were slowly working their way under his skin. Which was nuts, because he wasn't one of those guys who got off on unavailable women. And even if this whole game played out exactly the way he saw it, right down to Gwen letting Ted go for good, that's still what she was.

And now he was going to kiss her.

If he had an ounce of self-preservation at all, he'd be putting some distance between them. Taking a step back from the texts and talks and visits he couldn't get enough of. But he wouldn't. And not because he'd made some noble commitment to help her and he felt obligated to follow through.

No, it was because being around her felt so damn good, and no better judgment was going to be able to convince him to give that up.

—⁓—

Brody was going to kiss her.

Despite the fact that one of her favorite songs was playing and the man she'd been imagining herself with for most of her life had one arm slung low across her back as he moved them to the beat, all she could think about was Brody. What kind of kiss it would be. How much she would like it. Whether he would.

"I always forget how much I like dancing with you," Ted said close to her ear. Then pulling back, he smiled down at her. "We certainly do move well together."

Was that a wink? The lights were too low in the Back Room to get a good look at Ted's eyes, but from the way his hold around her waist tightened, she was pretty sure he was talking about something else. Before she'd agreed to this business with Brody, that kind of encouragement would have been all she needed to move a little closer herself. Slide her hands over his shoulders and her fingers into his hair. Let him know they were on the same page, and she was open to another night together. No big deal.

At least not for Ted. But for her, there had never been a time she hadn't on some level been searching for a cue that he wanted more.

Only now she couldn't help think that maybe Brody was right. Ted had seen what was happening with another man, and suddenly, he was there, trying to tempt her back with a dance and a look. Because that was all he thought it would take to pull her back in line.

She didn't want Brody to be right about this. She didn't want to think that Ted had been playing this game with her for years.

She didn't want to be his blanket.

And most of all, she didn't want him to be less than the friend she'd believed he was.

Ted slowed, releasing his hold around her waist so his hands rested at her hips.

"Gwennie, you okay?"

Stepping out of reach, she nodded, glancing away because she wasn't ready to accept it as truth yet, let alone talk to him about it. "I'm fine."

His brows pulled together. "You sure? Nothing about Brody?"

When she stared at him, he shrugged. "The guy seems like he's been hanging around a lot lately. And you're such a sweetheart, I'm not sure you'd tell him to kiss off, even if you wanted to."

Even if she wanted to? No, telling Brody to kiss off was the last thing on her mind. "No, I like Brody. A lot, actually."

Shoving his hands in his pockets, Ted nodded, giving her a tight smile. "Cool. Good. Just, you know, checking. Because we're friends."

After that, Ted rejoined a couple of the guys he'd come with over at the pool table, while Gwen returned to Claudia and the girls. Brody had a fresh drink delivered to her within a minute and a half of her leaving the dance floor, but the man was busy with his business to run, and it was almost an hour before she saw him again.

"Claudia, it's going to be beautiful. New Year's is the most romantic night of the year, and everything about the wedding is going to be magical." Gwen was busy assuring her friend when Brody emerged from the kitchen and started heading their way.

"I know, but they're talking about snow over the next two weeks," Claudia said, pulling up the weather app on her phone to check the trends, even though the wedding itself was well outside that window.

Gwen sent Bret a pleading glance, and he reached over and gently extracted the phone from his bride-to-be's clutches. "Come on, sweets. Don't make yourself crazy with that."

Claudia's attention was then fully on her fiancé. They could barely look at each other without practically ending up in each other's laps, and while most of the time that left Gwen with a warm, achy feeling deep in her chest, sometimes it made her desperate for an escape.

Fortunately, it looked like she had one in the form of a six-foot, lumberjack-strong hottie who'd promised her a kiss. Brody was standing a short way off, those muscle-packed arms crossed over his chest, his eyes fixed on her mouth.

She wet her lips, not because she was trying to look like a porn star but because she swore they'd started to tingle from the intensity of his stare.

He nodded toward the back, and her heart started to skip.

Was this it? Was he going to kiss her right now?

Pushing out of her seat, she crossed to him. Wrapping his fingers around hers, he led her down the back hall. "Where're we going?" she asked when they got to his office, and he grabbed her coat from the back of the door where he'd invited her to store it when she came in.

"You'll see."

———~w———

Fat flakes were drifting from the sky, falling in lazy spirals down around them, covering the city in a soft blanket of white. The first snow had started while they'd been inside, and it had already transformed the city.

Brody was pulling her down the alleyway to where it spilled out onto the sidewalk.

"Hurry!"

She was laughing as she ran behind him, her coat still open. Whatever he was up to, it didn't matter. Because his excitement and enthusiasm were contagious.

At the end of the alleyway, they turned out onto the sidewalk in front of Belfast, and Brody pulled her to a stop.

"Right here," he said, drawing her in a little closer. Those big hands of his went to the open sides of her coat, pulling them closed so he could button her up.

Brody was smiling, his ruddy complexion deepened by the cold, but this wasn't the usual let's-be-buddies grin he had for everyone.

"Are you ready for this?" he asked, searching her eyes as he stepped closer. Giving her a chance to back out if she needed one.

She shivered.

"It's not like I've never been kissed before." She'd been kissed plenty of times. Skillfully kissed. Thoroughly kissed. Passionately kissed. And yet there was something about the man in front of her, something about his confidence, his warning, the way he seemed to do everything bigger and bolder and—dare she even admit it—*better* than everyone else that had nervous butterflies setting off within her belly.

The corner of his mouth kicked up in that half smile he did so well. "You've never been kissed by me."

"And it's really that special? Like I need to brace myself or something?" she asked with a laugh, but a part of her was wondering if maybe she should.

Brody leaned closer, his breath washing over her ear. "Definitely brace yourself."

She wanted to laugh, but then those thick fingers were gently tucking the hair back from her face, smoothing the strands behind her ear. His thumb grazed her cheek, and her heart stuttered in her chest.

"You going to be okay with this?" he asked, giving her a last out.

She nodded, suddenly more nervous than she could account for. He was closing the distance between them, watching her until his nose brushed against hers and his breath warmed the scant space between them. And then that space was gone. His lips met hers in a slow press that was soft and firm at the same time. She didn't know what she was expecting, except it wasn't this rush of tingly sensation spilling through her at first contact.

This wasn't a real kiss. But that little gasp of breath between them warned that something inside her was treating it as if it was. Or at the very least, like she hadn't taken Brody's warning seriously enough. Because that bit of contact, brief as it was, made her quake.

She blinked, finding the dark green of Brody's eyes inches from her own, a furrow digging between them.

Was it over?

He cupped her face, his big palms warm against her cheeks, gentle as he tipped her head back.

No, not over…

And this time when his mouth met hers, she was ready for that well of heat pouring from his big body into hers, the dizzying rush from a contact that shouldn't have been so different from what she'd experienced before but somehow was. What she wasn't ready for was the way this second kiss completely blew away the first one. How the brush and tease of Brody's full lips against her own was like a sensual vibration rolling through her entire body, shaking her to her foundation.

"Gwennie, that you?"

Her eyes blinked open, and she found Brody a bare half inch away from her, his eyes locked with hers, that half smile pulling a little harder at the places inside her. "Told you."

"What?" she whispered, dazed from that kiss.

Voice low, Brody answered, "He's starting to think he might have something to lose."

His head jerked the barest amount to the side, and following the direction, Gwen turned and saw Ted walking up the sidewalk toward them. His overcoat was buttoned up, his scarf secure around his neck. He gave her a short nod.

"Was wondering where you ran off to," he said, adjusting his sleeves over his gloves. "I'm heading home, so if you're ready, I can walk you back."

She looked to Brody, whose eyes were filled with warmth, amusement, and something more. Something that made her belly do a little flip because wow, that was nice. He was nice. And big. And strong. And with those snowflakes dusting his russet hair and the broad shoulders of his peacoat, he looked—

"Unless you were staying?" Ted asked, bringing her attention back to him. Back to the way he was looking at her, then Brody, a not-so-small furrow between his brows.

Looking back at Brody, she whispered, "Am I leaving?"

He reached out and smoothed another bit of flyaway hair back from her face before brushing her chin with his thumb. It was a possessive, calculated move. Like running her out to the sidewalk through the back and making sure Ted saw them kiss when he rounded the corner.

"I'm still telling myself to take it slow," he narrated, putting the fictional inner dialogue of his actions into the quiet space between them. "And I'm worried if I get you back to your door, I won't be able to leave you there. So even though I don't want you to go, and especially not with him, I'm going to say I think you should."

Gwen laughed, pressing her forehead into the center of his chest. "Oh, to have this kind of insight in a real relationship."

She wanted to laugh at herself for getting caught up in the moment for even a second, but then she'd always been a sucker for the snow. For the romance. And Brody had just delivered something straight out of one of those gooey movies she couldn't get enough of.

"Gwen?" Ted asked again, now only a few feet away.

"Thanks, Ted. I'll walk with you," she said, stuffing her hands into her pockets. Grin spreading wide, she waved good night to Brody and fell into step with Ted, who cut her a sideways look.

"You into that guy?"

Chapter 6

THEY TALKED FOR HOURS THE NEXT WEEK—LATE INTO THE nights and on and off throughout the days. Gwen had been to Belfast on Tuesday, but Brody had been out with vendors that night, and with schedules tight, they hadn't seen each other since their kiss. Maybe it was better that way, because that kiss was sticking with her. Popping into her head at inopportune times and leaving her staring into space with her fingertips pressed to her lips. Not something she needed Brody to see when the guy was just helping her out.

And not that she'd suddenly fallen for him or anything... She hadn't.

Not really.

So the break hadn't been the worst thing. At least not for the first few days, but now Gwen was ready to see her friend again. She was ready for those big, strong arms to pull her to her side and to see the smile on his face when he laughed, because hearing it through the phone simply wasn't as good.

She missed her friend.

Unfortunately, before she got to see her friend and get her hugs and smiles and all the other good stuff, she had to get through this pre-wedding madness.

The club was fine. Spin Out was kind of a meat market, with its high-octane music blasting through speakers, smoke machines, strobe lights, and chrome.

And while it was a fun place to hit once in a very
rare while, Gwen preferred Belfast's warmer, more
welcoming vibe. The honeyed tones, glittering strung
white lights, and pressed copperplate ceilings. The
pub seating, Back Room, darts, and pool that always
offered her and her friends a variety of entertainment
as they hung out. But Bret and Claudia had met at
Spin Out, so it was sentimental for them, hence the
bachelor and bachelorette parties closing out the night
together there.

But until the guys showed up, it was the usual
shenanigans.

Glancing over her shoulder, she cringed at the sight
of Claudia wearing a candy-covered T-shirt and offering
some overeager stranger the opportunity to bite one off
her ass for a dollar. The guy was making a big show of
getting on his knees and wrapping his hands around her
hips to steady himself or some such nonsense while he
took his time pulling the candy free. Claudia loved it,
along with most of the girls there, but out of every part
of the wedding, including sorting the seating chart for
divorced families, the bachelorette party was Gwen's
least favorite.

Pulling out her phone, she texted Brody.

Gwen: How's the gentlemen's club? Are you going
to need a Lysol spray-down after you leave?

She'd figured she wouldn't hear back from him right
away, considering he was probably in a place as loud
and distracting as this one. Who was she kidding? The
distractions Brody was facing were probably of the

double-D variety and, she was guessing, with little to no coverage.

More than that, she imagined those distractions would be in his face. Not that it was any of her business or that she had the smallest right, but the idea of women from the club wanting to touch him—as women everywhere else seemed to—was putting her on edge.

The phone vibrated in her hand, and she grinned.

> **Brody:** Counting down the minutes until we get out of here. No Lysol required. I know better than to sit down in one of these places, and the girls know better than to waste their time with me.
> **Gwen:** Not into the dancers?
> **Brody:** Call me old-fashioned, but if a woman is going to "dance" for me, I sure as hell don't want fifty other guys getting hard watching her do it. Private type.
> **Gwen:** Says the guy who practically dragged me down the alley to make sure we got caught kissing.
> **Brody:** There's a difference. You're not mine.

Right. Of course not. It was stupid that she'd phrased it that way. She should have made sure he knew she knew that, because now… What if he thought she didn't know?

> **Brody:** If you were, things would have been different… And no way would I have let some other man walk you home after.

A smile that didn't quite make sense curved her lips. She wasn't his, and that's not how he'd felt, but still, there was something about the idea of Brody being the private, possessive type that appealed to her on a level she couldn't quite account for. She was about to respond when Tina caught her with an exaggerated hip bump.

The petite brunette had been throwing shots back like water since about an hour before they'd gone out, but somehow, she barely looked affected. Dancing in place, she asked, "What are you doing all the way over here, all by your lonesome?"

Gwen fanned her face with her hand. "Just taking a breather."

"Really? Because we were kind of thinking it looked like you were on your phone." She giggled, cupping her hand around her mouth, and then whisper-yelled, "And we want to know who you were texting with."

Another look back to where a handful of girls from the party were congregated, and Gwen saw all of them watching her with grins as wide as Tina's. Busted. Holding up the phone, she wiggled it in the air and mouthed over the heavy beat of the music, "*Brody.*"

A round of cheers erupted from the girls, and then they were bouncing over toward her, the questions coming rapid-fire.

"Oh my God, that is so freaking cute."

"You guys are adorable."

"You're so lucky, because he is, like, inferno hot."

"How did you guys hook up?"

"Oh my God, yes! Tell, tell, tell!"

Gwen took a step back, laughing as her hands came up in front of her. "Whoa, take it easy. This is Claudia's night. She's the one we want to hear from, right?"

But then Claudia was right there with them, half the candy missing from her shirt as she shook her head like Gwen was out of her mind. "Not a chance. Come on, spill it, Gwen. Details!"

This was the conversation Brody had been talking about when he'd asked her for her list. Was there anything the guy couldn't foresee?

"Here's the thing, girls. I'm not sure what's going on with Brody. I mean, there's something, but it's still really new."

"Yeah, yeah, we get it. Not at the planning-the-wedding stage. Disclaimer accepted," Tina offered, going to her toes as she tried to flag a passing waitress.

Claudia was rolling her hand in the signal for more information. "Come on already. The boys are going to be here pretty soon, and I've got more dollars to earn before they do. So spill. What got you thinking *Brody*?"

Giving in, Gwen grinned. "First, he's just an incredible guy," she answered honestly, her grin stretching to stupid proportions, because it was absolutely true and she loved saying it out loud. "He's got a heart even bigger than all those huge muscles, and seriously, the way he makes me laugh…" She closed her eyes, getting lost in all the outrageous things he'd done and said solely to get a rise out of her. "Honestly, he kind of snuck up on me. We were friends, and then all of the sudden, I found myself thinking about him when we weren't together." When she was at work and the kids said something adorable, while she was waiting at her L stop. Before she fell asleep at night. Every time she thought about the snow.

"And then I started wondering what he was up to.

Looking forward to the next time I'd run into him. Hoping it would be soon."

Claudia was shaking her head. "I love that you feel like Brody *snuck up on you*."

Gwen bit her lip. "I know…pretty funny, considering the man's not exactly hard to miss." It was more than his build or his looks. There was just something about him that drew the attention of nearly everyone in a room.

Tina leaned in, clutching her hands together. "Okay, so it started all stealthy. But when did you notice things had changed? That maybe you weren't exactly looking at him like a friend?"

The answer was on Gwen's tongue before she'd thought about it. "He laughed. That's what it was. We were talking on the phone over Thanksgiving, and I was lying back in my bed. My eyes were closed. And suddenly, he was laughing about something we were talking about, and *that sound*…" She pulled in a deep breath and shook her head, remembering the impact of that laugh the first time she really heard it. The first time she'd been listening enough to recognize how amazing it was. "It was this low, rumbling, rich sound in my ear, and I felt it all the way through me." She peered up from one girl to the next. "You know what I mean?"

Claudia was nodding enthusiastically, a starry look in her eyes. "I do."

If she'd been lying about any of what she'd just said, she might have been able to deny it a little longer. But she hadn't been. So fine. She'd developed a small but legitimate crush on the man who was helping her out. Big deal. Brody didn't have to know, and even if he found out, she was guessing he was used to anyone who spent more than five minutes with him developing at least a little crush.

Besides, it wasn't like she thought anything would come of it.

"That's really sweet," Tina said, elbowing the blissed-out bride-to-be out of the way. "But, Gwen, who cares about his laugh? The only thing I want to hear about is whether you've test-driven that criminally hot mouth of his…or anything else."

Everyone's focus went laser sharp as they crowded in.

"*God, yes*. Tell us about his mouth."

––––––

By the time they spilled out of the party bus at Spin Out, Brody was pretty sure most of the guys were going to be hating life the next day. Some more than others.

Bret elbowed Brody and nodded over to where Ted was trying to fish his phone out of his pocket—but his hand kept missing, and the confusion just kept getting worse.

"He's more fucked up than me," Bret grunted with a shake of his head. "Something's off. Tried talking to him about it, but he clammed up."

Based on the handful of times Brody had caught Ted giving him the side-eye throughout the night, he had a pretty good idea what the problem was. *Prick*.

It didn't surprise him Ted hadn't wanted to confide in Bret. While Ted was in the wedding party, that had more to do with Bret not having much family and needing to even out the lines than the two men being particularly close.

"Don't worry about him. Just have fun." Brody

clapped Bret on the shoulder, urging him up to the club entrance where he gave their names to the bouncer. A minute later, they were being led up to a VIP area where the bride's party was already waiting.

Gwen was standing by the private balcony that overlooked the dance floor. The girls were all wearing black dresses, mostly the kind that were tight and left less to the imagination than if they'd been wearing nothing at all. He had a deep and abiding affection for those dresses, but when he saw Gwen's, his heart started to pound in a way he couldn't remember happening before.

By comparison, her dress was conservative, with a skirt that flared to a few inches above her knees and a top that gathered across the chest and came together into a halter behind her neck. It was a dress that had his imagination working overtime, and in the best possible way. She was gorgeous. And with her hair pinned up like it was, showing off the smooth length of her neck, he could clearly see the hint of a smile playing on her lips as her thumbs blurred over her phone.

He wanted to know what that barely there smile was all about, and a second later, the vibration of his phone promised he would. A second after that, those whiskey eyes came up, finding his.

Damn, he liked the sight of that smile.

Then she was crossing the distance, meeting him halfway, and stepping easily beneath his outstretched arm for the hug that had become standard with them. The one he'd gotten hooked on like some kind of junkie and had been waiting to get again all week.

When she peered up at him from beneath her lashes,

his heart started hammering, and it took everything he had to keep his hands where they were instead of letting them coast over the bare skin of her back, then lower to the cut of her waist and curve of her hip.

"Miss me?" she asked.

"More than I should." He looked around and found Ted watching them from where he was holding up the wall. Someone had already gotten him another beer, and Brody didn't like the look in those eyes. Signaling one of the other groomsmen, he pointed to Ted and mouthed "water."

Then peering down into Gwen's upturned face, he asked, "What do you say we get out of here for a few?"

She nodded, her smile going wider still. "Perfect."

Taking her hand, he led her down the stairs and through the main part of the club. "Hope you don't mind, but I promised the owner I'd stop for a drink. He's a good guy. You'll like him."

Gwen shook her head, letting him guide her through the club to the back hall. "I'd love to meet him, but I would have been fine if you'd wanted a few minutes to catch up with him on your own."

She might have been fine, but Brody wouldn't have been. Not after he'd seen her. Not after he'd seen the way Ted was watching them.

"Call me selfish. I wanted my fix." But then he knew he needed to tell her the rest. "But so you know, Ted's had too much to drink tonight. It might be better if you give him a wide berth."

She stopped walking and turned to look at him. "Is he okay?"

Of course, she'd be worried about Ted. She wouldn't

be Gwen if she wasn't. "Yeah, but he's going to feel it tomorrow. And I'd feel better if you stuck with me."

Grant Wendel's office was in the back of the club on the second floor, and when they arrived, the guy took one look at Gwen and let out a low whistle.

"Come on, man. Ever heard of 'Nice to meet you'?" Brody demanded, giving Wendel a light jab in the shoulder while tucking Gwen closer beneath his other arm. To her credit, Gwen wasn't fazed and, once proper introductions were made, seamlessly joined their conversation. With Christmas only a week away and the wedding on New Year's, they talked about the usual things. Holiday plans and horror stories of weddings past. A half hour later, Wendel was in love, and Gwen was as oblivious as ever about how she'd affected the man.

They were passing the exit on their way back to the main part of the club when Gwen pulled Brody to a stop. "Hey, umm…one second." She peered up at him with apologetic eyes. "You probably ought to know it's been a bit of a feeding frenzy with the girls tonight. They've scented romance in the water, and when you get up there, they're probably going to eat you alive."

"That right?" Brody asked, not concerned at all.

She blew out a breath and rubbed the pointed toe of her high heel over a spot on the floor. "They're relentless."

Was that guilt he detected in her pretty eyes?

"Gwendolyn Sidney Danes, did you kiss and tell?"

Her neat white teeth bit into her bottom lip, and she glanced away. Definitely guilty.

"I held them off as long as I could. But they were determined."

He had no doubt. But now he wanted to know what she'd said.

"At least tell me you were complimentary." He was only half teasing and didn't expect her to blush so hot, he could see it even under the club lighting.

"Gwen, *that good*?" he pressed, his ego inflating to monumental proportions. "Now you've got to tell me."

Her mouth fell open in shock. "Brody!"

"What?" he asked, all innocence as she leaned back against the wall, covering her face with her hands. This was going to be good. "You're going to have to tell me what you said." He moved closer, bracing a hand at the wall above her head as he leaned in to speak into her ear. "You know, so we're on the same page."

Chapter 7

BRODY WANTED TO HEAR WHAT GWEN HAD TOLD THOSE girls for only one reason: so he could see her face when she told him about the kiss they'd shared. To find out whether she'd been as affected by it as he had.

He was a damn fool.

Because no way was Gwen going to get all breathless talking about a kiss that she'd only let him have to get another man's attention. More likely she'd recount the events in clinical detail for him, issuing the swift kick to his ego he deserved.

Or worse, she'd tell him it had been *nice*.

Maybe that's what he needed to hear.

But then she was peering up at him from that too-small space where he'd crowded her.

"I told them that even though I'd seen the kiss coming, known it was going to happen, and thought I was ready for it…it caught me by surprise."

Her whiskey eyes held with his, drawing him in until there was nothing but the two of them. Until he wasn't sure he was still breathing or if he even needed to.

He needed to look away. Step back. Get his shit together.

He didn't move an inch. "Because it was good?"

She shook her head, and he could feel the warmth of her breath against his neck. "No, I knew it would be good. I was ready for *good*."

Jesus, she was killing him. "What weren't you ready for?"

He didn't want to know. *He shouldn't know*.

"I wasn't ready to get caught up in it, to get a little lost in it, and forget why we were there. I wasn't ready to be disappointed when it ended. And I really wasn't ready for how much I would think about it after. Is that crazy?"

Not as crazy as how badly he wanted to thread his fingers through her hair, tip her head back, and kiss her again. Kiss her because he wanted her and not because he knew some unworthy prick was about to walk by. But whether Gwen had thought about his kiss or not, she hadn't given up on Ted.

So instead of taking what wasn't his, Brody brushed her soft cheek with his thumb and smiled. "Let's get back to the party."

Gwen was reeling as they made their way back to the VIP area. There was no way that had just been her. Sure, Brody flirted and teased, but the way he'd been looking at her…the way he'd all but boxed her in with his body? She pressed a hand to her belly. Forget butterflies, these had to be hummingbirds.

What just happened with Brody hadn't felt like it was for someone else's benefit. It felt private and right and like maybe despite how all this business started, they were getting to a place that was more about them than some age-old crush she wasn't even interested in anymore.

As if conjured by that thought, Ted stepped up to

them. The hand Brody had been resting at the small of her back tensed, and Gwen immediately recognized that Brody had been right. Ted's eyes were unfocused, his posture off.

"Been gon'a while, huh?"

And he definitely didn't sound right either.

"Everything okay, Ted?" she asked warily.

He looked away before meeting her eyes with a hostile glare. "Not so much, Gwennie."

Prickles of alarm skittered down her spine, and the flutters in her belly became a lead weight.

Brody's hand closed around her hip, as if he was preparing to hold her back. "Hey, man, you look like you should sit down for a break." The words weren't said with any malice, but there was a stern edge to them, and when she glanced back at him, Brody seemed even bigger than usual. As if each level breath he took was somehow filling him out more.

But Ted wasn't looking at Brody. Ignoring the suggestion completely, he stared at her. "The back alley? Really, Gwen?"

What? And then she remembered the EXIT sign they'd passed in the hall on the way to Wendel's office, and it clicked. "Ted, no."

God, this was embarrassing.

"That's enough, Ted," Brody said, stepping around her so his body was between them.

"Don't deny it on top of everything else. I saw you leave, pass the ladies' room, the dance floor, the bars," he accused, bordering on yelling. "Christ, Gwen, what would your parents think?"

She felt like she'd been slapped. Stunned, it took her

a second too long to register the menacing growl coming from Brody's chest or that his hand had shot out and was gripping Ted's shoulder in a hold that had definitely gotten his attention.

"Brody," she choked out, reaching for his arm. But she hadn't needed to worry.

"Ted, you're off base. You're drunk. And you're going to regret the hell out of this tomorrow. Understand?"

"I understand that Gwen's too good for some asshole with so little respect for her that he'd take her to the back alley behind Spin Out. What, did you have to wait for wall space beside the Dumpster?"

Ted was drawing more and more attention, and Gwen could feel her cheeks heating at being the center of it.

"Ted, Brody knows the owner. His office is upstairs. That's where we were."

He blinked and looked away, his face still twisted like he didn't believe her. But then a couple of the guys from the wedding party stepped in and, taking over, suggested they all grab a seat and sober up some.

When she turned to Brody, the muscle in his jaw was jumping, and his eyes were as hard as she'd ever seen them. "You deserve better than that guy, Gwen. When are you going to realize it?"

"Gwennie, you've gotta believe me when I tell you how sorry I am about last night."

Ted looked like hell, his usually neat hair sticking out at unflattering angles and dark circles under his eyes offsetting his sallow complexion.

She believed he was sorry, and if not for how he had

behaved with her, then for the sheer amount of booze he'd consumed. Because he looked wrecked. Still, there was no excuse for what he'd said.

"What were you thinking?" she demanded, uncrossing her arms to throw one hand out at him. "Even if Brody and I had been sneaking off somewhere, which we weren't…" she emphasized with a pointed glare. "What business is it of yours? What business is it of anyone's? You're not my brother, you're not my boyfriend, and to the best of my knowledge, you've never been on my father's payroll to keep me out of trouble."

Shaking his head, Ted ran a hand over the stubbled growth on his chin and looked at her with bloodshot eyes. "I know, I know. I'm none of those things, and whatever you do with O'Donnel is between you and him."

Head cocked to the side, she waited. Because she'd known this man all his life, and she knew without a doubt there was a *but* coming.

"But, Gwennie, him?" Ted looked pained. "You know the guy's got a reputation."

Gwen's brows raised, her voice following along. "Brody? Yeah, I'm pretty sure he does have a reputation. For a lot of things. Like being one of the nicest, biggest-hearted guys in the city."

Ted shook his head. "I know he's nice."

"And for being one of the most loyal men anyone has ever met."

"He's good to his friends. No question."

"Then what the hell else could it be, Ted?" she snapped, the temper she'd been trying to keep in check since he showed up at her door unannounced getting away from her. It was bad enough that he'd embarrassed her last night, but to come over here this morning and start in on Brody again?

"He's a heartbreaker, Gwen."

That stopped her. "What? No, women love him. He's friends with all his exes."

"Yeah, but you know he's not a forever kind of guy. He's a while-it-lasts guy, and the only reason I'm telling you this is because, deep down, despite the fact that you act like that's not what you want, I think you're a forever kind of girl. And I don't want you to get hurt."

Gwen stared, frozen in place. Unable to believe what she was hearing. That Ted...*Ted* was warning her off Brody.

"You've got to be kidding me." The words were barely a whisper, mumbled under her breath. But Ted had heard them.

Walking over to grab his coat, he shook his head. "Honestly, I wish I was. But either way, last night wasn't cool, and I know it. It was no way to treat a friend, especially not one who means as much to me as you do."

Ted really *was* a good friend. Even if he had made some bad choices, selfish choices, over the years. But the thing was, she wasn't nearly as hurt as she would have expected to be. Irritated? Absolutely. But nothing deeper.

She nodded. "Okay, Ted."

"You forgive me?" he asked, flashing the crooked smile that had been getting this guy out of jams for as far back as she could remember.

She nodded and waved him toward the door.

"Guess I have to. It's not like I can ignore you through Christmas."

He pressed a palm into his forehead and winced. "Plus there'd be the whole awkward drive home."

"We couldn't have that." She laughed and then walked over to the coffee table where she had a bottle of ibuprofen. Pouring two into her palm, she held them out in offering. "I forgive you."

———⁓———

"Gwen, relax. It's going to be fine," Ted assured her Thursday night from his seat at the high top beside her.

Brody looked out the front windows of Belfast at the snow that had been falling since ten that morning and was forecast to keep coming.

He wasn't so sure Ted was right about this one. But as usual, the smug prick thought he knew everything.

After what had happened at the bachelor party, Brody had been hoping Ted would crawl into a corner somewhere and never come out. But that hadn't been the way it went. He'd apologized to Gwen face-to-face, then stopped by Belfast on his way home from work Tuesday to scowl at Brody while he acknowledged he'd been unfair to Gwen at the party, while stressing that she'd completely forgiven him. *Great.*

The guy was such a dick. But the thing was, the few times Brody had talked to Gwen this week, he'd realized how much a part of her life Ted was. Even if she got over him completely, he would never go away. She wouldn't want him to. And that was starting to weigh on Brody.

Ted had made a fool of himself Friday, but no way

was it the first time in twenty-six years. Gwen wasn't the type to hold a grudge. She was understanding. She was generous. And she'd been in love with this clown for what Brody was starting to think might have been decades. And suddenly, Ted wanted her.

During the most romantic season of the year.

Surrounded by the family that loved them both.

While Brody would be back in Chicago with nothing to do but wait.

Unless they were snowed in.

Gwen shook her head, worrying her bottom lip between her teeth. "Ted, I want you to be right. I really do. But they're talking about up to two feet overnight. And with the wind—"

Blizzard conditions.

Ted reached across the table and took her phone, placing it facedown on the table. "They always exaggerate. Besides, even if we do get dumped on, I'll be able to drive it, no problem."

Until that point, Brody had been pretty quiet.

This was something between Gwen and Ted. But no fucking way was he letting Gwen get in a car with this cocky dipshit. Not for a three-hour drive in near blizzard conditions out to rural Illinois. He remembered what the roads had been like the last time the snow came down this way. And if he wasn't mistaken, getting stuck in that storm was what put Jase and Emily, former enemies, on the track to getting married.

His eyes narrowed as he looked back and forth between Ted and Gwen.

No way.

"Gwen, if it's not safe, your parents are going to

understand. And hell, then you can hang out with me."
He smoothed a hand over her hair, and when she turned
to look out at the street, he added, "I know it won't be the
same, but I have a party for friends who haven't got any
family in town. I do it every year, and it's definitely a
more-the-merrier event. I swear you'll have a good time."

"That's a nice offer," Ted said, his body language all
but screaming *not a fucking chance*. "But unnecessary.
We'll be able to get out no problem tomorrow."

"Guess we'll have to let Mother Nature decide."

Twelve hours later, Brody was staring out his front
window, grinning at more snow than he'd seen since he
was a kid as Gwen's sleepy voice filtered through the
line.

"I told him not to even try it, but he's so bullheaded.
He only made it about a block from the lot where he
rents his spot."

"He's okay though?" Brody asked, to make sure. He
didn't want Gwen to be worried about anything, and
while Ted was a dick, he didn't really want the guy to
get hurt. At least not seriously.

"He's fine. But it's going to be a few hours, if that,
before they can get a truck to tow him."

Brody still couldn't believe the fucker had tried. One
look out the window would've told any reasonable man
he didn't have a chance in hell of getting out of the city.
Ted *deserved* what he got. He hadn't just been willing to
risk himself; he'd been willing to risk Gwen's safety too.
And that had the skin across Brody's knuckles straining
tight around the fist he couldn't quite let go.

Pulling the phone back to his ear, he said, "So you're
coming to my party?"

"When do you want me over?"

Now. Last night for the whole night, definitely this morning.

Damn, he needed to shut that thinking down. But he'd been trying for weeks now, and it only seemed to be getting worse. And now Gwen wasn't going to be driving off with Ted at all. She was going to be with *him*.

"An hour give you enough time?" he asked, loving the bubbly sound of her laughter. "I'm serious, Gwen. I'll be over in an hour to walk with you. We can pack a bag with whatever you want to wear tonight."

Another warm laugh tickled his ear and warmed his chest. "Brody, it's ten a.m. Your party doesn't even start until seven, right?"

"Yeah, but you've got a VIP pass. Perks of being the girl I'm into," he explained, keeping his tone joking when deep down, he knew he was serious.

She sighed. "About that. Ted doesn't think he's gonna be able to make it tonight. Even though he's very appreciative of the offer... I think he, umm, has other plans, so you may be off the hook in terms of being *into me* for the evening."

If only it were that simple. Brody was pretty sure he was into her whether Ted was there or not. Just as he was pretty sure Ted didn't have other plans, considering the guy had been trying to drive out of town until twenty minutes ago.

Not that he cared. But because he knew *Gwen cared*, he added, "In case those plans fall through, let him know the offer stands."

"I will." Then after a pause, she asked, "Are you really going to be here in an hour?"

His grin spread wide. "Nah. Make it fifteen minutes. And keep your pajamas on. It's going to be a cozy, hot-chocolate-in-front-of-the-fireplace kind of day."

Chapter 8

SHE HADN'T ENTIRELY BELIEVED HIM, BUT FIFTEEN MINUTES later, Brody was there, kicking the snow off his gigantic boots and shaking his hair free of it when she opened the door.

Looking like some sexy abominable snowman, he grabbed her bag and said, "Let's go."

The snow was thick and deep, crunching first beneath their boots and then beneath just Brody's after he insisted on giving her a piggyback ride through most of the four-block trek. She'd expected him to wear out fast, but the guy kept chatting, laughing, and threatening to dump her into the snow the whole way. By the time they reached his place, she'd been laughing harder than she could remember.

Brody's home was amazing. It was an old, converted warehouse with high ceilings and heavy rustic furniture blended with modern accents. It was perfect for him. Everything a bit bigger, a bit sturdier, and a bit more inviting than the norm.

And then there was the kitchen. This guy had it all. Top-of-the-line range. Spacious marble counters, a fridge bigger than her bed, and an enormous island in the center with plenty of space for prep work as well as a buffet.

"I think I've died and gone to heaven." She sighed, running her fingers along the marble. "Was it like this when you bought it? Or did you have it remodeled yourself?"

Brody opened one of the upper cabinets and pulled out a couple of handmade mugs. Setting them on the counter, he retrieved a saucepan and then an assortment of ingredients from the fridge and cabinets. "Sam Farrow, this guy out of Wicker Park, did most of it for me. But the space had been partially converted before I moved in. We just fine-tuned it."

"Well, it's beautiful. In fact, now that you've let me into your secret lair, you may never get me out."

"Secret lair?" He shook his head, grinning. "Yeah, aside from this party once a year, guess I don't really have people over too often."

He poured milk into the saucepan and then added one ingredient after another. "It's not that I'm a super private guy. Or that I don't like the company. It's more that I do most of my entertaining at my second home."

"Belfast?" she asked as he grated some chocolate into the mix, gave it a stir, and then grated some more.

"I'm there so much. And the only time I'm not is when most people are at work."

She'd never thought about it before, because Brody was such a social guy. "Does that make you lonely?"

He stopped stirring, seeming to really think before he answered her. "It didn't use to. But sometimes." Satisfied, he divided the steaming, fragrant concoction between their mugs. "The good news is, when I find myself getting lonely, I've got this friend I call whose laugh always makes me feel like she's right there with me, filling up all the empty space."

She smiled. For as hard as it had been to say goodbye

to her kindergarten class the day before, a part of her liked the idea that for the next six months at least, she'd be sharing Brody's backward schedule. Maybe neither of them would have to be lonely.

As promised, they drank their chocolate by the fireplace in a deep leather couch so comfortable, Gwen thought it might swallow her whole. Brody sat at one side while she sat at the other, her feet pulled up beneath her.

"Tell me something I don't know about you," she said after a sip of the most decadent hot chocolate she'd ever tasted.

Brody's head dropped back as he looked up to the exposed-beam ceiling, thinking.

His hair had dried into a wild mess of curls, and it took everything she had to stay where she was, to not crawl over and run her fingers through them just once. It was no wonder the women could never stop touching him.

When he looked back at her, he grinned. "I wear a size thirteen shoe."

This time, it was her turn to laugh. "Okay, somehow I'm not surprised. But that wasn't exactly what I was looking for. Tell me something about *you*. About who you are and how you got to be this way."

Giving her a jut of his chin, he asked, "What way?"

"I don't know. So personable. From what I've seen, you can talk to anyone about anything."

His jaw shifted to the side, and he was looking at her as if he was trying to decide how much to say. For a man as talkative and open as he was, he kept some parts of himself very private, and she found herself half holding her breath, hoping he would open up to her.

"I like people. I like talking to them, getting to know them. Figuring out what makes them tick and what makes them different. My mother isn't that way, I don't think. And I never really knew my father, so it'd be pretty tough to say how much *nature* played into it. But with sixteen different nannies before I hit prep school, it'd be safe to say *nurture* had a hand."

Gwen could only blink.

"I know, kind of a lot of information I just unloaded on you," he said with a self-deprecating laugh. "Want me to break it down? Or maybe you're good."

"I think maybe you could break it down…but, Brody, only if you don't mind." Because suddenly, she could see how uncomfortable he was, and being the reason he felt that way was the last thing she wanted. "You don't have to."

His eyes cut to hers, and then he shook his head. "It's okay. I don't talk about my family a lot, so I'm a little rusty. But it's no state secret. Or maybe it is. I don't know that much about my father. I only met him once, and I didn't know for sure who he was until about seven years later after he'd died."

"You didn't know?" she asked, suddenly wishing she wasn't sitting so far away from him.

"My mother is an international corporate lawyer. I believe he was a client. A married client. And she was very serious about protecting his privacy. Probably her career too. It's important to her."

"But he knew about you?"

Brody nodded. "I think there just wasn't a place for me in his life."

What a sad thing to have to come to terms with. And

what a tragedy that his father had missed out on knowing this amazing man!

"You said you met him?"

There was a ghost of a smile on his lips as Brody nodded, his gaze lost in some middle space. "Yeah. My mother wasn't very accessible. She worked long hours and traveled all the time. But once when I was about ten, she came home from a trip, and instead of closing herself off in the office the way she usually did, she came and found me. Told me to get dressed because we were going out to dinner. I was freaking out, sure she was going to tell me Nina—I think that one was still Nina—was going to be gone when we got home. Replaced with whomever she'd hired to take care of me next. I asked her, but she said no. She just wanted to have dinner with me, and there might be one of her friends there, so if he came by, I should be on my best behavior."

"Did you know?" she asked, imagining this big, strapping man as a vulnerable boy.

"Not right away. But when he came to the table, I couldn't take my eyes off him. He didn't have the same hair or eyes… I got the Irish from my mother's side. But this guy was *big*, Gwen. And there was something about the way he looked at me, like I wasn't just *someone else's* kid he was being polite about meeting." He cleared his throat and looked at her. "He was probably only there for five minutes total. Never sat down. But he smiled at me before he left and told me I seemed like an impressive young man, and my mother should be proud."

"Five minutes," she whispered. That's all his father had given him.

He met her eyes, letting her see the acceptance in his. "It was a good five minutes."

"Do you think your mother loved him?"

Brody let out a short laugh, as though maybe he'd never thought about it before. "I don't think she loves anyone. I don't think she's built that way."

He didn't think she loved him.

"Gwen," he said, that deep voice gentle. "You look like you're about to cry, and I won't be able to take it if you do. I didn't tell you about my parents to break your heart. They didn't break mine."

"No?"

He shook his head. "My mother is cold and distant, and she wasn't around for me. But she made sure I always had someone who was."

"The nannies?" How many had he said there were... sixteen?

"She always hired girls in their early twenties, younger even than you. And they were without exception adoring. You want to know why I'm such a good listener and I like people so much? It's because I grew up going to their coffee dates and lunches and friends' houses, and when they weren't fawning over me, they were talking like women that age talk."

"But why so many? Why not just hire one that stayed with you through your youth?"

He shook his head. "She wanted me exposed to as many different people and influences as possible. Honestly, I think she was trying to do the right thing for me. But her brain just doesn't work that way."

Gwen was afraid to ask, but she had to know. "Were you happy?"

"I was." His grin spread. "Now ask me something else."

Something that wasn't going to break her heart even if it hadn't broken his. Something good. "How about the bar. How did you get into that?"

More relaxed, Brody made another of those considering faces before answering. "I grew up wanting my own restaurant. The plans for the bar came later. My grandmother owned this swank place in Manhattan, and I thought there wasn't anything better."

"Your grandmother?" Could this guy get any better?

And the answer was a resounding yes, because then he reached back, pushing his big hands through the untamed curls of his hair and making his shirt stretch tight over his chest and arms. *Nice.* Brody slid the elastic off his wrist to bind the hair that liked to fall in his face. It wouldn't stay that way for long. Within fifteen to thirty minutes, she'd bet all those wild red-brown curls would be back on the loose.

But for now, he settled back against the cushions. "Yeah, the story goes that my grandfather opened the place before he met her. And one day, she came in with a date who'd done her wrong. Big mistake. She had a temper and apparently wasn't afraid to show it. So when she finished chewing this date out, Fiona was getting up to leave, and my grandfather stopped her to offer her a job. He thought she could keep the kitchen running with that fiery Irish temper."

Gwen was getting that warm, swelly feeling in her chest as she leaned forward, eager to hear more. "And then he fell in love with her and taught her to run the whole restaurant?"

Brody coughed out a laugh. "Not quite. She told him

what he could do with his offer and suggested if he had a better one, he had until she was out the door to give it to her. So he asked her to marry him instead."

She was up on her knees, her chocolate set on the table behind the couch so she could clutch her hands over her heart. "Oh my God, no wonder you're such a romantic!"

"Oh, Gwendolyn. You give me those eyes and tell me *I'm* the romantic?" he asked with a shake of his head. "Hate to ruin it for you, but Fiona thought her husband had rocks in his head. Remember this is the woman who raised my *mother*. The happy ending to Fiona's story was her husband died within a year of marrying her, so she didn't have to leave him, new baby and all...plus she got the restaurant. Anyway, one summer, I got to stay with her, and she taught me to cook and—"

Gwen's brows crumpled, that warm, swelly feeling in her chest deflating in a rush. "Wait... What? *No*." She leaned forward, poking him in the shoulder. "That's the worst love story I ever heard!"

And now he was laughing for real, those sea-green eyes flashing at her as he wedged himself farther back into the couch cushions. "*Love story*? Sorry, but that's not really how the women in my family are. Hey!" he yelped when she poked him again. "Didn't anyone ever tell you not to poke the bear?"

Oh yeah, some bear. She'd heard people call him that before—because he was so big, she guessed—but the only kind of bear this guy could be called was a teddy bear. She poked again and again because... "Yes, love story! You totally set me up."

Poke. Poke.

"*Gwen.*"

She was pretty sure that was supposed to be a warning, but no way could she take it seriously when the big guy was literally trying to wiggle away amid those deep, rumbling laughs.

Poke.

But then, lightning fast, the world spun, and Gwen found herself laid out across Brody's lap, held in place by the strong hand still wrapped around her wrist and the solid arm supporting her back. She blinked up into Brody's too-green, too-deep, too-soulful eyes, caught there and held. The laughter died between them, and she swore that, even as tightly as he was holding her, the world shifted again.

A furrow dug between Brody's brows, and that dark stare cleared, going light in a blink. The corner of his mouth kicked up.

"Warned you," he said, shifting back on the couch and helping her to stand before getting up himself. Then after a wide-armed stretch, he grinned back at her. "Time to get cooking. You want to watch and be awed or help out? I'm happy either way."

Gwen stood where she was for a moment, watching as Brody headed for the kitchen.

He looked back, an easy smile on his face. "Gwen?"

She shook off the remains of a moment she hadn't quite been ready to let go and followed after. "I'll help. I love to cook."

~~~

It had been a perfect day, spent in the most perfect way. He'd given Gwen his present early, not wanting an audience when he made his excuses about why he'd bought her jewelry as if she were his girlfriend, even though she wasn't. She'd thrown her arms around his neck, pressing kiss after kiss to his cheek as she thanked him for the heart-shaped ruby earrings he hadn't been able to resist because they made him think of how sweet she was.

And then she'd tormented him, telling him about the present she had for him but refusing to let him have it, because she wanted him to have something to open on Christmas morning. He might have tried to work her for it, because he wanted to open it when she was with him. Opening presents alone on Christmas morning sucked hard. But this year, he thought maybe she'd stay. Not in his bed. Or maybe in his bed, but not naked in his bed. And maybe he would have someone to open gifts with in the morning. With that outcome in mind, he hadn't pushed.

They'd indulged in bouts of lazy, alternating with preparations for the party. They'd cooked together, working seamlessly side by side. Gwen stopping every so often to offer him a taste or lean close to take a deep draw through her nose and moan.

She was such a sensualist. Brody decided he could spend the rest of his life in the kitchen with her and never get tired of it.

When the food prep was complete, Gwen set out holiday decorations while he shoveled the walk and back terrace before setting up the restaurant-grade outdoor heater. Gwen had a glass of wine waiting for him when he came in, and with a few hours to kill before his guests started showing up, they'd put on a movie, watching until Gwen drifted off to sleep beneath his arm.

Her head rested against his chest...and then his

stomach…and then his lap. And yeah, sitting there stroking the soft silk of her hair as she slept offered the kind of contentment he could definitely get used to.

If he had the chance.

Hell, the way she'd been looking up at him when they'd been on the couch—her eyes wide and filled with the kind of surprise that didn't have anything to do with the way he'd caught her—made him think he would. Only then he'd thought about *fucking Ted* and that unrelenting crush that was the reason she'd been on his couch in the first place. She'd looked like she would let him kiss her if he'd tried, but what then?

She wanted Ted.

Didn't she?

She never brought him up anymore…but what if Brody was just seeing what he wanted to see?

Yeah, she might have let him kiss her, but somehow he'd scraped together enough sense not to try.

Looking down at her as she slept, he wasn't sure how much longer he'd be able to resist.

Gwen was embarrassed when she woke up, her cheeks pink and her eyes hazy. She was beautiful in her fluster as she apologized for falling asleep all over him—something he would be replaying on a loop in his head for time eternal—and then excused herself to get ready for the night ahead.

Guests didn't start showing up until seven, and it was probably seven thirty before he saw Gwen again. When he did, she was standing in the corner looking festive and beautiful in a red sweater dress with a thin black belt that matched her heels. She'd been talking with a group of his friends he was fairly sure she hadn't met before, laughing and chatting as though she'd known them forever. As though she could fit into his life without even trying. He probably looked like some kind of creeper standing there staring at her, but when her eyes met his, she'd given him a shy smile that did things to his chest he didn't fully understand.

He wanted to talk to her. Find out what she was thinking. Figure out what she was feeling, if maybe it was the same as him. He wanted to stand by her side and touch her hair, hold her hand, and smell her perfume. He wanted her to want him to be there, but not because they were playing at romance to get another man's attention.

He wanted her to be *his*.

But because of the convoluted way their friendship had grown, the physical affection they'd been sharing for more than a month, and too many other reasons to count, he still had no fucking idea whether she wanted that too.

Or whether the man she still wanted was Ted.

It was close to nine when he saw Gwen stepping out onto the terrace alone. She hadn't signaled him, hadn't made eye contact, just let herself out the back door.

He should leave her alone. Stay with his guests. He knew he should. But even as he thought it, he was excusing himself from the group, dodging past one friend and weaving around another. A moment later, he was closing the sliding glass door behind him.

Gwen was looking out over the back of his neighborhood. Her arms were crossed, her hands rubbing over them to keep warm.

"I brought you a coat," he said, stepping close as he held it open for her. "I think yours is buried under about twenty others. So this is one of mine." It was ridiculously big on her, but he couldn't help liking the sight of her wrapped in something that belonged to him.

"Thank you," she said, smiling over her shoulder at him. "It's colder than it looks out here."

"We could go inside."

She shook her head. "It's too pretty to go back in just yet."

He turned her around and started buttoning up the oversize garment. He rolled one sleeve past her slender fingers, and then the other, taking more time and care than absolutely necessary, knowing it was just an excuse to touch her without actually touching her. To break the rules. But only a little.

She was right; it was a beautiful night. The city was covered in a thick blanket of white, and while the wind had died down midday, the snow had started falling again about an hour before. *Beautiful*. But all he could see was the woman in front of him, with the snow-kissed cheeks and frosted lashes.

"I didn't mean to pull you away from the party," she told him, gesturing to the sliding glass doors behind them and the party beyond.

He ought to go back inside. Talk to her tomorrow. But he didn't.

"If I was into you, I'd have been waiting for an opportunity to get you alone."

"Why?" she asked softly, her breath fogging the air between them in soft puffs.

Jesus, he knew better than this.

She blinked up at him, and when those whiskey eyes met his, the only thing he knew for certain was he couldn't resist.

Chapter 9

IF HE WAS INTO HER...

He was giving her the words that had been behind every other bit of feigned intimacy between them. But tonight, Ted wasn't there. There was no one watching, no one to see. What Brody was showing her was for her and her alone. Gwen's heart was racing.

This was what she wanted.

What she'd been telling herself not to hope for but couldn't seem to stop wanting anyway.

"Brody."

He closed his eyes, looking almost pained before meeting hers again. And when he did, he took her face in his big palms, cradling it with such tender care, it made her chest ache. Finally, he lowered his mouth to hers, and she shivered at the bliss of that perfect lingering press. The soft cling of their lips and the brief, torturous break in contact before he was back again.

This kiss bolder, more intense. More demanding.

His fingers slid into her hair, closing around it as he urged her to open beneath him. His tongue pushed past her lips, and she gasped, then moaned around him as he thrust inside, giving her his taste as he *took* her mouth.

It made her crazy.

Pulling at him, she tugged at his shirt, his shoulders, his neck as he kissed her harder, deeper. Angling their mouths one way and then fusing them another. Each claiming lick making her more desperate than the last.

A deep, rumbling groan sounded from low in his chest, and then the world spun. When her feet touched back down, her back was pressed into the brick at the far side of the terrace.

The way he was kissing her was like he couldn't get enough. Like he didn't know how to stop. Like maybe he'd been waiting as long as she had.

Those big hands were everywhere—in her hair, touching her face, sliding down her neck, and teasing her breasts. She was burning for him, mindless from his touch, his kiss. And when his hand found the back of her thigh, his fingers flexing once, she whimpered against his lips.

He swore and, cupping the back of her knee, brought her leg up along his until she was open to him.

Oh…God…yes.

With the snow falling around them, he kissed her again—slower, harder, filling her mouth in time with the slow rock of his hips.

Tension gathered low in her belly, heavy and warm.

Her heel hooked the back of his thigh, urging him closer—

"Gwe… Oh shit, I… Sorry."

She jerked at the too-familiar, too-smooth, too-high voice coming from way too close.

No.

He wasn't supposed to be there.

In an instant, Brody had shifted so he was blocking her with his body. But not before she'd seen Ted ducking back inside. *Ted.*

Her stomach churned with the realization, *This wasn't what I thought*. That perfect moment with the perfect man was just another perfect act.

Not real.

She'd thought Brody had come out to be with her, but he must've seen Ted arrive and known that he'd come looking for her. Brody hadn't kissed her because he wanted her. He'd done it for the same reason he'd been doing everything else over the past month...to help her *get* Ted. A man she'd stopped wanting somewhere along the way.

Heat burned through her cheeks, and she turned away, pushing her dress back down her legs and using everything she had to fight the tears that wanted to come. He'd even warned her about what he was doing with that *If I was into you* talk...but she'd ignored it.

"Gwen, are you okay?" Brody asked from behind her, his voice strained and tight.

There was no way she was going to be able to hide that something was wrong. Off.

She cleared her throat and forced herself to turn around and face him. His expressive face was unreadable, his eyes shuttered.

"A little embarrassed, maybe," she said, working to keep the outward evidence of that monumental understatement under wraps. "I mean, it was perfect timing, right? So, yay, us. But—"

"But it went too far." He cleared his throat and took a step back, shoving his hands in his pockets. "I shouldn't have let it."

He'd been doing her a favor, because he thought she was his friend and not some psycho who was going to try to turn an arrangement with very specific rules into something it wasn't.

She shook her head, struggling for something to say to minimize the damage. "We wanted to make it count. And if that wasn't enough to do it, I'm not sure either of us is interested in whatever would."

Brody laughed, but it sounded as strained as his voice, and she hated it.

"We should go in. Get you back to your party. Ted's already seen us so…"

She closed her eyes, waiting, the part of her that never learned hoping Brody would tell her that he hadn't known Ted was there. That what had happened between them was real, and he wanted her.

"Yeah, we're good."

And that confirmed it. She was doing the same thing with Brody she had with Ted. Shifting her attention from one unavailable man to the next. What was wrong with her?

—–⁓—–

Brody followed Gwen, stepping inside the doors just long enough to hear Ted crack the joke that he had to stop meeting Gwen like that. And then the guy was all with the apologies, holding up a bottle of wine in one hand and a small gift-wrapped present in the other as he spoke to Gwen in the kind of quiet tones that made it clear what he was saying was for her alone.

After what had happened outside, it was just as well. Brody had gone off script, big time. But when she'd looked up at him, the only thing that had mattered in that moment had been kissing her. And then kissing her deeper. Harder. Getting lost in the taste of her. In the feel of her fingers in his hair, pulling him closer as she got lost in him too.

But that's not what it had been.

She'd been playing along, following his lead. And thank fucking God, Ted had shown up when he had. Because how else was Brody supposed to explain his actions when she realized that kiss hadn't been for anything or anyone except himself.

He was the worst kind of asshole.

Brody poured himself a few fingers of whiskey, tossing half of it back in one go as he watched Gwen step into Ted's arms for a hug. A moment later, the guy was standing beside him.

"Sorry I missed the dinner. Everyone's talking about how great it was." Ted handed him a bottle of wine before returning his hands to his jeans pocket.

"No problem, man. Just glad you were able to make it." Total lie. But really, what the hell else could he say? That he wished Ted was still stuck with his car in some snowdrift?

He nodded, glancing back toward where Gwen was talking with a couple of girls from the bar. "It's just really cool of you to have us."

Brody's focus boomeranged back to Ted, who was staring him in the eye. *Us*? Yeah, that look alone said it hadn't been an accident, and Brody understood Ted loud and clear. That possessive *us* was a statement. Fuck, it was a challenge… And it should've been exactly what Brody was waiting to hear. But it absolutely wasn't.

Ted wanted Gwen, and despite having witnessed

Brody all over her—or maybe because of it—he was more determined than ever to get her back.

Brody's breath whistled out in a rush. It sucked being right sometimes.

Counting back from ten, he reminded himself of all the reasons this was a good thing. That Gwen was going to get what she wanted…and then, God willing, she was going to realize she didn't want it anymore. Mission accomplished.

But in the end, what he said was, "Of course, man. You're one of Gwen's oldest friends, and any friend of Gwen's is welcome here."

Translation: *It's on.*

If it took this pencil-neck dickweed seeing Gwen with another guy to come around, no way was Brody going to make it any easier for him than he had to.

They stood watching each other a moment longer, and Brody started to wonder if Ted was going to whip his dick out for comparison.

Ted would lose.

Fortunately, the noisy arrival of several more guests prevented the confrontation from coming to that, and when Brody found Ted again, he was back with Gwen.

An hour later, everyone was dancing and singing along with the music coming through his sound system, the fire was going strong, and by anyone else's standard, the night would be considered a success. But there was no ignoring how badly he'd fucked up with Gwen. Even if she thought he'd known Ted was there, the way he'd kissed her—like he wasn't going to stop until he'd heard her come apart for him—had gone too far. He'd taken too much. Touched her like she was his. When she wasn't.

He'd forgotten the rules of the game.

Hell, he'd forgotten the game altogether.

And every time he'd tried to get close to her since, this fucking party had gotten in the way. He ought to be thrilled that she was laughing, having fun, surrounded by his friends and fitting in as seamlessly as she always did. But he couldn't shake the sense of foreboding that had settled into his gut. He couldn't stop searching for a moment when he might get her alone again and try to make things right.

And then his moment came. She was in the kitchen, stacking dishes on the side of the counter. Alone.

Cutting through the crowd, Brody made his way into the not nearly private enough space and came up beside her.

"Gwen, leave this stuff. Come back to the party and have some fun." He wanted to reach for that bit of hair that had fallen over her shoulder, wind it around his finger, and give the loose coil a gentle tug. But suddenly, there was a divide between them that hadn't been there before. And it felt like a divide he couldn't, or maybe shouldn't, cross.

"It's no problem. I didn't want to leave your kitchen looking like a train wreck after this was so nice tonight." She rinsed another plate, adding it to the stack. Still not looking at him, and he felt his heart start to pound, because that wasn't right. When she reached for another plate, he caught her wrist, pulling her around to meet his eyes. She was smiling up at him, but over the past months, he had become familiar enough with Gwen's myriad smiles to recognize there was nothing real about this one.

He pulled her closer, needing to apologize. "Gwen."

"Actually, I'm kind of exhausted and—"

"Gwennie, you ready?"

Brody closed his eyes in a plea for patience. *Fucking Ted*. Again. How in the hell did this guy keep stumbling upon them at the worst times? But when Brody looked back to the doorway where the guy was standing, he realized Ted wasn't just there to get Gwen to join in a game of cards or some quiet conversation. He was holding her coat over one arm, already wearing his own.

Brody's head snapped back to Gwen. "You're leaving?"

Her eyes skated away. "It's been a long day, and if the roads are clear, we'll be driving out early to get home."

Bullshit. Everything she was saying might be true, but that didn't change the fact that she wouldn't be leaving, she wouldn't be dodging his eyes like this if there wasn't something more going on.

Dammit, why did he kiss her like that?

He needed to talk to her, make sure they were okay, but he could fucking feel Ted standing there in the doorway. Waiting and watching.

To hell with him.

"Are we... Are we okay?" Brody asked, lowering his voice though he was sure Ted could still hear it.

Gwen gave him one of those *don't be silly* faces with a matching wave of her hand, but when her eyes caught his, she let out a quiet sigh. "Ted, could you give us a minute?"

The guy smiled wide, his eyes flicking to Brody's before returning to hers. "You bet, Gwennie. I'll meet you by the front door."

And then he was gone. And it was just the two of them. But before he could open his mouth to let the apologies and explanations and lies—if that's what it took—flow, Gwen had taken both of his hands in hers and was looking up into his eyes.

"We're fine. Thank you for everything today. I had the best time. But this thing with Ted…" Her voice trailed off, and Brody's breath caught in his lungs, holding while he waited for what she would say next. "I don't think he needs any more convincing."

Her words hit Brody like a blow to the gut, knocking him back a step. "So you guys are…" He tried to make himself say the rest, to ask if they were together. But he couldn't force the words onto his tongue, let alone past his lips. He cleared his throat and shook his head. "He's taking you home."

A small stitch pulled between her brows, the corner of the mouth he'd tasted only hours ago turned down. "He's walking me back to my place. And then tomorrow, we'll head back home to Dobson."

Home. The place that they'd been sharing since before they were born. The connection that would never be severed. The history he wasn't a part of. Couldn't compete with. Didn't have a place in.

He understood. He straightened his shoulders, then giving Gwen's hands one last squeeze, he leaned down and kissed her cheek.

"Hey, Merry Christmas. I'll see you at the bar when you get back."

That bit of strain left her face, softening her smile. She nodded. "Merry Christmas."

And then she was gone. Leaving him with a house full of friends, feeling as alone as he could remember feeling since he had moved out on his own.

The last guest left a little after one thirty. He wasn't worried about the mess, about cleaning up, or the mysterious single boot or stray glove that had been left behind.

He didn't want to think about anything, least of all what might have happened when Ted got Gwen to her door. Whether he'd looked at her beneath the falling snow and found himself caught up in that same pull Brody hadn't had the strength or sense to pull himself out of.

Throwing the dead bolt and turning off the lights, Brody headed back through the open space to the liquor cabinet. Ignoring the open wine and eggnog, he went straight for the whiskey. Hell, it wasn't like he had anything else to do tomorrow. The first shot was down before he hit the stairs.

If Ted tried to kiss her, would Gwen let him?

Reaching the second floor, Brody leaned against the rough wooden railing, looking over the living space below.

"Do you ever get lonely?"

Yeah, gorgeous. Looked like he did.

Flipping off the light so he wouldn't see the vast expanse of his empty home, he followed the hall down to his room where he stopped and stared at the silver-wrapped gift about the size of a shoebox in the center of his bed. It was beautiful, the bow a pile of shimmering coils tied around paper with glitter-encrusted snowflakes pressed into the pattern. It was so Gwen. He could practically imagine her running her fingers over it and making that little hum of appreciation that drove him wild.

She'd left his present for him.

He sat and took the gift into his lap, carefully running his thumb beneath one fold and then the other to preserve the paper. When he opened the box, all he could do was reach for the bottle he'd set by the table and take another long swallow.

Chapter 10

"NEW SCARF?" MOLLY ASKED, WALKING UP TO HIM MONDAY morning outside Belfast. Then being Molly, she reached for it like she was about to take it off his neck. "Ooh, so soft. This is gorgeous. Let me try it on."

But before she had a chance, he batted her little hand away, pointing his index finger in her face. "Don't touch."

Shooting him one of her signature glowers, she crossed her arms over her ever-expanding belly. "Geez, I just wanted to feel it for a second."

Brody did a double take, laughing, his brows raised as he looked down at her, because...*really*?

He'd lost more than his share of T-shirts to this girl, and as a rule, he didn't mind. She was a sweetheart, and he enjoyed making her smile, even if it was only because of some stupid saying on a T-shirt that would probably still be too big for her if she were nine months pregnant with triplets. But this was different.

"Hurry up. I'm freezing out here. *And I don't have a scarf*," she added with a good-natured jab. "What's so special about it?" she asked, following him back to his office to leave their coats. "The scarf, I mean. Aside from it being completely gorgeous and all."

"Christmas present."

Apparently not in any hurry to leave his office, she ran her fingers over the pattern.

"It even matches your eyes."

"Molly, I'm opening the kitchen an hour early because you called me up begging. You want this burger or not?"

For a second, her eyes glazed, and he could practically see the drool pooling in her mouth. "God, yes, I want the burger."

"Then come on."

Once they were situated in the kitchen and he had the grill going and the ingredients out, Molly pulled a chair over to crawl up on the counter. "So who's it from?"

No sense in playing dumb, but he didn't have to give Molly any more than she was asking for. At least that's what he was thinking until he heard that menacing little growl from behind him. With a big breath, he turned around and held out his hands. "Fine, it's from Gwen. It was a Christmas present. She knitted it for me, and I fucking love it, so no, you can't have it. Good?"

Leaning back on one hand, she slowly rubbed her belly with the other.

"She knit it for you? That's awfully sweet. *And time-consuming*."

He turned back to her burger. "It was very thoughtful."

He only wished he'd had the opportunity to thank her for it with more than a text he never got a response back from.

"Mmm-hmm. Very." Then, "You guys still pretending to date?"

The spatula clattered against the grill. He could *hear* her smiling.

"No. We're done with that."

"Did it work?"

"Yes." *Too well*.

He set the finished burger next to Molly, who promptly sank her teeth into an enormous bite and then, still chewing, demanded, "Eggsplng."

This was a woman Brody had known longer and better than any other in his life. She'd been like a little sister to him when she moved into the quad he was sharing with her brother freshman year. She'd been the girl he'd thought he might love a little years later, until he realized she'd been in love with Sean from as far back as they'd all known each other. She'd been the only one he could trust with his business, and through all those years, she'd become one of his best friends.

If he could talk to anyone about this, he could talk to her.

Growling at him around another monstrous bite, she snapped her fingers impatiently.

"She was at the party Saturday night, and I kissed her."

Molly nodded. "You've kissed her before though, right? Outside the bar or something?"

"Yeah, but not like this. There was a misunderstanding, and I got carried away."

The chewing stopped, and Molly raised a brow. "How'd that work out?"

"It made Gwen uncomfortable and Ted jealous. And now he wants her."

She nodded, taking another bite. "That's good, right?"

"Not good. Moll, this guy is so fucking blind and so unworthy, it makes me physically sick." And a little violent. "And now I don't fucking want him to have her, but I'm pretty sure that train has already left the station."

Molly stopped chewing and swallowed with a gulp that had him pulling his phone out to look up alternatives to the Heimlich maneuver for pregnant women when she asked, "You mean, *left the station* like the train is maybe already *entering a tunnel?*"

Brody scowled, not entirely following until she brought her hands together, one finger pointing into—

"Christ, Molly!" he coughed out, taking her hands and firmly pressing them back into her lap. But the damage was done, and now he could barely breathe, wondering if Ted was at Gwen's place right now. If he was in her bed and getting to hear her laugh against his neck, feel her hair sifting through his fingers. If he knew how loud those sexy little sounds she had made when they'd kissed could get when they were more than kissing.

"Well, yeah, that's what I was asking," she said. "I mean, I thought that was what you were saying, because yeah, the train definitely would have left the station then. But I can see it wasn't what you were saying. Only now you're thinking about it. So sorry about that."

She shifted in her spot on the counter, looked down at her half-eaten burger, and licked her lips.

"Just eat it, Molly."

"I didn't want to be rude…or insensitive." The burger was in her hands and then her mouth in a flash. "Ju gnow whaght I meang?" she asked, chewing around her words and making him laugh. Because yeah, that was Molly.

"I know what you mean."

The kitchen staff had started showing up by the time the burger was gone, so Brody helped Molly off the counter and walked her back into the bar. She poured herself an iced tea. "She love this guy?"

He wanted to tell her no. That he didn't believe it was possible to really love someone if you'd never had the chance to actually *be* with them. But they both knew better. Molly had married the guy she'd loved in secret for more than a decade.

"I don't know, Moll. I think he's a dick, so I keep telling myself she isn't seeing him for who he really is. Only I guess everyone else thinks he's a pretty decent, stand-up guy too."

"That sucks."

"Tell me about it."

They stood there a moment longer, Molly straightening things that didn't need to be straightened. "Any chance she'll find another bar so you won't have to see them all the time?"

"Not really. I gave her a job. She starts tonight."

⁓⁓⁓

Jill was showing Gwen the ropes when Brody came out of his office. She'd already been at work for an hour and was starting to wonder whether she would see him at all. And now, as he came up beside her, standing a polite distance away but still far too close, she wondered if maybe she'd been hoping he'd avoid her.

He was dressed up tonight, wearing a pair of charcoal trousers with a black shirt that was open at the collar and fit him so well that she'd be willing to bet her favorite pair of boots it'd been custom-made. His hair was down, those wild waves framing his face like a tempest. For now. It was only a matter of time before he'd have it wrestled back into a tie, and then only a matter of time after that before it would be free again. But as it was, it was the kind of finger-tangling temptation she really needed to stop thinking about. Remembering. Wanting more of.

"Hey, boss," she offered, going for friendly, even though her stomach was still in knots. "How was Christmas?"

There, she'd done it. Made some totally benign, completely appropriate comment, devoid of any innuendo or flirtation.

"Really good, thanks. How about yours?" he asked, his eyes on his phone. The only real distance between them in his posture.

She shouldn't take it personally. It wasn't personal.

It was business. Even if every other time she'd walked into this place, he'd always had a few minutes for her. Even when she knew he was busy, he'd joke about needing a break and her smile being a sight for sore eyes.

But now she worked for him. Now she'd be here a handful of days a week as an employee. Who he'd kissed as a favor, and she'd practically climbed him like a tree.

"Gwen?"

Oh geez, that's when she realized she hadn't answered his question. So much for playing it cool. Shaking her head with a laugh, she tried to cover. "It was good. Great." More nervous laughter slipped past her lips as she desperately scrambled for something else to say. "Exhausting. I could probably sleep for a few days, just to catch up from vacation."

Brody seemed to have stopped midmotion, stalling in place. Probably wondering what the hell was wrong with her.

Because seriously, *what the hell was wrong with her*?

Straightening, he cleared his throat and looked out over the bar crowd.

He was avoiding looking at her, and suddenly, she needed to see his face.

Reaching for his arm, she said his name and waited until finally, those sea-green eyes met hers.

Okay…and that…was a mistake.

Because her heart was pounding hard, and her skin was hot. She couldn't quite remember the right way to breathe or anything else, except how it had been when he'd kissed her. When his tongue pushed into her mouth and his hands tightened in her hair and… *Stop, stop, stop!*

"I just want to say thank you for this," she said in a rush, looking at her feet and then the ceiling. She tried his elbow, thinking it might be safe, but wrong again. How had she missed how incredibly hot that bend in his arm was?

Focus! "The job means a lot to me, Brody. So I—I really appreciate it is all."

He let out a breath and nodded. He lifted his hand as though he were going to wrap it around her shoulders the way he always did, but at the last moment, he let it fall back to his side. "Hey, anything for a friend. Besides, you're doing me a favor. I needed the help."

She didn't know whether to believe him, but it didn't really matter, because the man was already walking back toward his office.

"So, that wasn't awkward at all," Jill muttered, reminding Gwen they hadn't been alone.

Eyes wide, she turned back to her. "I'm so sorry. I—"

But Jill was already shaking her head, waving her off. "Don't worry about it. Not like I've never seen it before. I've been working with that guy long enough to see more than my share of these things end." Grabbing her tray, she added, "And don't sweat it. Within a day or two, you guys will be back to normal. He'll make sure of it."

Gwen nodded, wrapping her arms around her waist and wishing that somehow Jill's assurance could make her feel better. But it didn't.

———

Chickenshit that he was, Brody hung out in his office for most of the night. He told the staff that he was catching up on work, and he fully intended to do it. But the fact of the matter was, he hadn't done dick. All he could think about was Gwen. The way she'd wanted him to know that the job was important to her. As if she had to remind him. As if she'd been worried that he wouldn't want to keep her on.

Why? Because after he kissed her, his ego couldn't take the fact that she left?

It rubbed him wrong to know she thought her job might be at risk, but even that was nothing compared to the way his head was working overtime replaying Gwen's statement that she'd been tired. How great the holiday had been, but it had left her exhausted.

Was that because she'd been staying up late with Ted?

A sharp pain in his hand drew his attention back to the now, the present, the broken pen jabbing into his palm and bleeding ink all over his paperwork.

It didn't matter if Gwen was with Ted. No, that wasn't right either. It did matter. It was exactly what they'd been working for, so if it had worked out and she'd gotten what she wanted, he was going to be fucking happy for her. Not some dick who holed up in his office licking the wounds he'd known better than to let himself get.

Gwen was his friend, and that wasn't going to change.

Throwing out the ink-stained papers, he shoved up from his desk and headed into the men's room to see if he could get his hands clean. But the minute he pushed through the door, he was confronted with reason number one for having wanted to stay in his office.

Fucking. Ted. He was washing his hands at the sink before straightening to meet Brody with his smug smile.

"Hey, man, you ready for the big event this weekend?"

It took Brody a moment to remember that Bret and Claudia were getting married in a few days.

"Oh yeah. Looking forward to it."

As if he didn't have enough to feel guilty about. Now he'd forgotten about the wedding. Not like he'd missed it, but he was the *best man*. And best men were supposed to have their heads in the game, be checking in with the groom and doing all the shit that needed to be done to keep the guy from freaking out. They weren't supposed to be completely MIA because some girl had thrown them for a loop.

But Gwen wasn't just some girl.

Brody frowned, checked his watch. It was eleven thirty on a Monday night. What the hell was this guy still doing here?

"Pretty late for you, isn't it?" he asked, hoping Ted would take a look at the time, freak out, and run right home. But he shook his head.

"My company shuts down between Christmas and New Year's. Besides, I'm here for Gwen."

Keep it together, man.

"Gwen? So you're—"

"Killing time until her shift ends."

Right. Because then he'd be walking her home. And God damn, Brody didn't want to think about what would happen after that. Already, he could feel his muscles tensing, the seams on his shirt straining. The pop of one knuckle after another as his hand tightened into a fist and a haze of red covered his eyes.

Ted looked to the side and shrugged. "Well, I'll let you get to it. See you around, man."

Brody should have gone back to his office and stayed there the rest of the night. But damned if he could do it.

He'd known exactly what he was doing, parking himself on the stool closest to the door twenty minutes before Gwen got off. He was watching, like a stalker. Waiting, like the glutton he was, to see her leave. And sure enough, when the time came, Ted was right there by her side. Helping her with her coat and then wrapping his scrawny arm around her shoulders as they walked out together. Just like he was there the next day, dropping her off before her shift started. Nodding at Brody, who, yeah, sure as shit was sitting on the same fucking stool, as the guy pressed a quick kiss against her temple before letting her go with the parting assurance that he'd see her that night.

Hell.

Chapter 11

HAD THEY SPENT THE NIGHT TOGETHER? HAD THEY SLEPT IN the same bed and lazed around through the morning?

There was one thing Brody knew for sure. Whatever had happened with Gwen the night before was none of his business, and his smartest move was to let it go.

Because he had rules about this. He didn't go after unavailable women. Ever.

But smart seemed to have left the building, because then he was chasing after her as she went into the employee lounge. Following her in so he could… What? Now that he was standing in the small locker-lined room with her, those whiskey eyes watching his while her smile faded to a frown, what the hell was he going to say to her?

"Hey, so how's it going?"

Definitely the wrong thing. And now Gwen's frown was more pronounced, and she was shifting uneasily on her feet. Probably wondering again if he was there to fire her.

"It's going good, Brody."

He nodded. "Great. Fantastic. That's what I like to hear, you know, when I check in on all the new employees to make sure that they're not having any problems. Because you're not, right?"

Now he was on his game. These were totally reasonable things to say to someone who recently started working for him. Gwen pinched her lips between her teeth and turned back to her locker to hang up her coat. "No problems at all, Brody. Thanks for asking."

And that was his cue to go. Smile, maybe give her a pat on the back, and let himself out of the room. He could envision himself doing it, practically hear the door closing behind him, but instead, he was actually hearing his own voice, and he was saying the dead last thing he should.

"Hey, you want to stick around for a drink after close?"

And if he'd thought she'd looked uncomfortable before, it was nothing compared to this.

"Think I'll be pretty shot by closing," she answered quietly, not meeting his eyes at all.

He rubbed a hand over his face, wishing he could wipe away the last week. Go back to the way it had been before. Him falling for her, yeah, but not having done anything to ruin a friendship that had become as important to him as any he had.

"Get some rest then. Some other time."

She nodded and, eyes averted, headed back to the floor.

~~~

By Thursday night, Gwen wasn't sure how much more she could take. Everyone at Belfast was great, going out of their way to make her feel welcome. Never prodding about what had happened between her and Brody, even though they all seemed to know it wasn't happening anymore. They were wonderful, and she liked almost everything about the job.

But there was one problem, and it was getting worse every day.

Brody.

She could barely look at him, because every time she did, it was like her brain shorted out, and suddenly, all she could think about was that last kiss. The feel of his hand in her hair and on her leg. The heat of his breath against her neck and the way her body had all but ignited under his touch. How real and right it had felt to be in his arms. And how wrong she'd been about what it meant.

And then she'd be blinking back the tears and "accidentally" dropping her pen under a table or misplacing a check or something to save herself from Brody having to see her break down while she was waiting tables in his bar. But the excuses were running thin.

Brody being Brody, he was completely cool about it. Doing what it seemed everyone and their brother had assured her he would do—bending over backward to make sure they were going to stay friends. The thing was, no matter how hard he tried, it wasn't going to work. She couldn't act normal, and she couldn't go back to the way things had been before. Not the way she had with Ted.

Brody was different.

It didn't make sense. She'd known him for less than a year, but God, it hurt not to step under his arm the minute she saw him. She ached to be able to talk to him. She longed…

She was going to have to find another job.

If she'd been smart, she'd have done it already. But the same screwed-up part of her that had spent twenty years following around one man who didn't love her seemed to have shifted her attention to yet another man who wasn't interested.

What the hell did that say about her?

Nothing she wanted to contemplate right then.

She just wanted to do her job. Make her tips. Burn through the hours, and then hopefully through the rest of winter break. Because once winter break was over and school was back in session, they'd be deep in the heart of flu season, with every kind of disgusting bug a girl could wish for floating around. Stomach flu, strep, full-blown influenza. People would have been on airplanes over break, breathing the germs, passing them around, bringing them home. Students weren't the only ones to get sick. The hand sanitizer would only go so far, and pretty soon, the teachers would be calling in too.

They were going to need substitutes. And every day she could pick up at a school meant a shift she didn't have to take at Belfast.

But as she thought it, a wave of guilt swept over her. Brody hadn't given her this job so she could look for ways to avoid doing it.

"Hey, Gwen, you going on break?" Rob asked from behind the bar as she stowed her tray.

"About to, but I can hold off. What do you need?"

"Can you check the stockroom for me? I think the inventory's off on the Grey Goose. But take your break. There's no rush."

Preferring to skip her break altogether, she headed straight back. Anything to keep her mind busy. Anything to keep it off Brody.

Too bad nothing seemed to work.

She pushed through the door to the stockroom and stopped short as Brody looked up from one of the shelves and stared. He was wearing a gray button-down, rolled at the sleeves, with dark-wash jeans and a black belt. His hair was on the loose, hanging wild around the heavy bones of his face.

Her heart started to hammer, and she could feel the air in the room getting thin, her greater brain function starting to cease.

He looked good. Even better when he turned to her and the corner of that criminally skilled mouth curved up. "Hey, Gwen, you looking for me?"

"No," she answered, barely managing the single word, standing there staring back at him like a fool.

She needed to get out of there. But before she could take a step, Brody had set his tablet on the shelf behind him and crossed his arms.

"Any progress on the Ted front?" His smile was friendly, easygoing, but didn't seem to make it all the way to his eyes. Or maybe that was just her.

Of course he was asking her about Ted. Putting the reminder out there about how everything they'd been doing for the last month was supposed to have been about him.

It might have started that way, but for her, things had changed.

She owed him an explanation. At least partially.

"No. Nothing new there. The truth is, I think you might have been right about us from the start. We wouldn't be right for each other."

He took a step closer, his focus intense.

Probably because this was the first time she'd managed to string more than a handful of words together for him since she'd started. And it was killing her.

"What changed your mind?"

You. Those late nights on the phone, the texts that left

me laughing every day, the weight of your arm around my shoulder, and the smell of your cologne. Your eyes, your hair…your mouth.

She cleared her throat, which had gone uncomfortably tight, and searched the corners of a room that felt like it was closing in around her. "Must have finally realized it wasn't worth wanting a man I had to convince to want me."

Rubbing that big hand of his over his jaw, Brody let out a long breath.

"That's good to hear, Gwen. You can do better." Then raising his palms in offering, he suggested, "How about I take you out to celebrate? It's a slow night. We could take off—"

"Brody, I can't." She couldn't go with him and pretend everything was fine, that she didn't want something she couldn't have. And she couldn't keep doing this either.

"Of course you can. It'll be fun. Couple of friends."

"Friends," she repeated, feeling the word slice through her.

He wasn't going to quit.

"That's the problem, Brody. I know you want to be my friend, but I can't do that."

Something she swore was satisfaction flashed through his eyes, and then he was stepping into her space, anger sharpening his words as he demanded, "Why not? Hell, I thought it had to be about that dickhead Ted. If you were together, it would have made sense. He'd be jealous, and you'd respect his feelings, and what the fuck could I really say about it? But if it's not Ted, then it's got to be that kiss."

Her breath caught, and she stepped back, startled but not scared.

She was *relieved*. Because suddenly, there was nothing easygoing about the man standing in front of her. He wasn't comfortable or relaxed or *unaffected*.

"What happened on Christmas Eve, that kiss, it wasn't about being friends or you doing me a favor," she admitted, her eyes starting to water as the burden of trying to hide her feelings lifted. Now she and Brody were back to where they'd started. They were being honest, and even if these were the last minutes they had together—because there was no way she would be able to face him again after this—what she was giving him in that moment was real.

"Gwen, *I'm sorry*. I know I took it too far. It was a mistake, but what we have is *good*. And that kiss doesn't have to mean anything—"

"It wasn't you who took it too far. *And it meant something to me*." Turning away, she couldn't look at him. Couldn't handle the confusion in his eyes. "I wish it didn't. I wish I could go back to before this stupid charade with Ted and start from scratch. Be your friend without pretending anything else. Because then maybe…" What, maybe she could have gone on being his friend indefinitely? That's what she wanted to say, but even as the words jumbled around in her head, she knew they wouldn't be true. That it would only have been a matter of time before she'd opened her eyes and seen what had been there in front of her face the whole time. Brody. With his wild hair and his big body and his even bigger heart. Brody with his over-the-top compliments and deep, rumbling laugh. His candy-kiss cocktails and mischievous eyes.

Sooner or later, she would've fallen. Because with a man like him, how could she not?

"Gwen," he said, his voice almost pleading.

"I didn't even know he was there." The words were barely a whisper, but she knew he heard them. Shaking her head, she started for the door, needing to get out of there. But before she could get past him, his hand was on her arm, his big body cutting in front of her.

"What?"

She closed her eyes "It wasn't that I got carried away or caught up in the moment. It wasn't that I let things go too far or that you let things go too far and I didn't stop you or whatever you're about to argue next. I don't know when exactly it happened, only that it had already been a while." She drew a steadying breath. "I wasn't waiting for Ted, because I didn't think he was coming at all." For this, she needed to see him, to make sure he understood exactly what she was saying. That *she* was the one who'd made the mistake. "When you looked into my eyes and kissed me, I thought it was real. *I wanted it to be real.*"

Brody stood stock-still in front of her, not even a breath moving through him. It was safe to say he understood.

Which meant now she could run and hide and get on with never showing her face on this side of the river again. Or she could as soon as Brody let her go.

But that wasn't what was happening. In fact, the opposite seemed to be true.

He was pulling her closer, his grip firming where he held her arm. And the way he was looking at her, it couldn't be what she thought. It couldn't be...except that her every sense and nerve seemed to be firing up like she'd started to let herself believe it was.

"Tell me that's what you still want." His voice was low, urgent. Demanding.

She searched his eyes, showing him everything in hers. Trembling, she whispered, "I want you."

He swore, the sound deep and guttural, and in the next second, his mouth met hers in a searing crush. And then he wasn't holding her by her arms. He was holding her entire body, gathering her closer with those powerful arms and lifting her clear off the ground.

"Brody," she gasped against his mouth, her arms twining around his neck. She needed to hold him. Couldn't do it tight enough.

Burying his forehead in her neck, he bunched his hands in her hair and the stretchy fabric of her skirt.

"Gwen, I'm so sorry, baby. I should have told you while we were still standing in the snow. I didn't know he was there either, and the only reason I kissed you was because I couldn't stand not to. And then *he was there* and I felt like I betrayed you in the worst way, because you wanted Ted, and all I wanted was you."

She choked on a sob. *It had been real.* "You did?"

"I should have told you the truth, but I thought if I did, I wouldn't just lose you to the guy who didn't deserve you, I'd lose you as my friend too. And Gwen, I couldn't take both. Except that's what happened anyway, and I've been going out of my mind."

This time, her fingers were in his hair, burrowing deep, closing around the untamed waves and then releasing, only to close again. Pulling his head down to hers so she could take the kiss she was starving for. The one she didn't need to feel like she'd stolen. Brody's arms were around her, supporting her as he bowed her back with his body. His tongue thrust past her lips, and she moaned around the taste of him. Gasped at the sound of his deep, rumbling growl and the feel of it rolling through her. God, she loved that sound.

"I missed you," she whispered, her hand moving over the sides of his face and down his neck. She needed to touch him, feel that this was real.

"Baby, you can't even imagine."

Their eyes held an instant longer, and then whatever restraint had been holding Brody back must have snapped, because he was kissing her again, taking her mouth in a possessive claim that had her clutching at him tighter. He lifted her off the floor, and her legs wrapped around him. Her shoulders met the door, and he rocked into her.

Her eyes shot wide. "*Brody*."

She could feel him against her center, that thick, hard ridge running the length of her sex. It was like lightning shooting through her.

His hold on her thighs tightened, driving her wild.

"*Your hands*," she panted, meeting the motion of his hips with her own.

"Too hard?" he asked, immediately loosening his hold.

She shook her head. "No… So good… *More*."

He swore, rocking into her again, this time gripping in time with the motion, and she started to shake. Her inner muscles clenched and squeezed, and her breath nearly stalled in her chest.

"Like this?" he growled, rocking against that needy spot again and again. Then harder when she nodded, desperately clutching at his shoulders, his neck, those amazing arms and then back to his shoulders.

"Don't stop," she begged a second before he was back at her mouth, filling her with his tongue, his thrusts deep and hard, mirroring his hips.

She couldn't take it, couldn't get enough, couldn't keep going without... "*Brody!*"

Everything inside her seized as her climax slammed through her in hard pulsing waves that went on and on until she was boneless, limp against the door with Brody pressing his forehead to hers. She cupped his face in her palms, smoothing her thumbs over his heavy cheekbones. "I really missed you."

He closed his eyes, nodding once. "You too. More than you can imagine."

Knock, knock, knock...

Eyes blinking wide, Brody spun them around so he was the one with his back against the door that one of his employees was standing outside of. Knocking on.

Gwen could barely stand. Her knees felt like jelly, and the rest of her way too good for what had just happened not to be glaringly obvious.

"What are we going to do?" she hissed, looking around the stockroom for some magical back exit.

Brody grinned. And yeah, like that smile didn't have "guilty" written all over it. God, he was sexy.

"We're going to fix your skirt," he said, eyes hot as he ran his hands over her hips and thighs, returning the garment to order.

He kissed her again, a lingering press of his lips against hers, and she felt the tightening band of his arm around her back as he drew her in as close as possible.

She was smiling by the time he released her, that giddy sense of elation bubbling up in her chest.

This was real.

Eyes still locked with hers, Brody stepped over to the shelves and yelled, "It's open. Come on in."

Eric pushed through the door, tentatively looking into the space Gwen and Brody had been steaming up with their kisses minutes before. She was surprised the single window on the far wall wasn't fogged over. This was so embarrassing. There was no way someone would have knocked and then *waited* if he hadn't known what they were up to.

"And that's where we keep the mixers," Brody stated as if he'd been giving her some kind of grand tour.

Eric already had what he'd come for and was on his way out when Jill walked in.

Her brows shot up as she darted a look back and forth between Brody and Gwen. "Hey, guys," she said, looking more than a little amused. "Gwen, I was going to tell you to go ahead and take your break."

This was the stuff of nightmares. Four days on the job, and already she'd been busted with the boss.

Something told Gwen she'd be hearing about this for a while.

So why couldn't she stop smiling?

Brody was nodding, stepping toward the door. "So, you're good, Gwen?" he asked as if she was supposed to have any idea what he was talking about. "You know, with where everything is in here?"

Ahh. Right.

And now Jill had actually covered her mouth with her hand.

"Yes, we're good," Gwen replied, trying not to sound like some breathy phone-sex operator. "Thanks for helping me get it all figured out."

He was nodding, backing through the door now, a grin spread wide across his face. "Good, well, anything you need, my door's always open." And then as an afterthought, his eyes cut to Jill, who was deep in the study of her thumbnail. "For anyone, anytime."

And yeah, this couldn't happen again. Not at work. Because Brody had no game.

Jill looked up at Brody, an adoring smile on her face. "Umm, there is one thing, Brody." She waved her hand around her neck and chest before offering a small nod in Brody's direction. "You may want to button your shirt. Or not. I mean, whatever."

Chapter 12

SOMEHOW, GWEN HAD MADE IT THROUGH THREE HOURS without her shaking hands causing a tray to spill or her flustered thoughts to get in the way of taking an order right. There'd been enough business to keep her occupied but not so much that she couldn't keep up. Jill had teased her mercilessly, but in the kindest, most enthusiastic way. Same with the guys behind the bar and the other servers.

To his credit, Brody had pretty much left Gwen alone. Or not alone, since he'd been around and watching her most of the night, but he'd given her enough space to be able to do her job. His only direct contact had been catching her as she passed with a drink order to whisper in her ear that she should let Ted know he was off duty for the night.

The minutes and then the hours had ticked by, until finally, Jill tapped Gwen's shoulder and told her to clock out.

Gwen set her drink tray down behind the bar and scanned the crowd. No Brody. That was almost a relief, because she had no idea what she was gonna say. No idea what she would do. More kissing seemed like a good start, but there should probably be some kind of conversation between them first.

Cutting into the ladies' room, Gwen stared at her reflection in the mirror. She looked the same as she had when she had arrived at work, at least on the surface. But her eyes were a little brighter, her cheeks a little pinker, and even all these hours later, she could still feel Brody's kiss on her lips. Okay, she could feel him everywhere.

That was the problem. The reason she was standing in the ladies' room instead of already with Brody.

Yes, they'd kissed, and it had been amazing and wonderful and all the things Gwen had thought she wouldn't be able to have. And as far as relationship clues went, a kiss with the kind of happy ending she'd just had was about as much confirmation as anyone could ask for that things were a go. But no way was she willing to risk another misunderstanding.

So even though all she could think about was flinging herself into Brody's arms, she was going to do the right thing and walk calmly to his office. Knock on his door. And when he let her in, they would talk. And if everything went the way she hoped it would, then and only then would she see about seconds on the kiss that would forever remain *first* in her mind. And only once they'd left Belfast. Because this was a place of business, and as much as she needed to feel Brody's arms around her, and his breath in her hair, and everything else that she was driving herself crazy fantasizing about, it wasn't going to happen again at work. End of story.

When Gwen got to the end of the hall, the door was closed. She reached to knock, then gasped as the door swung open before her knuckles could make contact. Then gasped again as those sea-green eyes raked over her from head to toe, and one powerful arm reached out, circling her waist before hauling her to his body.

"Thank fuck," he growled above her head, holding

her close as he spun her out of the way and closed the door. "I couldn't wait another second."

Her breath left her lungs in a rush. "Neither could I."

And then her fingers were lost in his hair as his mouth came down on hers in a claiming kiss as hard and impatient as the last one. Her shoulders met the door with a *thunk*, and then she had the delicious weight of Brody's big body against her. Pressing her into the solid panels behind her as he kissed her harder. His hands were moving over her hips. Sliding up her ribs and down her thighs. Pulling her closer as he kissed her like he was never going to stop.

Desperate for more, she opened beneath him, moaning around the deep thrust of his tongue and roving touch. They were out of control. Desperate. Both pulling at each other as if they couldn't get enough, as if they weren't in the back office of a bar populated by a couple hundred people.

Wait, she'd had a plan. Hadn't she?

Who needed a plan when she had a kiss like this? One she'd been waiting for that was just for them and left no room for misunderstanding.

And oh God, it was so good.

Another clench of his hands at her thighs, and she was wrapping her legs around him, meeting the rocking of his hips with her own, groaning at the steely friction between her legs and the kiss that was burning out of control.

"Brody," she gasped against his mouth as they moved together. "I was going crazy. I still feel like I'm going crazy."

"Crazy good?" he asked, one hand sliding over her butt in a gripping caress that left her even more breathless. "Because to me, this is crazy good. Anything prior to five minutes ago was crazy bad. Insane bad. Asylum bad."

Right now, definitely crazy good. "Asylum good."

"We should talk." His mouth was working down her jaw to her neck, burning a path of devouring kisses. "I know we should."

Her arms tightened around his neck, her breasts pushing harder into his powerful chest. He was so strong. So broad.

"We are talking." Her legs locked tighter around his back. "We're totally talking."

The room spun, and her shoulders met another wall.

"We are," he agreed, his voice so deep and rumbly that she felt it as much as heard it when he spoke. "Be my date for the wedding."

"Your date?"

His hips rolled again, hitting exactly the right spot. The one that made her whimper and beg for more. "I know we're both in the wedding and already going to be there, but I want to know—I want *everyone* to know—at the end of the night, *you're mine.*"

Her fingers were in his wild mane of hair, tangling in the thick strands she never wanted to let go of. "I'll be your date. And I'm already yours."

Another dizzying spin, and this time, she was sinking into the soft cushions of the couch, Brody's weight pressing down on her from above. Her breath caught, and she blinked up at him. "You feel so good."

Those green eyes held with hers for an instant. "Fuck, we should stop. Tell me to stop."

Stop? Never.

Then he was kissing her again with an urgency and need that matched her own, that drove her wild. She couldn't get enough. Couldn't stop pulling at his hair, his clothes. Begging him for more of what he was already giving her. Moaning when his mouth found her breast through her clothes. Arching beneath him when he pushed her T-shirt up and pulled her bra down. Crying out as his lips closed hot around her nipple and he sucked.

"Brody!" Sensation shot from her breast to low in her belly, lacing tight through her center.

Her hands were all over his back, following the muscles laid in thick slabs as they shifted and rolled with every movement he made.

She'd only touched his body a few times, but even without her hands all over him, it was impossible not to have at least an idea of how incredibly he was built. Especially when the straining seams of every shirt hinted at the playground that lay beneath. She'd thought about it. What he might look like naked. Then she'd told herself it was better not to know. But now, as one muscle flexed against the next, his mouth covering her breast, his hand pushing up her skirt as his knee fit between her legs—she couldn't wait.

"Let me see," she gasped, pulling at the buttons of his shirt. "Please."

Brody pulled back, a furrow between his brows as he searched her eyes. "See what?"

Okay, and there was nothing hotter on the planet than Brody O'Donnel kneeling above her on his enormous leather couch. She swallowed, looking into his eyes. "This," she murmured breathlessly, leaning up toward him so she could push at the bottom of his shirt again. But that change in position shifted her closer to the heavy thigh notched between her legs, putting pressure on the spot that was already making her mindless.

Leave it to Brody not to miss the way her breath sucked in and her eyes lost focus.

One corner of his mouth hitched up as he flexed his thigh against her sex.

Another gasp from her, and a low, rumbling growl sounded from deep in Brody's chest.

"Is that the spot?" he asked, rocking his thigh in to her again and finding the answer in her fractured breath and parted lips. Then he did it again and again, and all she could do was nod and move with him. Lift her arms as he stripped her Belfast T-shirt and bra off the rest of the way.

His cheeks had turned a darker shade of red, and his eyes burned with need as he palmed her breasts and thumbed her nipples. "You're so beautiful. Like a fucking dream. *More*. Because I've been dreaming about you for too long, and even in the best of them, you never look like this."

She wanted to answer him, thank him, or say something in reply. But he was still rocking against that needy spot, and the combination of his rumbling voice with the contact and friction was taking her to a place where coherent speech was beyond her.

And when he reached over his head to grab a handful of the back of his shirt and started pulling it off…it was too much, too good, too everything she'd been missing for too damn long, and her body arched, pulsing against that perfect pressure point, making her gasp and pant as each new mind-blowingly perfect inch of taut, muscly torso was revealed to her.

He must've felt her reaction—seen it in her face or heard it in that desperate cry—because his eyes darkened, and the already-tense muscles across his abdomen flexed harder as her name passed his lips. He whipped the shirt off the rest of the way, and good God, it was enough to set off yet another wave of pleasure. Because *his body*...

He was built broad, with thick slabs of muscles across his shoulders and chest, and bands of defined muscles that tapered toward his waist. His jeans hung low, and she could see that sexy V and the smattering of red-brown hair that started at his chest and narrowed into a line that dipped lower than the denim would let her see.

He was incredible, a work of art. But she only got to admire him for a second before he was covering her with all that bare skin. Giving her the decadent press of his weight on top of her. And letting his urgent words scatter against her neck and jaw.

"Please," she said, panting, her knees shifting restlessly against his hips as she tried to reach the front of his fly with her hands. "Brody, I need you."

Like she'd never needed anything in her life. Like she was going to die if she didn't have him.

He swore against her neck, the sound guttural and raw. There was a beat of stillness between them. The quiet before the storm that signaled a frenzy of critical actions and ragged breaths. Brody pushing her skirt up, then catching her panties on the way down. His thick belt hitting the floor next to his open wallet. She had his jeans undone, the denim bunched around his thighs, as he handled the condom.

She was trembling, her heart racing as need pulsed hot within her.

And then he was there. Braced on one powerful arm above her while he fit himself against her sex. Their eyes met, and he pushed inside.

"Okay, baby?" he asked, searching her eyes as he held himself still.

She nodded, trying to find her breath. It was a fullness like she'd never known, one she wouldn't have thought she could take, but now that she had it, she never wanted to give up.

Sliding her fingers into those wild waves hanging around his face, she promised, "I'm good."

So good. And not just because of the new kinship she shared with all those shirts that were always straining around his bulk. But because he had filled her *everywhere*. Her heart was brimming over with him, he was spilling through her every thought, and his body—

He started to move, and every thrust touched a place so deep inside her that she lost her breath. Every slow, dragging retreat had her on the brink of orgasm. Again.

"Gwen...so good...so tight." Rocking into her, he pressed his brow to hers. "Baby, can you take more?"

Her eyes blinked wide. Because...*what*?

"*Yes*." Wait, had she said that?

Then she wasn't saying anything, because all she could do was moan through the exquisite stretch of Brody giving her all of himself. She'd known he was big, had felt the solid width of him in the storeroom, but this...this was died-and-gone-to-heaven stuff. Porn-star-noises stuff. Praying-he-never-stopped stuff.

But he wasn't even close to stopping. He was just

getting started, his pace picking up as he delved deep
and dragged all that thick length back out.

Every stroke spurred a new cascade of spasms
through her center and took her closer to that point she'd
nearly forgotten existed until the week before. Tension
was gathering fast in her core.

Brody pumped into her harder, deeper.

She couldn't take any… "Oh God, *more*. *Yes*, like
that!"

"Fuck, Gwen," he growled above her, gripping her
hip in his powerful hold and bringing her up to meet his
next thrust, then following her down with his body until
he was buried so deep inside her that his groin met the
spread of her sex in a hard kiss of flesh against needy,
straining flesh.

Her world came apart in wave after wave of aching
pleasure so intense, it seared her from the inside out.
Clutching at his shoulders, she buried her face against
his chest, using his body to mute the sounds she couldn't
stop from coming.

Brody stayed buried deep inside her, rocking slowly
until the waves started to ease and she was able to look
up into his face and see the intensity staring back at her.

"Don't hold back," she whispered, tipping her hips
to meet his.

He reached beneath her, gripping her ass in a way
that made her clench around him again. And then he
wasn't holding back at all, his big body moving hard
and fast and so very deep. The muscles along his jaw,
neck, and shoulders stood out in stark relief, and beads
of sweat were rising on his brow and chest. He was like
nothing she'd ever seen before.

Then, eyes locked with hers, he drove into her one last time and growled a single word. "Mine." And with that final claim, she followed him over the edge again.

―――

"I'm never leaving this office again." Gwen sighed from where he'd laid her back over his desk.

He dropped a kiss against the silky bare thigh draped over his right shoulder and then nibbled the one on his left. "Mmm, so I get to keep you in here. For whenever I want you?"

Yeah, that had way more appeal than it should. But damn, the idea of finding Gwen in here every time he walked through the door, laid out in his open shirt and nothing else… Fuck, he really hadn't thought he could get hard again that fast.

She propped herself up on her elbows behind her, meeting him with the sauciest look he'd ever seen.

"To use as you like?" Her teeth sank into the swell of that sexy lip, and yeah, he was definitely hard. Like ready to drive nails through a board.

Gently easing her legs from his shoulders, he reached over her and, catching the sides of that too-big shirt, used it to pull her up against him. Her arms linked around his neck, and her legs fell around his waist as he kissed her deeply, giving her a taste of herself. She pressed closer, moaning as she met his tongue with the soft stroke of her own.

Jesus, this woman.

He carried her back to the couch like that and then sat in the middle so there was room for her knees on either side.

"The bar's been closed for an hour. Everyone's gone by now." He ran his hands up her thighs and over the round globes of her perfect ass. "I could get us something to eat."

She shook her head, all that honeyed blond spilling around her shoulders. How had he ever thought he'd be able to limit himself to friendship alone with this woman?

"No, I think the CLIF Bar you dug out of the bottom of your gym bag two hours ago is going to get me through."

"Had to keep your energy up," he teased, working the buttons of his shirt closed and then opening them again. Damn, he couldn't stop touching her. "But if I'm serious about getting you to sign on as my personal office sex slave, I should probably stock up on provisions."

"At least a few more condoms," she teased, walking her fingers up his chest. "Though I have to say, a part of me was relieved you didn't have an economy-size box tucked in your desk drawer. Like this was some regular thing."

He didn't think anything could make him stop regretting only packing two rubbers in his wallet. But that did.

"Gwen," he said, bringing her face up to his. Needing her to understand. "Baby, there's never been a box of anything in here. But full disclosure, there probably will be starting tomorrow. I've never needed them. Hell, I've never even been tempted to bring a woman back here before."

Her eyes brightened, even though he could see she was tired. "So I was your first dirty office sexcapade?"

He laughed, loving the smile she was giving him. "Yeah, you were my first."

Another she'd taken.

She sighed and rested her head against his chest. "That's nice."

Not as nice as being able to hold her in his arms. They stayed like that for a while, Brody running his fingers over her hair as softly as he could, feeling her relax against him with every breath. More than anything, he wanted to keep holding her like that. Let her fall asleep in his arms and hold her the whole night through.

But he didn't want her to have a single regret about this night, and something told him if she kept nodding off through the rehearsal tomorrow, she would. So as much as it killed him to do so, he nudged her awake. "Come on, gorgeous. Time for me to take you home."

Chapter 13

BRODY SCOWLED INTO THE MIRROR ABOVE THE SINK AND adjusted his coat, getting ready for the rehearsal. Of all the days to be booked from dawn to dusk, it had to be this one. Gwen was finally, unequivocally his, but had he been able to call her up for breakfast as he had so many other days? No, because today, he'd had the inspector coming through and meetings with vendors he'd set up months ago. By the time he was free, Gwen was already mani-pedi deep in spa activities for the bride's side.

Yeah, he'd see her at the rehearsal soon, but they weren't even riding together, and Bret had asked if he'd be willing to hang out afterward. Only the biggest douche in the world would blow off the guy he'd sworn to be best man for because of a woman. Even if said woman was special and sweet and had been driving him out of his mind for so long, he could almost, *almost* justify doing it.

But damn it, best men didn't leave their grooms hanging the night before they made the biggest commitment of their lives. No matter how bad they wanted to. And worse? Playing extremely unfairly when he'd walked her to her apartment early that morning, Gwen had extracted his oath to behave over the next two days.

In other words, no epic displays of PDA.

That was already driving Brody nuts, and he hadn't even seen her yet. All he could think about was wanting to get his hands on her again. Wanting to taste her and touch her and hold her. He wanted to hear her moan his name and see her eyes when she came apart and figure out every different way he could get her there.

How the hell was he supposed to play it cool when he hadn't seen Gwen in almost twelve hours, and during the last minutes he'd spent with her, she'd been making all those sounds that had nearly pushed him over the edge?

Fuck, those sounds.

He was going to be thinking about them all night. Thinking about the hot rush of her breath against his jaw and the way she pulled at his hair when he bit her neck.

Great, not helping at all. And even better, Bret was downstairs waiting for him, and now he had a semi. This was going to be a long fucking night, and the part where he got to see Gwen? Not nearly long enough.

When they arrived at the church in Evanston, Claudia was already there with her family, chatting with the priest. Brody jogged up with Bret to shake hands, exchange greetings, and assure the mother of the bride that the worst of the weather was behind them and the forecast for the next day couldn't be brighter. That was true. They were looking at highs around forty-five with clear skies and plenty of sun. And with an end-of-December wedding date, you really couldn't ask for more than that. Soon, the cars started pulling into the lot. One bridesmaid here, another groomsman there. The grandparents and Bret's aunt. And then there it was: Ted's sedan with Gwen in the passenger seat.

Brody should've known they'd come together, and the sight of them shouldn't have made the muscles along his back tense and scream, but he hadn't, and it did.

Nothing had happened with Ted. Nothing was *going* to happen either. Gwen had stopped wanting Ted as anything more than the friend he'd always been. It was complicated and a little messy, but when it came to Gwen, the pencil neck was part of the package. So Brody needed to chill the hell out.

Of course, watching the guy hop out of the car and jog around to help Gwen, then keeping his hand at the small of her back as they walked up the shoveled walk wasn't helping. Jesus, he wasn't a jealous guy. Or he hadn't been. But this—Gwen, Ted, the crush too recently killed—was bringing out a side of himself that he didn't normally see. Didn't totally like. But couldn't seem to cool.

Brody met them on the front steps, using everything he had in him not to stare Ted down until the guy tucked tail and ran. Instead, he focused on the woman he'd been waiting to see. "Hey, gorgeous. Ted. You guys get up here okay?"

He asked the question in a general, nonexclusionary way, but he was looking at Gwen as he waited for the answer.

She nodded, a pretty pink pushing into her cheeks.

"I visited with Claudia a couple of months ago, so we knew where we were going." She glanced around, nodding down the street. "It's pretty up here. All these old houses and big trees. Can you imagine it in the fall?"

He could. He could imagine walking the lakefront with her, the falling leaves catching in her hair. Kissing her. And as enlightened a guy as he might be, he was still *a guy*, so he could imagine doing a hell of a lot more than just that.

"We'll make a date up here next year," he suggested, reaching for her so she fit under his arm. Which absolutely wasn't breaking any promises about *behaving*, so he wasn't going to feel guilty. Especially when she snuggled in to him, her arms coming around his waist.

This woman.

Inside the church, Brody started to help Gwen with her coat, but then Ted was right there taking it out of his hands, muttering something about keeping their coats together for when they left later. It didn't matter.

Ted could run off with Gwen's coat, no problem. Because that left Brody alone with her. Or as alone as they could get in the middle of a church filled with all the critical players from the wedding party. So really, it just left them together without Ted for a few minutes, and Brody would take that any day of the week.

Leaning close, he asked, "How'd you sleep?"

<hr />

Gwen could feel the heat of Brody's body from her shoulder all the way down to her heels.

She smiled and turned her head to answer over her shoulder, keeping her voice low. "Not at all. And you?"

"Not a wink. But I've got to tell you, it was the best night I've had in weeks."

She felt the brush of his knuckles low over her spine and bit her lip. "I get that."

She wanted to turn to him, run her hands up the solid expanse of his chest, and sift her fingers through his hair. Tell him that she'd been thinking about him from the minute he dropped her off until her alarm sounded, and it had taken everything she had not to call and beg him to come back.

So much for getting some rest before the big weekend.

"You girls have plans tonight after the dinner?" he asked, playing with the ends of her hair, his touch light and tender.

"Couple of us are going over to this pub with Claudia for a while. I guess it was one of her favorites when she lived up here. Tina and Janna are staying at Claudia's parents' place with her overnight, but Ted is going to drive Nat and me back into the city tonight."

"Sounds like fun. Wish I could join you, but Bret—"

"I know, I know. A best man's work is never done. I'm glad he has you as a friend."

Bret didn't have much family, and from what Claudia had told her, he didn't connect with people that easily. Heck, half his groomsmen were Claudia's friends or family.

She peeked back toward the front of the church where people seemed to be getting organized. The rehearsal was about to start. Still, she had one last thing to say. "I'll miss you tonight."

Brody opened his mouth, but then his eyes shifted past her, and his expression shut down.

"Time to line up, Gwennie." Ted was waiting with his arm out to the side, an open smile on his face. "You ready?"

He was such a good guy. A great guy. A true friend, but right then, he was the last man whose arm she wanted to take for a stroll down the aisle. What she wanted was another few minutes with Brody. Okay, another few minutes in the stockroom with Brody and the door locked and no one coming to interrupt them.

She pushed a smile to her face and stepped over to where everyone was lining up. "You bet."

The rehearsal went like they always do. A few people fumbling around, but for most, this wasn't their first gig. Brody looked like he could have handled it in his sleep. He was quick to help out, and by the time they were through, he was everyone's favorite person. Especially hers.

Dinner was at a little Italian place a few blocks away, and when Gwen arrived, Brody was sitting next to Bret. He shot her an apologetic look when she walked in, his eyes cutting to shriveled Aunt Doris who'd claimed the seat beside him and, despite being nearly ninety-five, wasn't immune to his physical draw.

The frail little thing couldn't seem to stop touching him.

Tim called to Gwen from the other end of the table where he was holding out one of two open chairs. The restaurant was noisy and crowded, but in a way that left them all laughing and having fun, even when they had to squeeze to get everyone seated around the tables that weren't quite big enough for their group.

After a half hour, she discreetly pulled her phone out to text Brody.

Gwen: Should I be jealous?

Brody: Yes. Save me.

Gwen: It's those arms. They're like a magnet... impossible to resist.

Brody: I know about the arms. I'm used to the touchy arm stuff. Even guys feel them up.

So he noticed. She'd wondered about that. But the guys too? Wow.

Brody: It's the leg where I draw the line.

Laughing, she peered over at him, ready to scold him for joking about a little old lady like that. Only then, she saw it. Brody going stiff in his chair. His ruddy complexion turning a deeper shade of beet as he retrieved Aunt Doris's wandering hand from what Gwen could only assume was the vicinity of his lap.

Doris looked delighted.

"Gwennie, you remember when we were kids? Stella Jackson and Mike Rychek's wedding?" Ted asked, leaning his shoulder into hers as he cut into his chicken Florentine.

Dragging her attention from Brody, she turned to Ted. "Sorry?"

"You were the flower girl, and I was the ring bearer."

She laughed. Of course she remembered. It had been one of those days that put the kind of fairy-tale notions in a little girl's head that were nearly impossible to shake out.

He winked. "Remember the dress? It was one of those pint-size replicas of the bride's."

"That dress!" She sighed, leaning back in her chair and pressing a hand to her chest. "I couldn't get enough of that dress. I think I wore that thing until it was disintegrating on my body."

Ted was laughing beside her. "Yeah, you were wearing it when you made me marry you in the backyard by the old oak tree." And then she was laughing hard enough that tears were squeezing out of the sides of her eyes. Because she remembered that screwed-up little scowl on his face as she told him what to do. "You were not happy."

Just then, Brody slid into the chair the wedding coordinator had vacated across the table from them.

"What's so funny?" he asked, his eyes fixed on hers in a way that made her heart catch.

"Just reminiscing with Gwennie about that time we got married," Ted explained, hooking his arm over the back of her chair.

Brody's eyes met with hers, his smile amused. "Married, huh?"

She grinned. "We were six."

Ted shook his head from beside her. "She says that like she thinks it doesn't count or something."

Brody's jaw shifted to one side as he shook his head. "I can imagine you all dressed up—"

"Covered in dirt and grass stains and bossing this poor guy around." Glancing back at Ted, she saw he was still watching her. Still smiling, and her heart warmed. Yeah, he'd been acting a little off, a little jealous about Brody maybe, but that would pass.

This guy was her oldest friend. They'd been through so much together, were so much a part of each other's lives—and for the first time since they were kids, she realized how truly lucky she was that it had never gone beyond that.

Chapter 14

"DOUBLE ESPRESSO PLEASE—NO, MAKE IT A TRIPLE."

Gwen handed her credit card to the clerk and wondered whether anyone would notice if she took a little nap in the limo. She was starting to feel like she couldn't even remember the last time she'd had a full night of sleep. And since she didn't plan on getting much that night either... a few *z*'s en route to the church hardly seemed like much to ask.

She sighed. If only.

After the rehearsal, Brody and Bret had taken off for a quiet last night of bachelorhood, and she'd gone with Claudia and a few friends to the pub. Turned out to be a great place, and more than a few of Claudia's high-school besties had shown up to help her celebrate before the big day. It hadn't been a long night. Gwen had been in bed by twelve, but once again, she'd been lying there, staring at her ceiling and thinking about Brody.

She should have dragged him off to the ladies' room at the restaurant when she'd had the chance. Not very romantic, but she'd been aching to feel his mouth on hers again. She wanted the tightening of his fists at her sides and—

Who was she kidding? She wanted to feel all of him, and she wanted to feel it everywhere, and while something quick would have been a start, she wanted it for a whole night. For longer than that.

She was sugaring up her order when Janna materialized beside her.

"Just a sip. We're T minus sixty, and the last thing we need are a bunch of bridesmaids crossing their legs during the ceremony."

Gwen forced a chuckle, hoping the sound was at least remotely sincere. There was something off about Claudia's maid of honor she couldn't put her finger on. Not that it mattered. By this time tomorrow, Janna would be on her way back up to Wisconsin, and hopefully Gwen wouldn't see her again until they had a baby shower to attend.

Gwen's sip was more like a gulp as she started to head back toward the rest of the girls gathered by the front door. But then Janna was beside her again, reaching out to touch Gwen's arm.

"So, you and Brody?" she asked, and if this was her idea of polite chitchat, she really needed to work on it. Because it felt forced. Uncomfortable.

Still, it was a simple question and one she didn't mind answering. Gwen took another less greedy sip and nodded. "He's a good guy."

"And what about Ted?"

Gwen blinked, not following.

But the way Janna's lips had pressed into a flat line and her eyes were all but shooting daggers said maybe she was. Did this have something to do with Ted and Janna hooking up after the shower?

"Ted and I grew up next door to each other. We've been friends forever, so we're very close. But that's all it is."

If it was possible, Janna looked even more pissed. "Friends. But not *just* friends. At least not always."

"What?" Gwen choked out, unable to believe what she was hearing.

There was no way Ted would have told Janna about their history. He wouldn't tell anyone, least of all some one-night hookup he'd been actively dodging at the pub the night before. Unless...no. He wouldn't.

Her gut churned.

Unless he'd been trying to brush Janna off with some tall tale about there being something between him and Gwen, just so she'd leave him alone.

"Isn't one man enough for you? Or do you really have to keep stringing Ted along too? He's a good guy, Gwen. And if you can't see that, you ought to let him go once and for all."

Looking like she was ready to break down and cry, Janna turned on her heel and stomped back to the bathroom.

Clearly, Gwen had entered some kind of parallel dimension.

She wanted to set Janna straight, but if Ted had gone to the effort to fabricate this story, the friend in her felt like maybe she ought to back him up. And then *set him straight* as soon as humanly possible about using her to handle his hookup problems.

Sixty minutes later, they were at the church. Every hair was in place, every lash thick and long, every bridesmaid buzzing with nervous excitement as they crowded around Claudia for one last hug. She looked beautiful, and the smile on her face was what you wanted to see from every bride on her special day. This woman was about to have her own happily ever after, and she knew it with her whole heart.

One by one, the girls lined up at the entryway, taking the arm of their assigned groomsmen. Gwen hooked her arm through Ted's, because of course they were together again.

"You are in so much trouble, mister," she whispered through a forced smile.

His head snapped around, alarm in his eyes. "What are you talking about?"

Like he didn't know. "Janna?"

Ted blanched, his expression every kind of guilty. In fact, he looked almost sick.

"Relax, Ted. I forgive you," she said, relenting. They'd both made their share of mistakes over the years. "She's a serious nutcase. But if you're going to make up that kind of lie, at least make up the girl you're hung up on too."

Ted ran a hand over his face and shook his head. "Gwen—"

"We're up," she whispered, starting down the aisle, her eyes locked on the far end of the church where Brody stood beside Bret.

She'd seen Brody in a suit, in jeans, in plaid pajama pants, and in Bears jerseys. The man looked good in anything he put on, but this? *This* was something else. Brody looked like the cover model for some Irish formal-wear magazine. The black single-notch tuxedo and crisp white shirt fit him to a T, emphasizing his build in a way that had her fingertips itching to touch—and probably half the women in the church drooling over him.

And when his eyes locked with hers, that low thrum

of anticipation shifted into high gear. Because even from across the church, she could see the way his face changed, and it did something to her. Made her confident, excited.

Somehow, she managed to hold herself back from sprinting the distance and launching herself into his big, strong arms, or maybe that was Ted keeping her in time with the music. Either way, as they neared the end of the aisle, Ted gave her hand a small squeeze and angled his head closer to hers. "When this is over, we need to talk."

She did a little double take, but then it was time for them to part. Ted stepped to the right as she stepped in line to the left. After that, the music changed, and all anyone could look at was the bride.

Brody couldn't take his eyes off Gwen. She was gorgeous, standing there on the other side of the aisle in that scarlet gown, her hair pinned up in a twist. Tears glistened in her eyes as Claudia and Bret exchanged their vows. She was soft and sweet and such a sucker for a good happily ever after. She was his every fantasy. And from the looks she'd been getting throughout the ceremony, maybe not just his. Probably half the guys and at least some of the girls had designs on his woman. Mostly, it didn't bother him. Gwen was breathtaking, and they'd have to be blind not to notice. But there was one set of eyes glued to his girl that was bringing out the chest-thumping caveman in him.

Fucking Ted.

Brody's molars ground down. Sure enough, the guy was still watching her. It was just like he'd told her it would be. As soon as Ted realized he was losing that undivided focus she'd been giving him for God only knows how long, suddenly, he couldn't take his eyes off her. He'd been all about those frequent touches and private whispers—and what the hell had that been when they were walking down the aisle? Something about the look on Gwen's face had put Brody's teeth on edge. Because Ted was making a play all right, but it was too fucking late. Gwen had wised up about him and, more importantly, about what her heart really wanted. Who the right man for her really was. Spoiler: Not Ted.

The pencil neck would get over it. If it had taken this long for Ted to figure out he wanted Gwen, then he didn't really want her at all. And he sure as shit didn't deserve her.

Brody didn't want to think about Ted anymore, not with Gwen standing there looking so beautiful and with only a few mere hours before he could get her alone again. He wanted to hold her while they fell asleep and wake up to her still in his arms.

Next thing, the priest was inviting Bret to kiss his bride. And damn, that first kiss as husband and wife was something else—enough to knock down any thoughts about Ted, that was for sure.

Especially when halfway through the lip-lock, Bret punched his fist overhead as if he'd just brought home the gold…or the girl of his dreams.

Way to go, man.

After the recessional, Brody found his way over to Gwen.

"Some finish," he said, stepping in close behind her where everyone had gathered by the doors leading out of the church.

She turned to him, her smile as wide as he'd ever seen, those whiskey eyes so bright, he was pretty sure they'd be burned into his mind forever.

"That was amazing." She sighed, closing her eyes. "Did you tell Bret to do that?"

Brody laughed. "No way. That was all him. All I said was when he kissed her, he ought to really kiss her. Think about what they'd done, what it meant, how he felt about it…and put it all out there. Hell, nobody likes a limp finish."

Gwen was laughing into her hand, her eyes darting around to see who was close. "A *limp finish*? Only you, Brody."

He leaned closer, resting his hand at the small of her back and giving in to the briefest indulgence of letting his fingers play against the fabric there. "Only me, huh?" he said, conveniently ignoring the context. "Not gonna lie, Gwen. I like the sound of that a lot."

Stepping closer, so there was barely an inch left between them, she bit her lip. "Do you?"

Yeah. And she definitely shouldn't be looking at him like that. "Enough that I may have to put some distance between us."

A stitch pulled between her brows. "What?"

All he wanted to do in that moment was to flatten his hand against her back and bring her flush against his body. Feel the press of her soft curves and sweet lines from his chest down to his knees. But instead, he forced himself to release her and settled for brushing that little furrow with the stroke of his thumb.

"Have you got any idea how badly I want my hands all over you? How hard I'm fighting to keep from sliding my hands into your hair? Fisting the fabric of your gown as I pull it up? Messing up all that perfect makeup with my mouth?"

He groaned, because all those things he was trying so hard not to do were even more tempting now that he'd said them aloud.

And that catch of Gwen's breath, like all of what he'd said had as much appeal to her as it did to him? Not helping the resolve.

"That would probably be bad," she answered a little too breathlessly. "We haven't even had the pictures yet." Her hand moved to his chest, her fingers playing with a button there. "So, if anything *were* to happen, we'd have to be *very* careful."

Brodie's mouth opened, but no sound came out.

She hadn't just… But the way those pretty, even white teeth of hers were sinking into her bottom lip and she was peering up at him through those thick dark lashes… Oh yeah, she totally was. He gulped, feeling the blood rush from his extremities inward, all of it thundering straight to his groin.

Because, *hot*.

He took her hand in his and was backing her through the crowded vestibule when a solid clap on his shoulder had him stopping in his tracks and jerking around to where Sean was grinning at him, an even-more-pregnant Molly giggling by his side.

"Sean, Molly, good to see you," he said stiffly, his mind still stuck on the thought of getting Gwen alone in that little room down the hall. He turned to Gwen, whose cheeks were burning a pretty shade to match her gown, and gave her hand a squeeze. "You guys have met Gwen."

Molly's eyes flashed down to where he was holding Gwen's hand and then back up to his. Leaning in, she mock whispered, "So I'm guessing the train hadn't left the station after all, huh?"

Molly.

Gwen arched a brow at him, but he shook his head and brought her hand to his mouth for a kiss. "Jase and Emily around?" he asked, changing the subject.

Sean rolled his eyes. "Yeah, but don't bother looking for them. You know how they get at weddings."

Brody straightened. *Shit.* He knew exactly how they got at weddings. Which meant it was just as well Sean and Molly had cut them off before they got to that little room, because he was willing to bet it was already occupied.

"How do they get at weddings?" Gwen asked, looking from one to the next of them.

Brody stared from Sean to Molly before looking back to Gwen and laughing. "*Sentimental.*"

Chapter 15

THE WEDDING PICTURES TOOK FOREVER, BUT THE PHOTOGRA-pher had some great ideas, so Gwen couldn't wait to see how the photos turned out. And now that they were through, there were still a couple of hours to kill before the next event. Not wanting to waste a minute, she was practically running to Brody's car when she saw him closing the front passenger-side door.

He turned, his eyes raking over her in one heated pass before his head dropped in what looked like tortured defeat.

"What's going on?" she asked, a sinking feeling in her stomach.

"Aunt Doris needs a ride."

That wasn't a big deal. So Gwen would have to keep her hands to herself for another ten minutes. No problem.

Only it was a problem, because the ride Aunt Doris needed wasn't to the hotel. It was back to her house on the far side of Skokie so she could feed her cat. *And then* a ride back to the hotel.

And not surprisingly, she'd asked Brody to drive her…because he was such a "nice boy."

Gwen couldn't help but laugh. "There's a cost to being everyone's favorite."

Brody pulled her in to his chest for a brief hug, tucking her wrap around her shoulders. "I only want to be yours."

"You already are. And this won't take long," she promised. "We'll still have some time to ourselves back at the hotel."

"Good. Because I've missed you."

She was smiling like a fool when Brody helped her into the car. She was smiling when they pulled into Doris's drive. She was not smiling forty-five minutes later when the old dear finally reemerged and, after locking up the house, returned to the car, full of thanks for accommodating her need to feed her cat who apparently got destructive when dinner wasn't on time.

Brody was as polite as ever, gently extracting Doris's hand from his leg time and again. And by the time they got back to the hotel, Gwen had the feeling if she didn't step in, Doris would be slipping Brody her room key. When all was said and done, it turned out to be a peppermint from her pocket, along with a series of adoring pats and a papery kiss pressed to his ruddy cheek. It was kind of adorable, but this broad had put enough moves on Gwen's man already.

Gwen knew she was being ridiculous. It wasn't like she was going to die if she and Brody didn't get some alone time. It wasn't like the world was ending.

But with how her heart was hammering and the skin across her arms and chest was tingling as if an electric current was running from one end of her body to the other and back again, it felt that way. She barely lasted until the elevator doors closed before flinging herself at Brody. He caught her up against him as if he'd been waiting and then, holding her close, kissed her senseless.

Vaguely, she was aware of the chime of the elevator,

the whirl of her surroundings, and then the quiet snick of the door opening and closing behind her.

"How long do we have?" she panted into the space between them. Brody checked that sexy, oversize beast of a watch, and Gwen was momentarily distracted by how hot it was that he didn't pull out his phone for the time. She was such a goner for this guy.

"Twenty-three minutes."

They couldn't be late. The wedding party and immediate family were meeting for cocktails a half hour before the reception opened to everyone. And missing that would be incredibly insensitive.

"Okay, that gives us ten minutes. No, wait. Fifteen minutes. Then five for me to fix myself back up, and three to get downstairs."

And then her fingers were in his hair, and she was pulling him closer. Returning to the kiss that hadn't been nearly enough. Brody's arms tightened around her back, and again he lifted her feet from the ground, moving her as if she weighed nothing. She'd never been with a guy who was so strong. So incredible.

She thought he would lay her on the bed, but instead, he turned, pushing her back into the wall across from the hall closet. Bracing one hand above her head, he used the other to slide over her rear, pulling her hips in close to his.

Yes, that was the kind of contact she needed. The kind of proximity she was aching for. Only she wanted more. God, she wanted everything. Her hands were all over him, coasting up and down the hard planes of his chest, her fingers sifting in and out of his hair, tracing the solid columns of his neck and the heavy line of his jaw. He was the most beautiful man she'd ever seen. Pure, rugged perfection.

And damn it, they only had—she peeked at the clock—twelve minutes left. She let out a small whimper, and Brody pulled back.

"What is it?"

"Not enough time." When they'd been together at Belfast, Brody had taken hours with her. He'd spoiled her rotten in the span of a single night.

The corner of his mouth hitched up, and she recognized the look in his eyes from that first kiss out in the snow. Pure confidence.

And wow, that look alone was doing things to her body most guys needed everything they had to make happen. If they could at all.

"Oh, baby, we've got plenty of time."

Lowering his head to her ear, he growled, "I'll have time to spare." And then he was kissing her and touching her with those big, capable hands. Telling her all the dirty, delicious things he was going to do to her... in detail.

And before she knew it, he'd reminded her of what was turning out to be a fairly simple rule. Never doubt that this man could do what he said. Because Brody delivered.

⁓

The doors to the private reception were opening as Brody stepped off the elevator. Flutes of champagne were set out on a table, and from the looks of it, most of the wedding party had already arrived.

They'd cut it too close.

He never should have given in, but when Gwen had

turned those soft, sexy eyes on him and murmured "again," there wasn't a chance he'd have been able to tell her no. And while he'd more than managed his part in the allotted time, he should have known Gwen wouldn't be in any shape to sprint into action the second he finished her.

He shouldn't have left her upstairs alone. He should have stayed and helped, since he'd been the one to mess her up the way he did. But what the hell did he know about touching up makeup or smoothing hair? And if he was perfectly honest, the only thing that would have happened if he'd stayed in that room another minute was that Gwen would have been even messier, and neither one of them would have made it down to the reception at all.

But damn, it might have been worth it.

"Save a glass for me!" Gwen ducked through the doors just as they were closing, laughter in her eyes and a smile on her gorgeous face.

Sweeping a couple of flutes from the table, Brody handed her one as she stepped up beside him and Claudia's father began making his toast.

Leaning closer to her ear, Brody whispered, "How the hell did you clean up so quick?"

When he'd left her, her hair had been wild, her eyes hazed with satisfaction, and her lipstick gone. She'd been as beautiful as he'd ever seen her, and not just because she looked that way *because of him*.

"Mad skills," she whispered back. "Though hopefully no one notices my hair is down and half my makeup is gone."

Her hair was a spill of silk down her back, and her face was flawless.

Just then, Ted stepped up to her other side. "Gwennie, you okay? You look a little flushed."

Without missing a beat, Gwen answered, "Just excited is all. Couldn't be better."

The first toast was made, and everyone raised their glasses.

—∿∿—

Hours later, the clock was winding down toward midnight. The food, the wine, the heartfelt and humorous memories shared by friends and family throughout the night…all of it had been perfect. Almost as perfect as the man beside Gwen at the table where he and his best friends had been seated together. Brody had one arm over the back of her chair and was threading the fingers of his free hand through hers as he chuckled at Molly's continued pleas for a hand-knit scarf of her own.

"But see, now we're totally friends, Gwen. And friends can ask their friends to make them things."

Gwen had already decided to start on a blanket for when Baby Wyse was born, but she was beginning to think Molly had earned a scarf of her own simply for how hard and long she'd made Gwen laugh that night.

Still, she wasn't going to make it easy for her. "Really? Oooh, fun. Okay, let me think about what I want you to make me."

Molly tried to sit up, but with her feet in Sean's lap and her belly in the way, that shocked forward motion stalled at the jut of her chin. "What?"

"Yes! How about you make me one of those precious little needlepoint pillows that says 'Best Friends

Forever' or something equally meaningful. Up to you. Surprise me."

Molly snorted a laugh and then narrowed her eyes as though she were about to go in for the kill. "How about I make you a perfect, precious little baby to babysit anytime you want?"

The guys were all covering their mouths, laughing, but Gwen knew she'd taken the hit, because already, she was thinking about itty-bitty baby toes and how there wasn't anything better on the planet than new baby smell.

Emily leaned forward on the table, smoothing her already-perfect strawberry-blond hair back with one hand. "I think you got her, Moll."

Molly reached into the top of her dress and pulled her phone out of her bra. A storage tip she'd been delighted to share with the group, along with the information that it was something she'd only recently been able to manage. Benefit of being pregnant or something.

She held it out in front of her, selfie style, and bugged her eyes, not even bothering to smile for the snap. "Okay, I'm sending this to you now so you'd be able to match my eyes like you did with Brody's scarf."

The photo popped up on Gwen's phone, and it was even worse than she'd imagined.

She turned the screen to Brody and felt him jolt beside her before muttering, "Jesus, Moll."

Meanwhile, Sean had commandeered his wife's phone to send the picture to himself and then take his own bugged-out, slack-jawed selfie. And then it was on. Everyone trying to outdo the others. Turned out Emily, of runway perfection, scored the win.

When everyone finally caught their breath, Brody leaned close to her ear. "It's almost midnight. What do you say to another dance?"

"Perfect."

They were halfway to the dance floor when she realized she and Emily must have switched phones.

"I'll take it back to her," Brody said, dropping a quick kiss at her temple. "Meet you at the bar."

She nodded and walked over, asking the bartender for a water while she waited.

"There's my girl!"

Gwen turned around, surprised to find Ted beside her. "You startled me."

He shoved a hand through his damp hair and nodded to the bartender behind her. He'd lost the tuxedo jacket, and his sleeves were rolled up with his shirt collar open. And when he reached past her for what she was guessing was a Jack and Coke, he swayed before righting himself.

He tipped the glass back, downing half the drink in one swallow. She could feel her smile falter. "You okay, Ted?"

"Hot in here," he said with a laugh, looking away. "They've got the balcony opened up though. You want to head out with me? Cool off some. Talk a little?"

"It's almost midnight. Shouldn't you be finding some pretty girl to kiss when the clock strikes twelve?"

Ted stepped closer. "What if I've already found a pretty girl? The prettiest girl here."

Gwen looked up at him, praying she wasn't reading this right. But the look in his eyes said she was. "Ted, don't."

"Why not? Because of Brody?" he sneered, his good humor gone in a blink. "You've been with that guy for what, *a minute*? And I'm pretty sure half of that time, you were broken up."

She shook her head. "It wasn't the way you think, Ted. He's a really good guy. And I like him a lot. Maybe more than I've liked anyone before."

Ted's shoulders slumped, and he started shaking his head. "Gwennie, please come with me. We need to talk."

They did need to, but not until he'd sobered up. Not tonight. "How about we get together for lunch on Monday? We can talk then."

Maybe it was time to tell Ted the truth about the feelings she'd had for him over the years. Why things were different now. Why when he got a little drunk or lonely or just plain sentimental, he shouldn't think about her anymore.

"No." He looked over her shoulder and swallowed before meeting her eyes again. He looked desperate. "Monday's too late. Gwen, this is important. This is about *you and me*. It's about twenty-six years of *us*. It's about more than a couple weeks with some guy you're not even going remember next year."

She started backing away from him. "You're not yourself tonight, Ted. Why don't you put the drink down and go back to your room?"

Giving her that crooked smile that used to set butter-flies loose in her belly, he said, "Come with me, and I will."

"Excuse me?"

Not a chance.

"You remember what it's like with us. What it's *always* been like." He bit his lip. "I can see it in your eyes. You're thinking about it."

"No." She took another step back but came up short, bumping into a solid wall of Brody.

His arm wrapped in a possessive hold around her waist. "Everything okay, Gwen?"

"He's drunk again," she said, worried about what Brody might have heard. Not because it was true, but because she knew hearing it would upset him almost as much as it upset her.

"Doesn't make it any less true," Ted countered, stumbling to the side. Then getting bolder, he stepped toward them.

She heard or maybe felt the low rumble coming up from Brody's chest as he pulled her further into his hold. "Watch it, man. You're getting a little close."

Ted blanched, but Gwen could see in his eyes he wasn't giving up.

"She tell you about us?" Ted demanded, looking back and forth between them as if he wasn't sure who he was angrier at.

"Ted, stop," Gwen pleaded, painfully aware of the eyes that were already on them. Ted was making a scene.

"Some," Brody acknowledged with barely a shrug, turning with Gwen to walk away. "But I guess I was more interested in where we were going than where you two had been. Something you ought to give some thought to."

She closed her eyes, letting Brody guide her, praying that Ted would let it drop. But that was too much to hope for.

"You don't care where we've been, huh?" Ted taunted, yelling over the DJ who'd started counting down to midnight. "You don't care that I had her first…that I had *all* her firsts! She gave them to me. One after another."

Brody froze beside her, and her heart sank.

Slowly, he turned to her. She thought she would see shock in his eyes. Hurt or accusation, maybe. But what she saw was apology.

Wrapping his hand around the back of her neck, he shook his head. "Baby, I'm so fucking sorry this happened tonight."

"Three…two…one…" The DJ bellowed, "Happy New Year," and Brody pulled her into a kiss so tender and sweet that it nearly erased the last fifteen minutes. And when they broke away, with eyes only for each other, he smiled down at her. "That's how we're starting off the new year."

Chapter 16

GWEN CAME TO SLOWLY. HER BODY WAS WARM, HER CON-
sciousness caught somewhere between dreamland and
reality. Still drifting, she shifted against the sheets,
only to be reminded she wasn't alone when the arm she
hadn't realized was around her waist tightened, pulling
her back into Brody's warm embrace. A low, satisfied
rumble sounded from deep in his chest as one soft kiss
touched her shoulder and then another.

She smiled, but her contentment was short-lived as
the events of the night before bombarded her.

"Don't think about it," Brody murmured against her
neck.

"Mind reader now?"

"Don't have to be when you go from all lax and
cuddly in my arms to stiff inside a heartbeat."

As if by unspoken mutual agreement, they hadn't
discussed what happened with Ted the night before.
Brody had given her the perfect start to the new year
with that kiss, and she'd taken hold of it with both hands.

They'd ridden up in the elevator together with their
backs to the wall, their fingers caught together in a
lazy hold they'd maintained until they were back in the
room. They'd showered together, Brody washing her
hair and body with such tender care that she'd felt a
little guilty when it was her turn and things had taken
a turn for the dirty. She'd laughed when Brody opened

his overnight bag and dumped out what had to be thirty condoms and a couple of sports drinks. And hours later, when she lay with her head on his shoulder, their legs tangled together, and Brody's hand coasting softly over her back, she found sleep beneath a blanket of peace and contentment so right, she wondered how she'd ever managed a night without it.

But she couldn't forget about what had happened any longer.

"Does it bother you? What he said?" she asked quietly, listening to Brody's slow, even breaths.

"Yes." Another kiss at her shoulder, and then he was rolling her to her back so she was looking up at him. "He hurt you, and…fuck, it made me want to hurt him for it."

"I'm glad you didn't."

He nodded. "I don't lose control like that, Gwen. I'm a big guy, and I understand the responsibility that goes along with that. But every now and then, someone makes it hard to remember. And hell, last night… I know how you felt about him. And that giving those firsts to him meant something to you. It pisses me off to know that you trusted him with those gifts—memories that should be special—and he didn't respect them or you."

Her heart hurt just thinking about the way Ted had thrown her secrets out there for everyone to hear.

"I don't understand what happened. I know he was drunk, but I've known him his whole life, Brody. I've seen him drunk before. I've seen him mad. I've seen him hurt and scared. I've seen all the different ways that Ted can be, and I've never seen him behave like that before this last month." She'd never seen him try to hurt her. "He's my best friend."

"Gwen, I know you think this guy walks on water. But—" Whatever he'd been about to say, Brody stopped. After another breath, he shook his head and offered her a sympathetic smile. "Maybe it's not you. Maybe there's something going on at work or home, and that coupled with not getting what he wanted from you pushed him to a place he wouldn't normally go." He stroked the hair from her face and so very gently tucked it behind her ear. "It doesn't make it okay. It doesn't make it any easier."

"Maybe." But she knew it wasn't either of the things Brody suggested. If there was something wrong at home, she'd probably know about it before Ted did. His mother would call her so Gwen could break the news to him, or at least make sure she was there when he heard it. And work? He'd spent half the ride up to the rehearsal the other night telling her about the promotion he'd gotten. He loved his job.

She pushed up on her elbows, looking out through the sheers to the late-morning sky beyond. "The thing is, even if there's no other excuse, how am I supposed to handle this with him? I can be mad at him. I can be furious. But no matter how shitty he's been, it's not like I can just write him off. Say 'That's it, we're done.'"

Brody sat up, resting his back against the headboard, and then pulled Gwen into his lap where he started playing with her fingers. "He's family to you. I get it. But, Gwen, being family doesn't mean you have to pretend nothing happened. That's not what forgiveness is. If he's really family, he won't stop being a part of your life if you call him on his bullshit."

"Pretty wise, O'Donnel," she said, relaxing into his hold.

"Yeah," he acknowledged with a cocky smirk. "You gotta be when you run a bar."

It was after five when Brody walked her back up to her apartment. He'd secured a late checkout, and putting the subject of Ted aside, they'd spent the day in bed watching movies, ordering room service, and making no small dent in that stock of condoms.

"I shouldn't be more than an hour at Belfast, faster if I can swing it, and then I'll be back to pick you up," Brody said, sliding a hand around the nape of her neck and drawing her in for a lingering kiss.

He was so good at that.

Leaning against the doorframe, she watched him go. "See you soon."

She stood there a moment after he'd disappeared down the stairs, her gaze shifting toward the next flight. Was Ted up there? Was he all right?

Shaking her head, she walked back into the apartment and closed her eyes. She could wait until tomorrow to find out. Heck, it might not be a bad idea to give it a few days before she faced him. Give him some time to think and her some time to cool down.

Sadie and Gail were out, so Gwen went straight to her room and started emptying her overnight bag, exchanging her clothes from the weekend for clothes for the next day. Panties, socks, pajamas, jeans, and a sweater for the next day, and her skirt and Belfast T-shirt for work the next night.

She had barely stepped out of the shower, her second of the day, when she heard knocking at the front door. Pulling on a robe, she practically skipped down the hall.

"That was fast," she said with a laugh, throwing the

door open. But then she wasn't laughing at all, because it wasn't Brody standing there, fatigue etched through every line in his face. "Ted."

She crossed her arms, frustrated not to have a single day's reprieve, but even as she thought it, she doubted she would have been able to wait if the tables were turned.

He looked like hell, with dark circles beneath his eyes and his skin an off hue.

"How are you feeling?" she asked quietly.

He shook his head, not quite meeting her eyes. "Like an asshole."

"If the shoe fits."

Eye contact.

"I deserve that. I know I do. And I probably don't deserve this—hell, I know I don't—but I'm asking if I can come in anyway."

Letting out a slow breath, she nodded. "Let me get dressed. I'll be right back." She got as far as the hall before she cracked. "Get yourself a glass of water and some ibuprofen from the kitchen. You know where it is."

She threw on a pair of yoga pants, a long-sleeved T-shirt, and an oversize wrap sweater. Then standing in her doorway, she stared down at her phone. She could text Brody, let him know Ted was there. But then he'd probably come straight back, and he didn't need to. This was Ted. *Sober Ted*. Her oldest friend, Ted. And whatever was going on with him, she could handle it on her own.

When she got to the living room, he was standing in front of the windows, peering down at the street. He looked miserable.

"You were lucky to catch me. I'm only here to grab some things before heading over to Brody's for the night."

"I was waiting for you to get home. Been sitting up on the landing so I wouldn't miss it when you came in." Ted turned back to her. "I waited a while after he left so I could talk to you alone."

He'd been waiting out there for her all day? "Ted, what's going on with you?"

"Gwen, you can't know how sorry I am about last night. I was drunk. And I know it's not an excuse and that the last time I was over here apologizing, it was for the same thing, but it won't happen again."

"What I don't understand is why it's happening at all. How could you tell a room full of people about those things? They were private. They were special. And you threw them in my face."

His shoulders came up in a helpless shrug. "I'm losing you. And it's making me nuts."

Losing her? She didn't know where to begin with that. Because it hurt to think of Ted the way Brody had described him. She didn't want to have to ask him why it suddenly mattered now, when for years and years, he could have had her. She didn't want the answer. She just wanted Ted to be her friend.

But he wasn't acting like her friend, and Brody was right. If they were going to get past this, she was going to have to call him on his bullshit.

"Why now, Ted? Why not two months ago, or two years ago?" Why not when he could have had her whole heart, because she'd still been saving it for him.

"Two years ago?" he coughed, as if he couldn't believe her nerve. "You tell me."

She didn't have time for this. "Because of Brody? Give me a break, Ted. I've had boyfriends before."

Whatever indignation he'd mustered drained out of him. He looked defeated. "Not like him. It's different this time. I can see it."

"It *is* different. But what I don't understand is why you're acting like you have something to lose when up until a month ago, you sure didn't. What I don't get is why you suddenly care."

His head snapped up. "*Suddenly*?"

"Yes, suddenly. Why are you saying it like that?" she demanded, at her wit's end.

This wasn't going anywhere. All he was doing was playing games with her.

Throwing her questions back in her face.

Apologizing while acting as though somehow he was the injured party.

Ted shoved his hands through his hair. "You fucking know, Gwen. You've always known."

Only no. She hadn't. It wasn't until he looked up into her eyes with such longing and despair that she finally did know. That she saw what he'd been trying to tell her. That she understood what he was losing.

"No," she whispered, taking a step back. "Ted, that doesn't make any sense. For God's sake, a month and a half ago, you were all over Janna while I was twenty feet away. Single, available, and—dammit, I know you know—watching."

"*Gwen*."

"Or how about last year, when I walked in on Tammy Samson on her knees in front of you *in my bedroom… during my party*?" Her voice was rising, her finger jabbing at the air to punctuate each word.

Ted was still shaking his head, saying her name

again and again. The pleading sound of it more than she could stand.

"What was that all about, Ted?"

"A reaction. It was stupid. I was stupid. But I thought if I pushed…" Blowing out a frustrated breath, he pulled at his hair. "What about *us*, Gwen? What about all the times it was you and me?"

Those times had been few and far between. Always outside her control. And never something that ended in a way suggesting Ted was interested in more.

He reached for her hand, brushing his thumb over her knuckles. "What about your first kiss?"

His. They'd been talking, sitting in the tree house between their two yards, even though they were years too old for it. Ted had asked if she'd ever been kissed, and her heart had skipped a beat. When she told him she hadn't, he asked her what she'd been waiting for. And then she'd asked him to show her how.

"That was just two friends, Ted."

"Yeah, I remember. That's what *you told me*. And so that's what it was."

That's what *she* told *him*? Was that right?

She'd always remembered it another way. That Ted was the one who'd put them back on friendly ground. Was it possible she'd been wrong?

"How about your first time, Gwennie? Down by the lake that summer?"

"I remember," she said uncertainly.

"It was you and me. Everyone else had gone home. We were talking into the night, laughing like we always did. It'd been two years since I kissed you. And I was thinking I couldn't go another minute without doing it again, so I did. And then you were kissing me back, telling me you'd thought about this. That you wanted me. And I was the happiest fucking guy on the planet. Until the next second, when you told me you weren't looking for anything serious. But that I was the only one you trusted to be your first. And that when we were done, it wouldn't change anything."

Her heart had stopped beating, the breath stilled in her lungs. Because no, that's not how it was. That wasn't how it had happened. Sure, she'd tried to make sure she wasn't risking their friendship by making him think she didn't expect—

"I swear to God, Gwennie, I almost got up and left. But then I looked into your eyes, and what I saw there wouldn't let me go. I could see... I could *feel* there was more between us. So I stayed. Because even if you weren't ready to love me, I was the only one you trusted. I was the one you kept giving your firsts to. And I could wait."

He could wait.

He. Could. Wait.

Her heart was breaking for the girl she'd been. She wanted to pound her fist against Ted's chest and scream at him that she was the one who had been waiting all those years. But what good would that do, except to hurt him? Because now, as he stood in front of her, offering her everything her teenage heart had wanted, she realized the woman she was had stopped waiting. Yes, she had been in love with Ted, but she wasn't anymore.

"Ted." She hadn't known he'd been waiting. But now that she thought about it, about the women it almost felt like he'd been dangling in front of her, those times she wondered how he could be so insensitive, so blind...

Maybe what he'd been looking for hadn't been from those women at all. Maybe he'd been trying to force the same reaction from her that she'd been after from him when this whole business with Brody began.

Ted stared at her a moment longer, searching her eyes before his face cleared. A humorous laugh escaped his lips. "After I talked you into moving up to Chicago, found you an apartment in the same building…started every damn day by coming by to see you first. You really didn't know?"

"I'm sorry," she whispered, meaning it with her whole heart.

He let her hand go and took a step back. "So here's the thing, Gwennie. You might not have known then… but you do now. This thing with O'Donnel is new. It's not too late for us."

That was where he was wrong. It was too late. Over the years, she'd never been able to put her feelings for Ted aside completely. Through every relationship, he'd still been this little wish in her heart, keeping her from getting too involved or too invested.

But with Brody, it was different.

Maybe she'd already been letting Ted go, or maybe it was Brody and how being with him felt so *right* in a way it never had with Ted. Whatever it was, something had changed inside her.

"Ted, it kills me to know that you've been hurting. That you've been waiting for something I can't give you."

"You can." He pressed her, a hope-filled smile breaking through. "You love me."

"I do." Tears pricked at her eyes. "But I'm not *in love* with you."

Not anymore.

He cleared his throat and wiped a hand over his face. "Were you ever?"

Yes. For years and years. It was another first she'd given him. But what would knowing that do for him now? Hurt him. Give him false hope. Hold him back when he should be moving on.

"I'm sorry, Ted." She wouldn't do any of those things to him. "No."

For a moment, he just stood there, staring at her. And then slowly, he walked to the door.

"Ted, wait."

He laughed again and gave her the crooked smile that only hurt to see now. "Hell, I've waited this long. What's a little more?"

She'd mostly gotten herself together by the time Brody finished at Belfast, but he knew within the first minute something was wrong.

"Ted again?" he guessed, glaring up at the ceiling as if he was thinking about paying a visit to the man on the other side.

Resting a hand on his chest, Gwen waited until he was looking back at her. "Yes, but not the way you think. We talked. He apologized. And you were right… There were some other things going on with him. Stuff I didn't know about."

"It's still not okay what he did."

"No, it's not." But she certainly understood it better. "He knows that. And now that we've talked, I don't think it'll happen again."

Stroking his thumb over her cheek, he searched her eyes. "You okay, Gwen? Is *he* okay?"

She nodded, once again wowed by the man in front of her. She knew how he felt about Ted, but she could see the concern in his eyes, and it was genuine. He cared about what happened to the guy who pissed him off to no end, because he knew she cared. And there went another little piece of her heart.

"He'll be fine." They all would be. But she imagined it would take some time and space to get there. She and Ted were going to need to reframe their relationship. Establish new boundaries. And let go of old expectations.

"Do you want to talk about it?" he asked.

"Are you okay if I don't? It's just that I feel like it wouldn't be fair to Ted." She knew how it felt to have her secrets exposed to people she hadn't chosen to share them with, and despite everything, she couldn't do that to Ted. What he'd told her was between them. It was private.

Brody pulled her in to his chest and closed his arms around her so she felt safe and sheltered. Protected beyond the physical. "Yeah, gorgeous. I'm okay with it. There's a lot of history between you guys that I'm not a part of. I get it." Resting his chin on the top of her head, he stroked a hand down her back. "But I'm always here if you change your mind."

Chapter 17

ANOTHER NIGHT WITH GWEN IN HIS ARMS, AND BRODY wasn't sure he'd ever be able to go without again. It was too soon to try to talk her into moving in with him. He knew it was. But seeing her toothbrush on his bathroom counter, finding her swimming in his T-shirt and a pair of his socks while she flipped through the paper at the kitchen island, knowing that his sheets smelled like her…it was doing something to him. Something different from what he'd experienced with the women he'd had relationships with in the past.

"Morning, gorgeous," he greeted, detouring past her on his way to the coffee machine so he could touch her hair and maybe see if he could make her blush once or twice.

"Morning, *again*," she replied with a soft laugh, that pretty, pink heat he couldn't get enough of already pushing into her cheeks.

Mmm, what was she thinking about?

"You snuck out of bed without me."

His coffee maker was one of those industrial-grade high-end deals, but he'd shown her how it worked the night before and was glad to see she'd been able to work it this morning. A glance at his watch confirmed, yeah, still morning, but barely.

One honey-blond brow arched in his direction. "I thought you might need your rest."

He would've happily survived without it, but the thought was sweet. Besides, he'd gotten to wake with her in his arms earlier that morning. Not that they'd made it out of bed that time. But what a way to wake up.

"I can't believe you get the actual paper," she commented absently, flipping through the pages.

When his coffee was ready, he settled in behind her, wrapping one arm around her waist while he read a few headlines over her shoulder. "Guess I'm an old-school kind of guy."

"That's not what your coffee maker is saying. It looks like it came off an alien spaceship." She turned her head, peering back at him over her shoulder. "But now that I think about it, you really do use your phone less than almost anyone else I know. Heck, you don't even have it with you right now."

Why would he need it, when the only person he wanted to talk to was right in front of him?

Those whiskey eyes went wide, and one pretty hand covered her mouth. "Wait, is it because of your fingers? Are they so big it makes it hard to use the apps on the phone?"

There was that too. But come on, he wasn't a gorilla. He could use the damn thing, just not as quickly or as easily as someone with delicate little fingers like she had.

Setting his coffee aside, he held up his hand in front of her and dropped his voice as he whispered in her ear.

"I thought you liked my fingers. In fact I was almost sure of it... But maybe I should check again."

Then he was sliding his hand between her legs, finding his way beneath the hem of that overlong T-shirt so he could touch the silky bare skin of her inner thigh.

"Brody," she sighed as he roamed higher, higher, higher...

"Fuck," he ground out when he discovered she wasn't wearing any panties. It was nothing but soft, tender, bare flesh. "Open for me, gorgeous."

Her breath caught, and then she was stepping her legs further apart, giving him what he asked for. Pressing that perfect ass of hers back into him as he teased his fingers over her folds.

So wet already.

He stroked through her slickness, groaning at the feel as he eased one finger inside her heat. "You like that, baby?"

"Yes," she hissed as he curled the digit forward, stroking over her favorite spot.

Another sweet shudder, and this time when she pushed her ass back, he rocked forward, grinding against her just that much.

He pumped in and out of her and then carefully pressed a second finger in with the first. "Do you like my thick fingers inside you?"

He knew she did, could feel her need and desire spilling over his hand and the clench of her body around him.

"Brody, *please*."

Man, he loved the way she said his name. And when he got that breathy, little *please* tagged on the end, it was nearly enough to push him over the edge.

He wanted to fill her with his body. Tell her to put her hands on the counter and brace as he took her hard and deep. But the condoms were upstairs, so he'd enjoy giving her what he had. Slowly, he wedged another finger inside. Damn, it was so snug, but he knew she liked it, because she was moaning and gasping. Her hips bucked against the heel of his hand as he stroked in and out, again and again. Twisting and spreading, curving and stroking, he played with her until her knees buckled and, shuddering, she cried out his name.

Brody took her in his arms and, kissing her hard, cut through the first floor and took the stairs up two at a time. He needed her in his bed.

Hell, he needed her like he'd never needed anyone before.

When he finally made it to his room, he laid her against the sheets, shucking his clothes and grabbing a rubber while she tossed his T-shirt aside. Then she was inching back, opening her legs for him as he crawled over her. Peering up at him with those gorgeous eyes as he took her body like she'd taken his heart.

There was something primitive and powerful boiling up inside him. Something that hadn't been there before. Something he didn't want to fight.

"Never want to let you go," he growled, rocking inside her, buried as deep as he could get.

It was too soon for promises. His. Hers. But with that warm whiskey gaze still tangled up with his, promises were all he could think about.

Gwen had known she was going to have to return to the scene of the crime eventually. It was either that or find a new job and a new watering hole and a new place to meet up with her boyfriend. Belfast had turned out to be something of a one-stop shop for all things vital in her life. So yes, she'd been prepared to go back. But apparently, it had been in a deep-denial way, because when she actually found herself standing on the sidewalk that first Tuesday after the new year…*no freaking way* was she ready to face her coworkers after getting busted making out with the boss the last time she was there. Making out with her boss and then disappearing into his office until after the bar closed.

It was move-to-Canada time.

"Oh no you don't," Jill sang in her ear, coming up behind her and all but shoving her through the door.

"Jill," she squeaked, laughing and burning with shame all at once.

When the other woman released her and walked past, Gwen gawked. "What were you doing out there in your T-shirt…in January?"

Jill shrugged. "You were standing out there for ten minutes, Gwen. Ready to bolt. Figured my best chance was to go around from the alley and sneak up behind you. Get you inside quick, so I didn't end up having to train a *new* new girl."

"Well, thanks for that," Gwen said, meaning it more than Jill could appreciate.

"Go put your stuff away, and get back here. I can only be cool for so long before I die of lack of details, and Brody says you're the type to kiss and tell."

Gwen coughed out a laugh, her eyes going wide. "I am not!"

Tying her apron around her waist, Jill shrugged. "We'll see."

Turned out, she totally *was* the type to kiss and tell. All it took was three and a half hours of Jill shadowing her, making one outlandish guess after another, each more obscene than the last, until the actual events

from the previous week seemed so bland by comparison that Gwen cracked and gave up the first detail.
And then the next, because Jill's excitement was over
the top, and the truth was, Gwen was dying to talk at
least a little bit about the guy who'd turned her world
upside down.

After that, it wasn't so much that she was telling
Jill…and Maria and Zari, but that they'd gotten so good
at reading the color of her blushes, they were nailing
down details she never would have given up. But as if it
wasn't bad enough getting busted making out with her
boss, she had to go and get busted by her boss dishing
details about it. Though based on the way his arm had
circled her waist and he'd pulled her in to whisper a few
of his favorite highlights in her ear, she was guessing he
hadn't minded too much.

The only problem was those highlights had made
her favorites list too, and now all she could think about
was Brody and how hot it had been, watching him
prowl toward her as he whipped off his shirt. Or how
he'd just picked her up and moved her any which way
he wanted when they were in bed. Or what it had been
like when he'd skipped a day of shaving and then given
her the biggest, longest, deepest kiss of her life…for
almost an hour. These were NSFW thoughts. Not even
a little bit safe.

And worse yet, she seemed to have developed a sixth
sense about when he entered her proximity. It was like
a low charge, this subtle pull and aching awareness that
had her peeking over her shoulder as she was just then.

Sure enough, Brody was checking in with Rob. Or at
least she figured that's what he was going for. But those

sea-green eyes were focused on her, and the bartender must have realized it too, because he laughed and turned away to help a customer. And then Jill was at her ear, amusement in her voice as she nudged. "Pretty sure it's time for your break."

Gwen nodded, glancing at the time.

That would be good. Maybe she'd step outside and try to cool off. Except Brody was headed her way.

The butterflies were getting aggressive.

"Break time, gorgeous?" he asked, coming up beside her as she headed down the back hall. His hand was low on her hip, his arm warming the skin across her back.

The employee area was straight ahead, but Brody stopped to turn at his office door on her right.

"Wait," she said, her feet digging in, suddenly feeling a dozen sets of eyes burning into her back. "Everyone's going to know what we're doing if we walk in there."

Brody hummed, crossing his arms and turning to face her.

"What exactly do you think we're going to be doing in there?" he asked, coming a step closer so he was looking down into her face and she could feel the heat of his big body and the pull between them that had become almost unbearable to resist.

"You know exactly what I think we're going to be doing in there."

The corner of his mouth hitched higher. "Do I?"

She blinked, her mouth dropping open. But before she had a chance to reply, Brody had swooped down and caught her mouth with his. The kiss was brief, posses-sive, and sweet—and over as quickly as it had begun. She started to turn back to check and see who'd been watching, but Brody's hand was firm at the base of her spine, urging her forward with him.

"They already know. They're delighted. And they're going to see me kiss you like that about a dozen more times tonight alone. So how about we head back into my office? Because if we don't, I'm thinking they're going to see a hell of a lot more than that little kiss."

"Bossy," she groused under her breath, but there was nothing convincing about it.

Brody grinned, leaning closer to her ear. "Good thing you like it."

He held the door open and then closed it behind them. The sound of the latch engaging sent a sharp stab of anticipation through her.

Brody stepped toward her, closing the distance between them.

She wanted his kiss. Needed it.

Her hand came up between their mouths.

"Gwen?" he mumbled from behind the press of her fingers.

"Brody, we need to come up with some rules."

Taking her hand in his, he kissed it and then pulled her toward the couch. "What kind of rules?"

Dropping into the corner, he tugged her down onto his lap and adjusted her so she was exactly the way he wanted her.

God, that drove her wild. "The kind about work."

"There are lots of rules about work already. I'm pretty sure we've got more than enough."

"I'm talking about the kind where we *don't mess around* at work."

He scowled, and she laughed, shaking her head. "Don't

look at me like I just told you we're never going to do it again. All I'm suggesting is that maybe we hold off until after hours. You know, so your employees aren't afraid to knock on your office door if they need something."

His hand was already on her knee and coasting toward the hem of her skirt. "They text me."

"Brody, we could talk. Save the rest for tonight."

"We could," he agreed. "Did I tell you I'm going to be up in Wisconsin for a couple of days next week? I could tell you about the meetings I've got scheduled."

Then those thick, long fingers were teasing beneath the edge of her skirt, smoothing over the bare skin of her inner thigh without pushing any higher. Her pulse skipped, and her body started heating from within.

What had he been saying?

"If you don't want me to do something, gorgeous, all you have to say is stop."

She knew she should tell him to move his hand, that what he was doing was too tempting for her weakening resolve.

His mouth was at her ear, his lips brushing the shell. "By the way, my friends want to grab dinner on Saturday. Come with me."

Her eyes were fixed on his big hand halfway beneath her skirt. He was wearing that sexy oversize watch and the leather ties around the solid width of his wrist. So hot.

He was doing this on purpose. His fingers were big. Really big. Long and thick and, ooh, she loved what he did with them. He knew seeing his hand like that was nearly enough to make her combust.

"What do you say, Gwen? Saturday?"

She swallowed, trying to focus on his words rather than the shift of bone and muscle with each soft stroke of his fingers against her skin.

Dinner…

Saturday…

Another stroke… Had he inched higher, closer?

His friends… His friends. The man had more than he could probably count, but she knew when he said "my friends," he was referring to a specific core group. Molly, the guys from college, and Emily and Sarah.

Another stroke… Mmm, that was definitely higher.

"Yes," she said breathlessly, watching her skirt bunch as it caught on that wide leather band. *So sexy.*

"Yes to Saturday…" he growled, his thick fingers grazing the lacy edge of her panties once before dipping beneath. "Or yes to *this*?"

Her breath caught, and need spilled hot through her center.

"*YES!*"

In the blink of an eye, he had her beneath him, his arm under her hips, holding her up to him as she buried her fingers in his hair and pulled him down to her.

"Just for a minute," she gasped against his lips.

Teasing her open mouth with his, he gripped her hip tighter. "Anything you want, baby."

All of him. Everything.

And then he was kissing her in earnest. No teasing. Nothing held back.

She was desperate, panting, her body burning for him. But it was her heart that was out of control.

"Fuck, baby, I'm going to—"

Beep, beep, beep.

They froze where they were. She with her hand down the back of his jeans, her fingers splayed wide over what was most probably the most perfect male ass she'd ever encountered, and his hooked around the damp panel of the panties he'd just pulled aside.

"You're beeping," Brody stated, looking down at her with a puzzled expression.

Snapping out of her sensual haze, she started pushing and shoving at his immovable mass.

"It's my alarm. My break is over in sixty seconds. *Brody!*"

Climbing off her with a pained groan, he rubbed a hand over his mouth. "Gwen, slow down."

Reaching for her, he pulled her into his lap with her T-shirt only half on.

"I have to get back. My break is going to be over and… Oh my God, Brody, look at me. Can you tell what we were doing in here?"

She'd really wanted to be better than this today.

That sea-green gaze skimmed over her face, lingering at her mouth before moving on and finally settling on her eyes. "No. No way."

Her chin jerked back, and she gaped at him. "You are a *terrible* liar." Only she couldn't stop to tease him about it, because apparently *sexy times* was written all over her face, and she had less than twenty seconds to fix it.

Pulling her T-shirt on the rest of the way, she scrambled out of his lap and then staggered a bit when her knees weren't quite ready to hold her.

Brody was off the couch in flash, one big hand at her waist as he looked down into her eyes.

"You okay, gorgeous?"

She shook her head. "No way. Not even a little."

He laughed and ducked, catching her mouth with his for a kiss it nearly killed her to pull back from. Still, somehow, she managed it. "Break's over."

And then she was adjusting her ponytail and making sure her boobs were back inside her bra.

"You can take a few minutes, Gwen."

He reached for her hand, but she danced out of reach.

"I know you're the boss, and everyone is cool here. But as much as I want to crawl back over you right now, it's one thing to fool around in here when I'm on my break, and it's something else entirely for me to leave them hanging when I'm supposed to be on the floor."

Giving him a meaningful look, she added, "If this is going to work between us, we have to have *some* boundaries for work." And clearly, the no-messing-around plan wasn't going to take.

His brow arched. "*If?*"

"You know what I mean."

Shaking his head, he started following her out the door. "Don't think I do. You should come back and explain it to me. Better yet, show me. I've been wrong about us before. Don't want to chance another misunderstanding."

Gwen laughed and tried to pull away, but Brody caught her by the side of her hip and pulled her around and into his kiss before she had time to react.

When he let her go, setting her back a step, it was with a smile on his face that matched the one in her heart.

"Have a good shift, gorgeous."

Chapter 18

"OKAY, OKAY...SO LET ME GET THIS STRAIGHT," GWEN said, setting her beer on the table beside her mostly finished dinner. "Emily, you and Jase have known each other since high school. Sean and Molly since freshman year of college, and Max and Sarah since your last year of college?"

Emily slid her shoulder against Jase's, giving him a wink that had Sarah letting out a delicate snort. "That look is because they've known each other the longest. Don't mind Em. She just likes to win. A lot."

Emily tucked one shoulder to her chin and fluttered her lashes. "The most. I like to win *the most*." Then after a good laugh, she clarified, "But only about the really important stuff. Like bragging rights."

Gwen grinned, loving how much fun everyone had together, how easily they could all laugh at themselves and with each other. There was no mistaking how tight this group was.

"That's a long time. So when you met, did you just know?"

Now Emily was holding up her hand. "Yes and no. Jase and I had some chemistry, and I absolutely had a killer crush on him in the beginning. But things were complicated with us."

"She hated me," Jase chimed in, popping a chip into his mouth.

Shooting him an adoring look, Emily shrugged. "He deserved it. But eventually, we found our way back to each other."

Molly had an enormous piece of cake she'd brought in a Styrofoam carryout box from another restaurant in front of her. Stabbing up a bite, she pointed it at Emily.

"They're nauseatingly in love. Almost as much as Sarah and Max here."

Sarah clutched her hands in front of her, beaming back at Molly.

"Aww, you sweetie!" Then turning back to Gwen, she added, "Complicated is sort of the requirement around here. Max and I didn't see each other for ten years, and when we met back up"—she leaned in, whispering across the table—"I only wanted him for *one thing*."

Max crossed his arms, that stern look lost on his wife as she blew him a kiss. Then turning back to Gwen, she confided, "I read on the ladies' room wall *he was good at it*."

Straight-faced, Sean deadpanned, "I wrote it. It's true."

More laughter from around the table. This was how it had been all night, everyone joking with everyone else. Brody's friends sharing their stories with her, making her feel welcome. Making her wish she'd known them as long as they'd known each other.

She loved it.

Brody sat back in his chair, "Your turn, Molly. Tell her about you and Sean."

Molly looked as though she wasn't totally comfortable having all the eyes on her, but then she started mushing up a corner of her cake with her fork, an almost shy smile replacing her usually surly expression.

"Ours is the most romantic story of them all," she started.

Sean choked on his beer, earning him a killing look before the hearts were back in Molly's eyes.

"I had it bad for Sean from when I was fifteen. He was my brother's best friend, my roommate, and the dirtiest dog on campus, and I completely loved him, but he wouldn't let himself see me the way I wanted him to until last year when we started watching the knitting channel. He knocked me up, and I let him marry me. But not right away, because of the complicated business Sarah was talking about."

Sarah was wiping a tear from her eye, shaking her head. "I love that story."

Max was muttering about Sean getting his little sister pregnant. Jase was giving his wife a lovestruck smile while she held her hand over her heart as if she'd just heard the greatest love story of all time.

Gwen figured this must be one of those lost-in-translation situations, something you could only fully appreciate if you'd lived through it. Because…knitting?

But when she saw the way Molly reached out to touch her husband's tie, getting a bit of chocolate on it in the process, and their eyes met? Well, Gwen started getting a little choked up too. Because the love in that look alone was overwhelming.

Next thing, Sarah was tapping the table, leaning in toward Gwen.

"Okay, now you. How did you and Brody get together?"

Gwen's cheeks started to burn.

"Us?"

Why had she thought they'd be safe in this? "We've

only really been dating a little while," she hedged, suddenly anxious about being in the spotlight. Especially when their story—the one where she'd been hung up on another man and barely noticed Brody until the fact that she had suddenly, inexplicably fallen in love with the guy all but slapped her in the face.

She stilled.

Because there it was. The unconscious admission of a truth she hadn't been willing to let herself accept until that very minute.

She loved him.

But it was too soon for that, wasn't it? Yes, things felt incredibly right, but she didn't want to risk saying something that would freak him out or—

Brody's arm settled across her shoulders, his hand rubbing her arm.

"So I saw her the first time at a wedding a few years ago," he started, and she rolled her eyes, expecting another one of Brody's freakishly convincing if-I-were-into-you tales. The man could make up the most believable stuff.

"I couldn't stop looking at her. I mean, with the hair spilling down over one shoulder and those *eyes*. I couldn't do anything but stare."

He really was good.

He turned to her, giving her his cockiest grin. "She was wearing this deep-chocolate dress that wrapped across the front and left most of her back bare."

Gwen had stopped breathing, her skin prickling as she turned slowly in her seat.

He wasn't making it up.

This wasn't just some story.

"I finally caught her over by the bar and introduced myself, but then I realized the gorgeous girl who'd blown me away couldn't take her eyes off this pencil-neck chump dancing with some other woman."

There was a round of laughter, table slapping, and cries of protest, but Gwen could only stare.

"I knew it that minute. She was into him, and a little charm and a few well-placed lines weren't going to be enough to get her into me instead."

"Unavailable." Jase sighed, shaking his head.

And Sean added, "Brody's kryptonite."

"You guys know I'm a pretty practical man. As a rule, I don't get caught up in stuff I can't change. But fuck, I was kicking myself after that wedding. I kept thinking about her and wishing I'd tried a little harder to get her attention. Something. Hell, I didn't even know her name. She was just 'Gorgeous' in my head, like some kind of dream girl."

Sarah had both hands flat on the table out in front of her, leaning forward as if she was literally on the edge of her seat. "How did you find her?"

This time, it was Molly who answered.

"She showed up at the bar like a year later, right?"

Brody nodded. "Turns out she was friends with Bret's girlfriend, and they all started coming to Belfast once or twice a week."

Gwen's heart was pounding so hard and loud, she could practically hear her own whisper, "Why didn't you tell me?"

He shrugged, giving her more of that cocky smile of his. "Playing it cool." But she could see in his eyes there was more. *Ted.*

Emily narrowed her eyes. "Wait, so what happened between then and now?"

Gwen looked back at the tenderhearted, romantic beast of a man, waiting to hear how much he'd reveal.

"Complications, Em." Then grinning down at Gwen, he added, "See, baby? We've got just as many complications as all these guys."

Her throat was thick with emotion when she answered, "I guess we do."

"You lonely without your man?" Jill asked a few days later, setting the laptop up to do the schedule.

"He's only going to be gone two days," Gwen scoffed, passing her a glass of iced tea and then wiping up some imaginary spot so her manager wouldn't see what a pathetic liar she was. Because there was nothing *only* about it.

Based on Jill's disbelieving snort, she wasn't fooling anyone.

"You guys going to talk tonight?"

Giving in to a heavy sigh, Gwen crossed her arms on the counter, settling into a deep slump. That was the other thing. After an unfortunate incident involving a guy on a bike and a *Journey to the Center of the Earth*–sized pothole filled with rainwater, her phone was currently sitting in a ziplocked bag of rice in her locker. "I called him from his office line when I got in to let him know about the phone." They'd talked for all of about thirty seconds, because his first meeting was starting, and she didn't want to keep him. "The gist of it was, we'll see each other tomorrow night."

They'd been spending so much time together that she'd barely been back to her apartment in nearly two weeks. So it felt strange, knowing she wasn't going to be seeing him for another day. She wouldn't be sleeping in his bed or spending the next morning with him. And the low rumble of his voice wouldn't be the last thing she heard before she fell asleep. If she slept at all.

It had never been that way for her before. Not with any of her boyfriends. Heck, she'd usually been itching to get back to her own apartment after a date or the rare overnight. More interested in unwinding with her own friends than killing time with whomever she'd been out with.

Even with Ted, it hadn't bothered her to go a few days or even weeks without seeing him. They'd text here or there, and that was plenty.

But with Brody, it was different.

With Brody, it was as if he'd started to feel like *home*.

And with that little ache in her chest, she glanced at the clock behind the bar. Almost four. They'd had a heavy lunch crowd, but now there were only customers at two tables, and she'd checked on them less than five minutes before. This day was never going to end.

The door opened, and she turned, hoping for a party of sixteen to get her through the afternoon.

"Ted?"

He hadn't been in to Belfast since before the wedding, and aside from seeing him in the stairwell the week before, they hadn't crossed paths since New Year's Day. But all it took was one look to know whatever brought him to the bar that afternoon wasn't about them.

"Jesus, Gwen, you haven't been answering your phone."

Ted was crossing the bar toward her, a strained look on his face and an urgency in his step.

"What is it?" she asked, already coming around to meet him, a queasy feeling in her stomach.

"There was an accident at the store. Your dad was on a ladder. Your mom doesn't know what happened except he fell."

Jill had come up beside her, resting a light hand at her arm. "Gwen, I'll get someone to cover you."

Lips numb, throat tight, she croaked, "Is he okay?"

"They think yes," Ted started, and she threw her arms around him, forgetting in that moment that he was anything other than her oldest friend in the world.

His hand pressed into her back, holding her against him. "But, Gwen, his leg's pretty bad. When I talked to your mom twenty minutes ago, he was still in surgery. My parents are with her, but she's freaking out. We've got to go."

Chapter 19

BY THE TIME BRODY CHECKED INTO HIS ROOM, HE WAS BEAT. After some serious juggling and no small amount of running to make it work, he'd managed to get enough done in the first day that he'd be able to head home by two the next day instead of six. He couldn't wait.

Loosening his tie, he toed off his shoes and walked into the bathroom to get the water going for a shower. The room was small, built for an average-sized man, and the fit was going to be tight.

He pulled out his phone, checking again for any texts from Gwen. He'd broken down early that afternoon and ordered a new phone for her. The one she had was old, and no way that thing was going to work right after taking a swim in six inches of gutter water. The new one should have been delivered to the bar before she left for the evening, and then all she had to do was take it to the storefront down the block and they'd transfer her information.

Maybe she'd had something else to do.

No big deal. The way he'd been monopolizing her time, she was probably looking forward to a night off. But, damn, he would have liked to talk to her before knocking off. To have told her about the guys trying to talk him into opening a Belfast in Milwaukee and another in Madison. The contract he'd signed with the microbrewery outside—

His eyes locked on the six voicemails from unknown numbers that had come in during his dinner meeting.

Gwen didn't have her phone.

So if she'd been trying to get in touch with him, she'd have had to use someone else's.

The instant he heard her voice in the first message, he knew something was wrong. By the third message, he was sliding the key cards back to the girl behind the desk. The fourth message almost killed him. She was crying, still on the road home. There were complications with her dad's surgery, and it was still going on. By the last message, Mr. Danes was out of surgery and doing well. Gwen sounded exhausted and relieved, and when she laughed, despite it being the weariest, broken-down laugh he could remember hearing, he felt it straight through the center of his chest.

Christ, it gutted him, knowing he hadn't been there with her. That he hadn't even been there to answer the phone when she called him over and over.

Throwing his bag in the passenger seat, he started the car. It was already ten, and when he called the number she'd left him for her house line, it rang through to voicemail.

"This is Brody O'Donnel for Gwen. Could you ask her to call me? It doesn't matter what time."

If she called back tonight, he'd be on the road. If she called tomorrow, he'd already be there.

It was 7:00 a.m. before Brody was able to wrap his arms around Gwen. He'd gotten in to the hotel around three, managed a few hours of sleep, and been awake by five thirty thinking about her. Hoping she'd gotten some rest. Praying that nothing had happened with her dad overnight.

And when his phone finally rang, he was walking out the door of the bakery on Dobson's Main Street. They stayed on the phone until he pulled into her drive, and then she was coming down the front steps, a cordless phone still in her hand as she walked into his arms and buried her face against his chest.

"I can't believe you're really here," she murmured within his arms.

"I'm so damn sorry I didn't listen to my voicemail earlier. I'm sorry I didn't pick up." He was sorry he hadn't been there for her in any way that mattered during what had sounded like the scariest hours of her life.

She shook her head and peered up him with a watery smile. "Brody, you didn't know. You get half a dozen sales calls a day. More probably."

But he should have thought it through.

Gwen led him into the house, past the living room where her family watched movies and played trivia games at Thanksgiving, the stairwell where she'd carried him with her on the way to her room that same day, and into the kitchen where her mother was sitting at a round table beside Ted.

A guy Brody was trying like hell not to resent for being there for Gwen when he hadn't been. But Christ, it was always Ted.

When he looked up, Ted's expression was every kind of not-happy-to-see-you, man, but he stood anyway, extending his hand. "You finally made it."

Asshole.

Mrs. Danes was coming around the table while Gwen made the introductions. Her mother was friendly and warm, asking him to call her Wendy, thanking him for the coffee cake, for making the drive, for being there for Gwen. She looked rattled, as if she hadn't slept a wink, and he could hardly blame her. If it had been Gwen in the hospital… He couldn't even think about it.

"We're getting organized for the day ahead," Wendy explained, pouring him a cup of coffee as she listed all the different people they needed to meet with at the hospital that morning.

Brody sat beside Gwen, his hand on the back of her chair as she flipped through a stack of paperwork she'd brought home from the hospital the night before.

"Anything I can help you with in there?"

Tired eyes met his, and she gave him a grateful smile. "Maybe. At this point, I'm not even sure what I'm looking at."

"I can help with it." Ted stood up and took his empty mug over to the dishwasher. "We went through all of that stuff when my mom was in the hospital two years ago."

Wendy nodded, quickly getting up and shooing Ted away from the sink. Then giving him one of those what-am-I-going-to-do-with-you maternal looks, she pulled him in for a hug. "Thank you, Ted."

It was clear how deep her affection ran for the guy. He was like a son to her.

If only he could have been like a brother to Gwen. It sure as hell would have been easier to like the guy.

Gwen headed upstairs with her mom to finish getting ready. Which left Ted and Brody staring at each other from across the table in Gwen's parents' sunny kitchen with the pale-yellow wallpaper and garden motif.

"So how long you sticking around?" Ted asked.

"Not sure. As long as Gwen needs me."

"So you're leaving now, then?"

Brody forced a short laugh. This guy wasn't going to get to him. "Good try."

That washed-out stare met him from across the room. "Pretty sure she could have used you yesterday."

Having Ted remind him of his failures wasn't Brody's favorite thing, but he deserved it. Like Ted deserved credit for what he'd done.

"You really came through for her." And even though he didn't want to say it, Brody knew it was true. "You're a good friend."

Ted nodded, his mouth twisting into a frown. "Gwen and I are a lot of things to each other. She calls... I answer. We're always there for each other. That's how it is with us."

Right.

Grabbing his keys, Ted shrugged into his coat. "I'll get the car warmed up. Whenever the girls are ready, tell them to meet me out there. You can follow us to the hospital."

Brody closed his eyes, drawing a deep breath in through his nose. Ted was pushing his buttons, and yeah, not a lot of doubt as to whether he was doing it on purpose. But everyone was tired and a little raw, and just because Ted was using epically bad judgment, that didn't mean Brody was going to make it worse by reacting.

"Everything okay?"

Brody opened his eyes and smiled as Gwen stepped into the room.

Holding out his arm as she stepped in to his side, he dropped a kiss at the top of her head. "It is now, gorgeous."

"My mom's about ready, and then we can go."

He nodded. "Ted's warming up his car to give her a lift. But we can head over now if you like."

Pushing up to her toes, she pressed a kiss beneath his jaw. "Perfect."

Yeah, he thought so too.

The next few days were filled with appointments and errands and calls to medical supply companies to get the house outfitted for Gwen's dad's recovery. The Daneses' house had a guest room on the first floor where they could set her dad up. His recovery was expected to take some time, and even though they were hoping to get him up on crutches as quickly as possible, the stairs would be rough to navigate and a risk he shouldn't be taking.

By Friday, Mr. Danes was in good spirits. They had his pain managed, and his release was scheduled for the next day.

Brody couldn't blame the guy for itching to be ready to go home, but he knew what that was going to mean for Gwen. They'd already talked about it, and instead of driving back with him to Chicago, she would be staying in Dobson to help. It made sense, and Brody wouldn't have asked her to do it any other way…except for one thing. He would have liked to stay and help too. At least for a while. He hadn't been there for her when she needed him the first time, but he could be there for her now.

Yeah, he had his own business to run. But he had people he trusted to do it for him. He could take the time off, and he wanted to.

He'd offered, then offered again last night at the hotel. But Gwen had rested her head against his chest, playing with the buttons of his shirt like she always did, and said no. Things were going to be chaotic when they got her father home. They'd have nurses in and out for the first few days to help Gwen and her mom take care of him, and there wasn't going to be much downtime. What she hadn't said—but he could guess—was that the Daneses didn't know him well enough to feel comfortable with him hanging around the house, getting in the way while he was trying to help out.

He got it. But he didn't like it.

And he liked it even less the next morning when they were standing beside his car in Gwen's parents' driveway and Wendy gently patted his arm, reassuring him that Ted would be there through the end of the weekend to help, so they'd be fine.

Gwen had stepped into his arms, hugging him tight. "Sorry we can't say goodbye in private," she whispered.

"It's okay, gorgeous. Keep your new phone dry, and I'll call you tonight."

She laughed, burrowing closer. "Promise."

And then as if getting into his car to leave wasn't fucking hard enough, he wasn't even out of the driveway before Ted was walking out the front door to come down and wrap his arm around Gwen's shoulder. Fucking standing there with her while Brody drove away.

Chapter 20

"GWENNIE, SO HELP ME GOD, IF YOU AND YOUR MOTHER don't stop fussing, I'm calling the ambulance to take me back to the hospital."

Gwen's hands snapped back from the pillow she'd been fluffing behind her dad, and her mother let go of the throw she'd been adjusting across his good leg. Exchanging guilty looks, they each took a step back from the bed.

It wasn't the first time this had come up. Gwen had been trying not to hover, but this week had done a number on her. Seeing her dad—her hero, the strongest man she'd known growing up—hurt like this was killing her. She'd been more scared the night of the accident than she'd ever been in her whole life. And now all she wanted was to take care of him. Be close to him. Do what little she could to make things better.

Though right now, doing a little less was what the man needed.

"Sorry, Dad."

He waved her closer and pressed a kiss to her head. The scruff from his usually clean-shaven jaw prickled against her forehead. It was so weird, seeing him like this.

"Don't be sorry. But you know, there is one thing you could do for me."

Her mom perked up. "Sweetheart, what do you need? I'll get it. Let Gwen sit with you."

He laughed, wincing a little when he moved wrong.

"Wendy, how about you keep me company, and maybe Gwennie here could run over to Shelby's and grab me a slice of pie for later."

Pie? "What kind do you want? I'll make you one."

Patting her hand, he shook his head. "The kind that comes from the pie case at the coffee shop, Gwen. That kind. And as it happens, I know a guy who's waiting to give you a lift over."

Gwen let out a small laugh. "He's waiting?"

Leave it to her dad to recruit Ted into giving her a break. Any other time in her life, she would have been delighted, but now? It made her nervous. When Ted had driven her from Chicago, they'd spent hours alone together, but with the uncertainty of what had been happening with her dad and the flurry of calls back and forth from her mom and his parents, the last thing either of them had been thinking about was the state of their relationship. And in the days since they'd been there, sure, Ted had been around almost nonstop, but again, it had been about him being almost as much a part of this family as she was.

She'd been so grateful to him. But in addition, she'd been grateful for the reprieve from having to take the next steps in hashing out their relationship. But with an hour ahead of them at the coffee shop where they'd spent their first paychecks together, she feared that reprieve might be at an end.

Still, the last thing her dad needed was to be worrying about what was going on with the two of them—which he would if she started making excuses to avoid spending a few minutes alone with the guy she'd spent half her life making excuses to get closer to. And even if it made her uncomfortable, the least she could give Ted before he headed back to Chicago the next morning was a slice of pie.

She gave her dad a kiss, told her mom to call if she needed anything, and walked the familiar steps from her back door to Ted's.

"So, I guess you're the man assigned to getting me out of my dad's hair, huh?"

"Looks like," he said easily, buttoning his pea coat as they walked to the car. They made small talk on the short drive over to Shelby's, chatting about the usual things they discussed when they were home together. The restaurant out by the highway that had changed hands again, which of their high-school friends they'd seen so far, how weird some of the stuff their parents kept in the fridge was. But there were definite omissions among the usual topics as well. She didn't tease him about whether he was going to hook up with Sally Daniels this trip, and he didn't tease her about marrying him to get his parents off his back about "starting to think about settling down."

They didn't talk about Brody.

And they didn't talk about them. Not at first.

"So, you want pie?" she asked, scooting into her side of the booth. Ted always wanted pie.

"I want a lot of things, Gwennie," he answered, scanning the laminated menu in front of him. "But how about we start with the pie?"

And there it was. The moment she'd been hoping to avoid, when she couldn't pretend they were just two friends out for a bite.

"Ted, don't."

She didn't want to talk about this again. She didn't want to hurt him anymore. But then he was leaning across the booth, reaching for her hand. Laughing when she pulled it away before he could touch her.

"Tell me you never felt anything for me. Look me in the eyes, Gwen. Tell me so I believe it, and I'll drop this altogether."

Their waitress came to the table, her pad out to take their order.

Gwen would have told her they needed a minute, or maybe she would have just asked Ted to drive her back to the house, but he was already ordering. A slice of cherry for him, chocolate banana for her, and apple à la mode to share. Coffee for both of them. Same as always.

When they were alone again, Gwen spoke quietly. "You know I can't. But things change, Ted. People change."

"When did you change?" His eyes were intent, his mouth curved to the slightest degree. Like he thought he had her. "Because I've been thinking about it, and I'm betting it wasn't so long ago."

She looked away. "It doesn't matter."

The when, the how. None of that was important. The only thing that Ted needed to understand was *not now*.

"It matters to me," he said quietly. And then when the silence had stretched so long, she was sure the only word they would have left between them was *goodbye*, he asked, "Did you love me?"

He'd asked her before, and she wished the answer she'd given him had been enough.

Throat tight with emotion, tears pushing at her eyes, she shook her head. "No."

Their waitress was back, and one plate of pie after another was set between them. When she left, Ted straightened in his chair, picked up his fork, and met Gwen's eyes. "I don't believe you. I can't."

By Thursday night, Brody was going nuts. He'd talked to Gwen every day, usually more than once. Sunday night, she'd sounded terrible, but when she'd told him it had been a long day, he'd had to accept it. Or at the very least accept that she didn't want to talk about it. She'd wanted him to make her laugh, and even though she'd sounded like she was ready to cry when they first started talking, by the time they hung up, he'd had the melodic sound of her voice teasing at his ear and tugging at his heart for half an hour.

Tuesday had been better. Her father had had another appointment with the doctor, and the relief in Gwen's voice was undeniable. They talked after she'd had dinner and then again after she'd been up with her dad around two. The second call had been brief, but man, it did something to him to know that she'd wanted to hear his voice before she went back to sleep.

But tonight, she was killing him. He was driving back down in the morning, and all day, she'd been sending him texts with little notes detailing what she missed the most right then. It had started out innocently enough, that first *ping* bringing him a picture of her ear…because she missed resting her head on his chest and hearing his heart beat. *Ping*. A picture of her pretty painted toes…

because she missed how they sat at opposite ends of the couch when they were having coffee and he held her feet in his lap. Sweet stuff. The kind that made his heart ache to be with her.

And then, *ping*, he opened the message with the picture of her mouth. Her lips were glossed and parted, so he could see the hint of her tongue behind her teeth… because she missed when he made her a cocktail and then tasted it from her mouth.

Yeah. That one had caught him by surprise, and he'd liked it so much that it took him nearly fifteen minutes to get his junk under control.

Ping, the shot of her shoulder with all that honeyed blond pulled aside so he could see the strap of her burgundy bra and the warm tones of the skin beneath… because she missed when he *bit her there*.

Fuck.

It had gone downhill from there…shadowy valleys, creamy swells. Dips and curves. Scraps of lace. *Ping, ping, ping*. He hadn't left his office for over an hour… and then she'd really done it.

It was close to midnight when the text with no image at all came through.

Ping.

Just a few words, and he'd practically vaulted his desk to lock his door.

Gwen: I can't send you this one.

Holy hell.

It had taken him seven tries to get the damn call to send, but when it did, she picked up on the first ring.

"Send it," he growled.

Her laughter was soft and warm. Teasing and light.

"Mmm, I really want to," she purred from across so damn many miles, it hurt. "But I can't."

She wanted to play.

Leaning his back against the door, he closed his eyes and listened to the sound of her breathing.

"Why not, baby?"

"Because it's so…*naughty*."

He swallowed hard, his dirty mind sifting through a thousand possibilities in a flash.

"Naughty is my favorite. You should send it."

He could hear the rustling of her shifting around. Lying back in her bed maybe. Across from that Jonas Brothers poster. Her hair a spill of silk over her pillows.

"Where are you, Brody?" she asked quietly. His eyes popped open.

"Why?" Jesus, had his voice cracked, it had gone so low?

Another soft sigh and more quiet rustling. "Because I'm into you. And I want to be able to imagine where you are while I'm talking to you, what you're doing right now."

There was no way this was what he thought it was. There was no way it was going *there*.

"How about this," she purred again. "You tell me… and I'll tell you."

It was totally going there. Oh, *Gwen*.

"Office," he croaked, and then reminding himself he wasn't fifteen fucking years old, he tried again. "I'm in my office, with my back against the door." Because it was the only thing holding him up.

"Mmm…I love your office. I *love* that door."

It had seen some good times between them, that was for sure.

"Are you dressed up or down tonight?"

"Down. Jeans and the black pullover you like. What's in the picture, baby?"

"My fingers," she whispered. "And…"

He groaned. He knew it was part of the game. That little *And* trailing possibilities in its wake.

"Will you touch it, Brody?" The sultry whimper nearly cost him his manhood. "Right there against the door, will you wrap your big hand around yourself and tell me how it feels?"

His palm was already flattened over his fly, pushing against the need straining beneath.

"One condition, baby."

"What?"

"The picture."

Ping.

Twenty minutes later, Brody was panting, sweat dotting his brow. His back was still against the door, but he was sitting on the floor, legs wide, shirt half open.

"Send it, baby."

"*I can't.*" After what they'd just done, he never thought he'd hear Gwen sound shy again, but then he'd gotten her to take that *one last picture* for him. And fuck, he wanted it.

"Send it, or I'm getting in my car and driving down there tonight."

"Are you okay to drive?"

"After what you just put me through, not even close."

Another quiet laugh, this one sweeter, softer. Like

maybe she was close to falling asleep with him in her ear. And it hit him.

Jesus, he loved her.

"I'll see you tomorrow, Brody."

"See you tomorrow, gorgeous."

Ping.

Chapter 21

BRODY PULLED INTO GWEN'S PARENTS' DRIVE FRIDAY AFTER-noon, and like the last time, they were on the phone when he cut the engine. Skipping down the steps to meet him, she threw her arms around his neck, giggling as he caught her with an arm around the waist and swung her in a dizzying circle.

"Missed you, gorgeous," he said, setting her back on her feet and pressing a quick kiss to her lips.

"You too," she answered a little breathlessly, taking his hand as they walked up to the house.

Her mom was waiting by the door, a warm smile on her face, a hug at the ready.

"Brody, how was the drive down?" she asked, fussing over him as she led him back to the kitchen. Gwen followed along, laughing at her mother's inter-est in the traffic on the way down there, whether he'd had anything to eat, if he'd like some water, and about thirty other questions all in the span of about five minutes.

It was as if her mom realized she'd missed something significant the last time he was there and was looking at him, really looking for the first time. And liking what she was seeing too, because her smile just kept getting wider and wider. And like all the girls, Mom couldn't stop touching him.

Gwen and Brody sat at the table, her chair pulled

closer to his and their hands together in his lap as her mom buzzed around the kitchen, chattering away.

"The coffee will take a few minutes. And I know you said you weren't hungry, but Gwennie tells me you have a sweet tooth, and this is my favorite brownie recipe." Pulling the plate from the counter, she set it in front of Brody before patting his arm and then sitting down opposite.

"Thank you, Wendy. These look delicious."

"Dennis is resting, but I'm sure he'll be up soon. He was sorry he didn't get to spend more time with you last week."

"I'm looking forward to getting to know him better." Then taking a bite of one of her brownies, he paused, looked back and forth between Gwen and her mom, and then pressing his free hand against his heart, he rocked back in his chair.

Gwen laughed. "I know, right? She bakes like whoa."

"*Wendy*," he half groaned, shaking his head as if he'd never tasted a brownie before. And then he was praising the richness, the consistency, the quality of chocolate, and so on. It was over the top and pure Brody, but Gwen had seen him be polite, and that's not what this was. One bite, and the guy was legit in love with her mother's baking.

And her mom was eating it up as she hushed him, blushing and then patting his arm again and then his cheek. A minute later, she managed to touch his chest, and a minute after that, his hair.

Gwen shook her head, enjoying the Mom-feeling-up-Brody show immensely.

It was a perfect moment where everything seemed to fit.

The back door opened behind them. For an instant, she forgot her dad was upstairs and turned, expecting him to be walking in after a day at the store.

"Ted!" her mom exclaimed, standing up in a rush. "I didn't think you'd be home again so soon."

Neither had she.

"With all my best girls in Dobson, I couldn't stay away." Pulling her mom into a hug, he met Gwen's eyes over her shoulder before stepping back and giving Brody a nod. "O'Donnel."

"Ted."

There was nothing hostile about their exchange, but the temperature in the room felt as though it had dropped twenty degrees.

Then holding up his phone, Ted started down the hall. "Dennis texted he's awake. I'm gonna pop in and say hi."

Gwen frowned. "He knew you were back?"

Ted shrugged, disappearing around the corner.

She looked to her mother, but it was clear she'd had no idea.

Brody smiled like maybe he should have seen this coming. Or maybe he had.

She should have.

Her mom was waving them out of their seats. "Let's all go."

———✺———

Brody had had a feeling that guy would show up. Hell, it was the weekend, and while it normally wouldn't have been the most opportune time for Brody to get down there, it was the soonest he'd been able to get the management team coordinated so they'd have backup in case anything came up. For Ted, if he didn't want to take any more vacation, the weekend was the obvious choice.

Damn, Brody had been hoping to have at least a little time with Gwen's parents before Ted blew in. At least the chance to shake her dad's hand before the *other man* started making moves. But it didn't take more than one look from her father when they walked in the room to see the first move had already been played. Probably days ago.

Ted was sitting in the chair pulled up beside the bed where Gwen's dad was propped against the headboard, their heads bowed together as if whatever they'd been saying wasn't for public consumption. And then Dennis turned, his expression cool as he looked Brody over.

Definitely a new experience, because with the exception of his own, parents freaking loved him.

But not this guy.

Not when it finally mattered.

"Nice to see you again, sir," Brody offered, stepping past Gwen and her mother, who were both wearing matching looks of surprise. Dennis shook his hand.

There were a few minutes of strained small talk, and then Gwen's dad asked, "Brody, you checked in at the hotel yet?"

"No, sir. I came straight here." No sense in explaining that he hadn't been able to wait another minute to see Gwen. "They've got me down for a late check-in."

He sat a little straighter. Ted looked down at his hands, a smirk playing on his lips.

What the hell was this?

"How about you go get yourself situated? Take a

shower and clean up after the drive. Gwen, maybe you and your mother could help me get cleaned up some before dinner?"

Brody wiped a hand over his mouth and took a step back. It was obvious how uncomfortable Gwen was, and he knew from talking to her earlier that she'd had every intention of going with him to the hotel when he checked in. But her dad was making it clear: If he had a thing to say about it, that wasn't how it would go down.

This was his house. No way would Brody disrespect him in it.

Especially not with the conversation he was hoping to have with the man.

"Absolutely. Good idea."

It was more of the same that night. Subtle snubs. Gwen's dad asking what time Brody had to be heading back to Chicago the next day and then looking none too pleased to hear he was staying until Sunday. Wendy would ask about the bar, and then Dennis would ask Ted if he'd thought any more about the offer from the company one town over, elbowing the guy as he added that he'd have to talk *Gwennie* into moving back too.

So much for his big plans to impress her father. From the look of it, the only thing he could do to impress her father would be to get the hell out of Ted's way.

Not happening.

When the night wrapped up, Gwen walked him out to his car. Stepping into his arms, she shook her head.

"Brody, I'm so sorry."

He brushed a thumb across her cheek. "Don't be. He's feeling protective of you, and he's not really sure about me yet."

She was embarrassed, but she didn't need to be. Brody got the protective thing; he felt the same way about her. Unfortunately, her dad couldn't be more off base. If he had the first clue about the shit Ted had pulled with his daughter, the years of games? Well, Brody had a feeling things would have gone very differently.

"I tried to talk to him. But"—she glanced away—"it must be the medication. He's still taking some painkillers. Or maybe it's being so cooped up like this. He's not used to being the one who needs help. Still, I'm sorry."

Tilting her face back to his, Brody pressed a kiss to her lips.

They were sweet and soft and already opening beneath his when he pulled back. Damn, he wanted more, but if he got it, even a little bit, he'd never be able to make himself leave, and he needed to go. "I'll see you tomorrow, baby."

He waited until Gwen was back in her house before leaving. And when he got to the stop sign at the first corner, he pulled out his phone and dialed. After the second ring, she picked up.

"Hi, Mom, it's me."

~~~

If Brody had hoped the situation with Gwen's dad would improve, he was wrong. Saturday brought more of the same. *And then some* once Ted's parents joined the fun.

The Normandys seemed to love Gwen even more than her parents loved Ted, if that was possible. And under different circumstances, Brody might have liked them a hell of a lot. But as it was…

"You've been dating our Gwennie for less than a month," Mr. Normandy said, handing Wendy a glass of wine as he returned from the kitchen. "And you've broken up for a week already. What's that about?"

Gwen choked on her wine, hacking on the couch beside him. *Not cool.* But not enough to get under his skin either. Nothing could. Not today.

He smoothed his hand over her back until her airway was clear and then met the other man's questioning stare. "A misunderstanding. My fault more than hers. And not exactly a breakup, as we weren't really together in an official capacity yet."

This time, it was Gwen's mom choking on her wine and her dad planting his hands on the arms of his chair as if he were about to launch out of it, cast and surgical pins be damned. "So you were just *casual* at that point."

Brody met her father's death glare with a smile that came from the depths of his heart. "I haven't been casual about your daughter since the first time I saw her. We were *undefined*. I wasn't sure she felt the way I did, and if she didn't, I wasn't willing to risk losing her as my friend. So I wasn't as clear about how I felt or what I wanted as I should have been. It wasn't fair, and it almost cost me my chance with her."

Gwen took his hand. "But we figured it out."

Brody looked around the room, waiting for the next go at him, but it didn't come. And when his eyes landed on Ted, that smug look had been wiped clean off his face. Christ, the guy almost looked pained. Like maybe he felt guilty, except that Ted was too selfish, too self-absorbed for that.

After years of taking Gwen for granted, of *taking*

advantage, the only thing a guy like Ted would be able
to process was that he'd lost something, and he'd sink
to any low to get it back.

Wendy asked Ted's mom if she was going to try out
for the next community theater production, and everyone
followed the change in topic.

Ted wiped a hand over his face and stood, a defeated
slant to his posture that might have stirred some sympathy
from Brody if he'd believed for one second the guy was
sincere. That he'd ever actually been serious about Gwen.

"I'm going to head home," he said, his eyes on Gwen
with an almost pleading look in them before he turned to
everyone else. "See you guys tomorrow."

Ted took off, and the conversation continued until
Gwen's dad announced he was going to call it a night
as well. Using the crutches, he headed toward the guest
room and told everyone else to stay as long as they liked.
But then Ted's dad was stretching his arms wide.

Maybe this was it. His chance to get a few minutes
alone with Gwen. He wanted to pull her into his lap and
hold her for a while, bury his nose in her hair, and twine
their fingers together. Talk without an audience and feel
her relax in his arms instead of sitting there like she was
bracing every time someone opened their mouths.

But then Ted's dad clapped Brody on the shoulder.

"Okay, folks, think it's time we cleared out of here so
Gwen and her mom can get some shut-eye. Brody, you
need a lift back to the hotel?"

Subtle.

"Thank you, Bob, but I've got my car. And I think
I'll hang back." He wasn't going to put any qualifier on
the end, not *if you don't mind* or something along those

lines, because he wasn't asking. Not Ted's dad anyway. Gwen's mom, however, was another story. Turning to her, he said, "It'll only be a few minutes. I promise not to keep Gwen up, but since I'll be leaving tomorrow, I'd like to talk to her for a while."

Gwen didn't wait for her mother to answer, though the smile on her face suggested she wasn't about to protest. Instead, Gwen took his hand and started leading him back to the kitchen.

"Absolutely, Brody. I'll see the rest of you guys tomorrow," Wendy called from over her shoulder as she started up the stairs to her room.

When they were alone in the kitchen, Gwen stepped into his arms, pressing her head against his chest. "I'm sorry. That was…nothing I could imagine happening."

"They aren't used to me." Running his hand over her hair, he breathed her in.

Damn, that was what he needed.

What he'd been waiting for. Just this. The feel of her in his arms, the smell of her hair, and the soft sigh she made when she relaxed against him. He could put up with Ted and the rest of them all day every day, so long as he got a few minutes of this each night.

He could do it forever.

They spent a few more minutes like that, locked in each other's arms, enjoying the quiet and alone between them.

He kissed her at her door, one long, sweet press of his lips to hers before he let her go and told her to lock up behind him.

The temperature had dropped during the evening, and he pushed his hands deep in his pockets. He was halfway to his car when he noticed Ted waiting there.

Chapter 22

"TED. WHY AM I NOT SURPRISED TO SEE YOU OUT HERE?"

Ted pushed off from where he'd been leaning against the car. "Figured you should know I wasn't going anywhere."

Yeah, he was getting that sense. "Sounds like you're trying to tell me something."

Ted nodded. "Let's call it fair warning."

So, they were laying it all out there.

"You want Gwen."

A nod.

It wasn't like Ted had been making any secret of it, but damn.

Brody blew out a frustrated breath, shaking out the fist that was begging to land in this guy's face.

That was the last straw. He'd had a long day of keeping his mouth shut while getting the shaft from the people Gwen loved best, and he'd willingly done it for her.

But this, with Ted? No way. He was done.

"Ted, you need to back off, man. You had your chance, and you blew it. Gwen's with me, but even if she wasn't, you're the dead-last guy she ought to be with."

"*The dead last?*" Ted's brows shot high, and he took a step back with an incredulous laugh. "How do you figure? Because the way I see it, I'm her oldest friend, the guy who knows her better than anyone on the planet. Especially you. I'm the one who's been there for her through everything that's mattered. For our whole lives."

Did he really have to spell it out?

"You guys go way back, sure, and I know when the chips are down, you've been there for each other in ways most people can't even imagine. But her friend?" Brody stepped closer, letting Ted feel the months of pent-up aggression he'd been keeping at bay. "You're lucky I haven't dragged you out into the street and beat the hell out of you for the shit you've pulled with Gwen."

This was the part where Ted was supposed to piss himself and cower. Apologize for being a selfish fuck and then slink back into his house.

Instead, the guy jutted out his chin, looking...*pissed*? "What the hell are you talking about, O'Donnel?"

"I'm talking about all the years and all the chances you've had. I'm talking about how you fucking wasted them. And when she's finally moving on, *now* you want a real shot with her. I fucking told her this would happen."

Ted took a step back, shaking his head like he didn't understand.

"Now?"

The guy couldn't be that stupid. "*She was in love with you.* For years. For her whole damn life, man. She would have given you anything, everything. But all you wanted were those firsts you like to brag about so much, when any one of them could have been first, last, and always."

If Brody had been the one she'd given her firsts to, that's how it would have been.

"Through all those opportunities, Ted, you never wanted her. And *now* that she's found someone else, *now* that she's not hanging on your every word or watching your every move or waiting to see if this would be the night you'd want something more from her—*now* suddenly, you do. *Now* you're standing here, waiting for me by my car like some kind of stalker, laying it on the line so I know what's coming. Fuck that, and fuck you too. I've been telling Gwen she deserved a better man and a better fucking friend since the first day. And guess what? *Now* she's got one."

He waited for the bullshit to come back, the excuses, whatever pussy retort Ted had to offer, but instead, the guy just stood there staring at him, a smacked look on his face.

"She was… Gwen…" He shook his head, turning toward the Daneses' house as if he were about to run up and pound on the door. When he turned back, his eyes were wide with something that looked a whole hell of a lot like hope and—

Jesus, he couldn't even think it. Wanted to reject it. Deny it.

"She *told* you that?" he whispered, reaching for Brody's arm before he seemed to realize what he was doing and stepped back.

There was no right answer. No choice but to tell the truth, so Brody did. Barely. Practically choking out the concession. "Not lately."

"Not since she decided to give things a try with you?"

Give things a try.

That's not what this was with them.

Another look back at the house, and so help him, if

Ted took one step toward her door, Brody was going to tackle him on the front lawn.

"Since she stopped waiting for you to become the guy you're never going to be."

"Yeah." Ted turned to him, his pained smile so completely out of place after what Brody had said, it set his teeth on edge. What the hell was wrong with this guy?

Ted bent at the waist, bracing his hands on his knees. "It's hard to wait so long."

And that's when the ground rocked beneath Brody's feet and all the *know better*, *be better*, *do better* superior bullshit he'd been standing on gave way.

Ted Normandy really was that dumb.

The fucker was in love with her, and he'd had no idea that Gwen had been waiting for *him*.

Brody's heart started to slam, his blood running cold with panic.

"What I told you… It doesn't change anything."

Ted was shaking his head, a stupid smile spreading across his face. "That's where you're wrong, man. It changes *everything*."

No. "She's happy. I'm sorry." And this time when he said it, he truly meant it. Because suddenly, Ted wasn't the selfish prick Brody had thought he was. Suddenly, everything Gwen had said about him all those months ago was right. "We're together, and what we've got is good."

Straightening again, Ted let out a curt laugh. "What you've got isn't even a blip on the radar, O'Donnel."

Brody was going to be sick. He knew he shouldn't ask, but he had to know.

"Have you told her?"

Ted rubbed at the back of his neck, looking out at the street when he answered. "Not yet. But what do you think she's going to do when she finds out I've been in love with her since I was six, that I've been waiting for her since I was sixteen, and now that I know she's been waiting for me, I'd wait for her until I was sixty, if that's what it took?"

What did he think she would do? Christ.

Brody felt like he was dying inside.

Ted had started walking back to his house. When he got to the door, he stopped and looked back, his brows pulled together.

"Look, I know you care about her, man. Gwennie's got a tender heart, and it's going to be hard enough on her when she has to choose. She isn't going to want to hurt you, so just…hell, don't make it worse than it needs to be, okay?"

Standing there on the drive, Brody watched as Ted went inside, closed the door behind him, and turned out the light. Gwen's words from earlier that afternoon echoed through his mind.

Not really a place for you, huh?

～～～

The next morning, Gwen rubbed the sleep from her eyes and threw back the covers. No lazing around or hoping for five more minutes. Brody was going back to Chicago, and after the way her dad had worked him over, she wanted some time with him. And she wanted it *alone*.

It was still early, but she could smell the coffee, and when she got downstairs, her mother was sitting at the kitchen table reading her paper.

"How's Dad?" Gwen asked, pouring a mug for herself.

"Good. He was up earlier, some trouble sleeping, so we watched a movie together. But he fell asleep about half an hour ago. I'm guessing he'll be out for a few hours at least. You could take the car if there's anything you'd like to do."

Gwen nodded and crossed to her mom to give her a squeeze. "Thanks, Mom. If you don't mind, I'll run over to the hotel. Maybe hang out there a while, but I'm sure Brody will stop back with me to say goodbye before he goes."

Her mother nodded, a knowing look in her eyes. "A woman needs a little alone time with her boyfriend once in a while. Or at least some time without Ted doing everything but throwing his body between you guys."

After Ted's behavior the weekend before, her mom had known something was going on, and Gwen had needed someone to talk to. As it turned out, her mother had understood better than Gwen had expected. "I still can't believe that in all this time, I didn't know."

"You've been friends for so long, honey. There are so many layers to your relationship that sometimes I didn't even know, and I've been watching you two together since before you could crawl."

"For years, I thought he was all I wanted. But when I met Brody, everything changed. It's like suddenly, I could see things more clearly and"—she let out a heavy breath and met her mother's compassionate gaze—"what I want now is something else entirely."

"Love is like that, honey."

Ducking her head, Gwen smiled into her coffee and

headed back upstairs for a quick shower before she went to the hotel.

After the shortest shower in history and a blow-dry that was more for show than anything else, she threw a scarf around her neck and pulled a thick knit hat down over her ears to compensate for tempting fate with wet hair in January. Dobson wasn't that big of a town, so getting to the hotel only took about five minutes, another three up to his room, and then she was knocking at Brody's door, butterflies in her belly and that wonderful too-full feeling deep in her chest.

When he opened the door, the sight of him was almost more than she could handle. His hair was falling in damp waves around his bare shoulders, and all he was wearing was a pair of well-worn jeans with the top button undone. Her mouth went dry, her throat tight as she took in the sight of the sexiest man she'd ever seen. And he called *her* gorgeous.

"Gwen, I wasn't expecting you. Everything okay?" he asked, taking a step back into the room so she could come in.

His duffel bag was open on the end of his bed, his clothes and toiletries neatly stacked within. She glanced into the bathroom where he'd been getting ready, and her heart sank at the site of the empty countertop.

"You're so efficient, getting all your stuff packed up like this," she commented, trying not to advertise the fact that he'd be gone in a matter of hours, and it was hitting her hard. "I'd be pushing checkout time before I even thought about packing my stuff."

God, she was going to miss him.

All she wanted to do was throw herself into his arms

and have him hold her. But when she turned, he was already pulling a shirt over his head and then zipping up his bag. "Yeah, I've got to get back earlier than I thought today."

"Wait, what? You're leaving now?" She thought they had at least until after lunch together. He couldn't be going yet.

"It's Belfast. Couple issues came up overnight."

She waited for him to tell her more, but when the details didn't come and Brody continued his last check for stray items around the room, she realized mentally he was already on his way out.

"Well, I hope everything's okay," she offered quietly, wondering why he wasn't looking at her. Or touching her.

Then telling herself not to read too much into it.

Belfast was his baby. And if something was going on, it made sense that he'd be distracted and focused on getting back. But they hadn't even made any plans about when they'd see each other again. She knew he couldn't keep taking off to drive down to see her, but at least they might talk about it.

"Brody, you think we could sit down for a few minutes before you have to go?" she asked, stepping into his space so she could press her forehead into that spot between his shoulders. After a beat, his arms came up and closed around her, holding her tight and close. But all too soon, he'd taken her shoulders in his hands and set her back a step.

"Yeah, we can do that. Why don't we head downstairs to the restaurant? I was going to grab something to eat before I took off anyway. We can do it together."

"Oh, sure. The restaurant sounds good."

They were seated by the windows at a table for two. Brody was distracted, checking his phone and taking care of a few messages while they waited for the waitress to bring their orders.

Gwen understood she couldn't be his priority every minute. She didn't need to be. But there was something else. Something was off between them this morning, and it was making her stomach knot to think it might have something to do with the crappy way her father had treated him.

When he set his phone down, she reached for his hand. "I'm really sorry about this weekend, Brody. I thought we'd be able to have more time together. I thought things would be different with my dad."

Brody was staring at where their hands met. He was always the one trying to maximize the contact between them, looking for a way to hold her closer, tighter. But now, it was like he was only letting her touch him to be polite.

She cleared her throat. "I think my parents are going to need me to stay down here for another few weeks." Please, God, she hoped it wouldn't be longer than that. "I know you've already taken too much time off, but maybe I could come up for an overnight next weekend."

Brody wouldn't meet her eyes as he refilled his coffee from the carafe.

"Probably too early to make plans," he said, shifting back in his seat. "I'm already behind with Belfast. And you don't want to leave your mom overnight when your dad still needs help. How about we see how it goes?"

Gwen stared at him a moment longer, the tension that

had been building since she'd arrived to find him mostly packed now almost more than she could bear. Because this wasn't right. This wasn't Brody. And even if they hadn't been together all that long, *this* wasn't how things were between them.

She blew out a breath and shook her head. *No.* She was being dramatic, making a big deal about nothing. He didn't know what his schedule was going to look like yet. That's all it was.

She hoped. But when he still wouldn't look at her, she let out a nervous laugh.

"You aren't about to give me the asparagus talk, are you?" She was mostly teasing, but when he didn't answer, the laughter dried up in her throat, and she could barely manage to ask, "*Are you?*"

Brody's jaw tensed, the muscle flexing twice before he met her eyes. There was nothing in them. No light, no joking, no invisible pull holding her so she felt like she'd never be able to let go.

"Gwen, we've both got a lot on our plates right now, and neither of us really needs any unnecessary obligations."

Unnecessary obligations?

What was he talking about?

"Brody—"

"We've had such a good time, Gwen."

This wasn't happening.

"But we don't even know how long you're going to be down here."

"A few weeks," she said weakly, realizing he hadn't even been listening to her when she'd told him the first time. "Maybe a month."

"Yeah, see?"

No, she didn't. Not even a little bit. Where was the man who'd kissed her as if she were his next breath when he'd arrived on Friday? Where was the man who'd held her in his arms the night before like he never wanted to let her go?

"Is this because of my father?" she whispered, emotion already clogging her throat.

She couldn't believe it was. Brody wasn't the type to hold someone else's bad behavior against her or to let a parent's disapproval run him off.

"Did something else happen last night?" It had to have, because when he'd left, she'd felt like they were on the brink of something. She'd thought they were in—

"Nothing happened, Gwen. This is just a little more than either of us thought we were signing on for. That's all."

No. It wasn't. Not for her.

At last, his eyes met hers. "You deserve to have all the things you want, gorgeous. You deserve the guy who's willing to wait more than a few weeks or a month. You deserve the guy who'll love you *his whole life*."

A chill ran the length of her spine.

"What are you talking about, Brody?"

"I'm talking about you finding someone who isn't waiting for the first natural breaking point he can use to get out, Gwen. I'm talking about someone who stays when things get tough." Brody rose from his chair, reaching into his pocket for his wallet so he could pull a few bills out for the table. Their food hadn't even come yet, but he was ready to leave.

She was too stunned to move, to do anything but blink past the tears that had already started to fall.

Brody looked down at her, apology etched into every line of his face. "You want to know what happened last night? I realized I wasn't that guy, so I'm trying to do the right thing here. I'm letting you go."

---~~~---

The wheel gripped tightly with both hands, Brody stared out at the seemingly endless stretch of frozen farmland before him.

He hadn't expected it to be easy, but goddamn it. Sitting across from Gwen, forcing himself to act like it wasn't gutting him to let her go, had been the hardest thing he'd ever done.

She didn't understand. How could she?

Just like he hadn't understood about *fucking Ted* all those months ago when he'd started his campaign to get her over the guy he'd deemed unworthy. She'd been right all along. Ted was the good guy. The good friend. The one who'd been in love with her for as long as she'd been in love with him. The one who hadn't given up.

Now she'd have her chance. Once Ted told her how he felt, there wouldn't be any more secrets left between them, and the jackass who'd only been able to see what he wanted to would be out of the way.

And no matter how badly he wanted to crank on that wheel, turn the car around, and floor it back to her so he could beg her to pick him instead, Brody wasn't going to.

Another mile marker, and the wheel creaked beneath his grip.

It wasn't like he'd expected her to look relieved, shove out of her chair, and thank him before sprinting across town to get to Ted. But *those tears.* Fuck. They were chewing him up, making sure he felt the loss down to his soul. Reminding him that she cared, and that the affection and chemistry between them was deep and real. Even if the only reason it had been able to take root was because he'd cheated to get it.

Yeah, there'd been something between them all right, and it had been more than he'd ever shared with another woman. It had been special. And if *fucking Ted* hadn't been part of the picture, if Brody had met Gwen and there hadn't been anyone else, then sure as shit, things would be different now.

He wouldn't be driving away with no plan to see her again, with his gut twisted into a sick knot, her tear-streaked face etched into his mind. He'd still be there, making one excuse after another to put off leaving. Booking his room for another night whether he planned to stay that long or not, just in case he found a moment to get Gwen alone again. He'd be running his fingers through her hair, holding her in his arms, and plotting how the hell to win her dad over.

But that wasn't the way it had gone. He'd taken Gwen's chance at the happily ever after she'd been dreaming of since she was a girl, and fuck, he loved her too much not to make sure she got it back.

Chapter 23

TWO WEEKS LATER, GWEN'S MOTHER SAT ACROSS FROM HER at the kitchen table, her hands clutched nervously in front of her. "Honey, I don't need to go. We get together all the time, and if anyone should be getting out of this house, it's you."

Her mother wasn't talking about what had happened with Brody and how Gwen was taking it. It had been a long week for everyone. Her dad had developed an infection, and while they'd identified the problem and quickly gotten it under control, that fear had taken a lot out of everyone.

Gwen shook her head. "Mom, we've already talked about this. I have been getting out."

Coming around to her mother's side, she tugged to get her up.

"You went to the grocery store twice and the pharmacy once. That doesn't count."

"It counts as three times more than you've been out, Mom. Trust me, I'll be fine. Dad's doing better, and you need a break."

Still, she could see her mom was going to fight her on this. So she pulled out the big guns. "If you don't go, Dad's going to think he held you back. And then he's going to feel guilty on top of already feeling like crap. You don't want to do that to him, do you?"

Her mom's chin pulled back. "Wow, you want me to go that bad, huh?"

She did. One of them should have a life. One of them should have some fun.

And the truth was, even if Gwen went out and hit every bar in town, saw every friend she'd ever made, she still would've been miserable. It had only been a couple of weeks since Brody had ended things between them, but she hadn't heard from him once in all that time. No call, no text. Just this aching emptiness inside her that was getting worse every day.

Maybe she'd been silly to expect some kind of contact, but after the way everyone had talked about Brody and his borderline compulsive need to friend up the women he used to date, some small part of her had been holding out hope that he'd do the same with her.

And just like that, her throat tightened, her eyes blurred. Turning away from her mom, Gwen went to the fridge and buried her head within the cold shelves, pretending to look for something. If her mom saw her start to cry again, there was no way she was going to leave this house.

"I'm going to have some of these leftovers for dinner. Maybe watch a movie with Dad." At least until her dad fell asleep, and then she'd end up in her room, on her bed, staring at the walls and telling herself to get over this business with Brody. To stop trying to figure out what happened. Why he'd left.

The front door opened and closed, followed by the sound of chatter down the hallway.

"Look, Mary's here. Just go. We'll be fine." But when Mary Normandy appeared from the front hall, she had her husband and son in tow.

Ted had been back the weekend before, though Gwen

barely saw him. And while her mom had mentioned he was back again, she was surprised to find him smiling at her from the doorway as his dad walked past and set a paper bag on the table.

"What's this?" Gwen asked, looking from one of them to the next.

Ted answered. "There's been a coup." Shoving one fist into his pocket, he shrugged. "Your dad's starved for male attention, and he recruited mine to come bail him out."

Bob withdrew a sack of Gardetto's, a six-pack of near beer, and three ancient tapes for the VHS player she couldn't believe her dad wouldn't get rid of.

"*Full Metal Jacket*, *Predator*, and *Commando*. The classics," he announced with relish, staring down at the lot.

"The moms have girls' night, the dads are staying in, and I'm assigned to get you out of the house for a while. And before you say no, because I can see on your face that you want to… If you stay here, you'll be stuck listening to death screams for the next six hours at least. Choose carefully."

Gwen let out a defeated laugh and shook her head. "So where are we going?"

Ted clapped his hands, rocking back on his heels. "Lady's choice. We can head over to Winger's for a beer, Shelby's for pie, or the rec room at my house. Pick your poison."

She didn't even have to think about it. Two hours later, Ted was popping the tops on another couple of Fantas and pushing one into her hand as he flopped down on the sofa beside her. He picked up the remote from the coffee table they'd been propping their feet on since grade school and turned off the credits from *Scary Movie*.

"Gwennie, you look like hell."

She laughed quietly, plucking at the pair of Dobson High School sweatpants she really should have retired after graduation and her dad's oversize flannel shirt. "And here I didn't think there was a dress code for your basement."

"That's not what I mean. I always think you're beautiful, and those sweats have been a favorite since they were new. But you look like you haven't slept in weeks."

Focusing on her pop-top, she twisted the metal tab until it broke off, then dropped it into her drink. "Rough week with my dad. I'm fine though."

Ted licked his bottom lip and shook his head. "Come on, Gwennie. We've been friends too long for this. I know you feel like what I told you after the wedding changes things, but it doesn't. All that stuff has been the same for as far back as we go. The only difference is now you know about it. I'm the same guy you've been talking to since before you were making real words. And while I know this stuff with your dad has been a lot, that's not it."

No. It wasn't.

Her eyes cut to the man sitting beside her. He hadn't asked her about Brody since they'd broken up. He'd known, of course. Probably within an hour of it happening. Her mom had seen her when she came home, and no way had Gwen been able to get past her without some kind of explanation. Word spread fast from there. And that night, Ted had texted her from back in Chicago: *I'm here if you need me.*

"I can't talk to you about Brody, Ted. I just can't."

Nodding, he set his can on a coaster and queued up another Netflix classic they'd watched a dozen times before. "You're not ready yet. But I'll be here when you are."

She closed her eyes and thought back to that day after the wedding. To the words he'd said before he left.

"I don't want you to wait for me," she said quietly. "I don't want you to wait another day for me."

She could hear the click of his throat as he swallowed and the long stream of his breath. The movie started to play.

"It's only been a couple weeks, Gwen. I know you're still feeling kind of raw. But give it time. Give *me* time."

"Molly. It's not even dirty. Knock it off."

She was standing behind the bar, her round belly pressed against the lower shelf while she wiped a rag in wide circles like she was working at some old-time saloon.

"Restless," she said with a shrug, as though that explained why she was polishing his bar down to the floor.

Blowing out a heavy breath, Brody got up from the stool where he'd been reading through the mail and stretched out his shoulders and neck. Yeah, he might be feeling a little restless too.

He jutted his chin at her. "Is it working?"

Another shrug, this one he took as a no.

Not much was working for him either. He'd been trying to keep busy, keep his mind occupied. He'd even pirated half the jobs he'd hired Jill to do, hoping it would be enough to get his mind off Gwen. Off how she was doing back in Dobson. If Ted had told her how he felt. How she'd reacted.

Whether he was going to open a goddamned invitation to her wedding one of these days while sorting the mail.

Shit. He needed to give the mail back to Jill.

"Yikes, get a load of this one," Molly muttered under her breath as the chimes over the door sounded behind him. "Sorry, ma'am, we're not open for another twenty minutes."

Brody was about to tell whoever it was they could have a seat and wait when he was met with a cool, upper-crust voice not nearly as familiar as it should have been.

"I trust you don't mind I stopped by without calling ahead. I wasn't certain I'd have the time."

Molly was staring, her eyes bugged wide and shifting slowly between the two of them. Brody ducked his head and turned around, rubbing at the back of his neck.

"Mom, what brings you to Belfast?"

Maureen O'Donnel stood near the door, her ginger hair cut in a severe bob around her jaw, her lips slicked with blazing red. There was nothing soft about her. Not that there ever had been.

Tugging one finger at a time free from her gloves, she turned in a neat circle, surveying the bar she'd never visited before with a critical eye. When her focus landed back on him, she stepped forward.

"I realize you changed your mind about the ring. But I'm in town on business and figured I could save us both the hassle next time if I just gave it to you."

Opening her stylish clutch, she crossed to the table

where he'd been working and held out the heirloom he'd called to ask for the night before he'd found out about Ted.

He didn't want it. Didn't like that she was there. But since she was, he didn't have much choice but to take it from her.

"Thank you." He picked up the slender band of metal adorned with three diamonds and pushed it deep into his pocket.

It was awkward between them, but he knew he had to say something. "How long will your business keep you in town?"

"I actually wrapped it up this morning. I'm flying out in a few hours."

Of course she would put him at the very end of her trip. A last priority, only to be tended to if everything else worked out. *What a mom.*

But who was he to judge when thirty seconds ago, he'd been mentally praying she wouldn't have time for even a glass of water.

"I appreciate you finding the time to drop this off for me." Even if the effort was calculated to avoid the inconvenience of being forced to speak to him at some later date.

His mother nodded and gave him her cool smile, the one that paled next to the warm greetings her clients and business associates earned.

He hated that smile. But he returned it nonetheless and walked her to the door. There was a car waiting at the curb, and by the time his mother reached it, she was already on her phone. She didn't look back.

Jesus, this wasn't what he'd needed today. Or any day, for that matter.

He turned from the door and stopped to find Pregosaurus rex six inches away, her mouth hanging open in a typical Molly gape.

Here it comes.

"That…was your…*mother*?"

"Yeah, that was Mom." He could pretend it wasn't a big deal that she'd been there, or that Molly had actually laid eyes on her, but he knew it was. "Sorry I didn't introduce you."

Molly shook her head in utter disbelief. "She exists. And she's even worse than you said."

Yeah.

He started around her, wanting to get the ring into the safe in his office, but then Molly was back at his side, her steps doubled to keep up with his.

"So, umm…Brody. She gave you a *ring*."

"It was my great-grandmother's."

"She said you didn't need it anymore. Does that mean you'd…umm…asked her for it? Because if you had, that might go a long way toward explaining why you've been so off these past weeks." She grabbed his sleeve and pulled him to a stop. "Brody, were you going to ask Gwen to marry you?"

He shoved a hand through his hair and wrapped a good chunk in the elastic from his wrist.

"I got ahead of myself."

"Is that why you've been so clammed up about this? Cripes, Brody. A *ring*?"

"It doesn't matter. I didn't ask her—"

"And you're a wreck. I've been trying to stay out of your business because you usually talk to me about stuff when you're ready. But it's been a month, and you seem pretty messed up. You're hardly available at all, and even when you're around, you've got this someone-stole-your-puppy look on your face. You look worse than Max and Jase did before they sorted everything out with Em and Sarah."

"Molly, there's nothing to tell."

"You have a ring in your pocket. Don't give me that *there's nothing to tell*. There absolutely is plenty to tell. And I think it's time you sat down and did it."

Molly filled a half pitcher of iced tea and lined up empty shot glasses along the bar.

"If I were one of the guys, I'd get all liquored up with you to get you to talk. But since I'm a million months pregnant, we'll stick to the soft stuff. But you're talking."

Half an hour later, the bar was open, and the first lunch customers were placing their orders. Molly's chin was propped up on her hand, and Brody was slumped over the bar. "Things were happening so fast. It was never like that for me before. And it felt good. I didn't want to slow it down."

Blowing a few strands of blond from her eyes, Molly sighed. "Why would you?"

Because he'd only been seeing what he wanted to see. "There were some fairly obvious signs that I might not have been the right guy for her."

Like Gwen's unwavering belief that Ted was the most decent guy on the planet. Her twenty-year crush. Brody never considering that Ted might actually be all that and a bag of chips. Even though he trusted Gwen's judgment in almost every other way, seeing Ted as a villain was the only way Brody could justify his own feelings, his own actions.

"Cryptic much?" Molly straightened up and rubbed her back. "Signs like what?"

"It doesn't matter."

"Looking at you, it seems like it might. What about Gwen? Is she as bad off as you?"

"I haven't talked to her."

Molly coughed, looking at him like he'd grown a third leg. "It's been a month…and you haven't… What the heck happened with you guys? Because this isn't normal, Brody. You don't get bent out of shape about women. You don't sulk. And you don't ever go a whole month without starting to work the friend angle." Molly's brows furrowed, and she slapped a hand to her chest. "Did she cheat on you?"

This time, it was his turn to cough. "Gwen? No. Never."

She let out a huff. "Brody, then what?"

"Look, remember how we were sort of pretending to go out before we actually were?"

"Yeah."

"She was involved with someone else. Only things had sort of stalled between them. Anyway, I basically talked her out of the guy. I convinced her he wasn't any good for her, that he'd been playing her, and she needed to move on."

Molly's eyes had gone saucer wide. "But?"

"But it turns out I was wrong about this fucker. And even though things were amazing with us, she's been in love with him forever."

"She…she picked *him*? Over *you*?"

And he had to hand it to her, Molly's shrieky outrage was exactly what his ego needed. Even if it was misplaced.

"It didn't come to that."

She was staring at him, her head cocked to one side. "What do you mean?"

"I mean, the writing was on the wall, and I cared about her too much to put her through the big scene."

"Yeah, but, Brody, maybe she would have picked you."

"She's loved him for twenty years, Molly. She'd stopped waiting, but she never said she stopped *loving* him. I know what she felt for me was real, and I know it was good. Which meant that if I hadn't broken up with her, she'd have agonized about it. It would have torn her up."

"So you set her free. So she didn't have to choose. Are you even sure she still loves this guy?"

"Twenty years, Molly. You had boyfriends before you and Sean finally got together. What would you have done if you'd found out he'd been in love with you that whole time...while you were serious about someone else?"

She chewed her bottom lip and looked away.

He threw back another shot of iced tea.

They both knew.

Chapter 24

LEANING INTO THE KITCHEN COUNTER, GWEN STARED AT the far wall, getting lost in the winding pattern of roses and garden bugs that had been staring back at her since she was a girl. She was sleeping again. The seemingly bottomless well of tears had finally dried up the week before. And the sharp ache in her chest? Well, it hadn't gone away, but it had dulled, receding to the background most days.

She wasn't getting over Brody. Her heart was as raw and fresh a wound as it had been the day he'd left. But at least her heartbreak wasn't as obvious to everyone else. And sometimes that was as much as a girl could ask for.

From the stove beside her, the kettle began to whistle. She pulled it off the burner and filled the teapot, dunking in a couple of bags of chamomile vanilla.

The doorbell sounding had her checking her watch as she hustled down the hall. It was just before noon, and her parents were watching a movie in the guest room. They didn't have any plans until later that night with the Normandys since Ted was in town again that weekend.

She knew it wasn't any of them, because neither Ted nor anyone in his family had used the bell in probably twenty years.

"I've got it," she called, passing the guest room, her heart doing the same pathetic little skip it had every time there'd been an unexpected visitor, call, or text for the past month.

Maybe it was Brody.

She knew it wasn't. Even if he'd decided he wanted to be friends after all, he wouldn't drive three hours each way to do it. He'd wait until she was back in Chicago and offer to buy her a beer the next time she was at Belfast.

Still, she couldn't entirely tamp down that rebel surge of hope.

Swinging the door open wide, she shook her head in bewilderment. "Molly, what in the world are you doing here?"

And even as she asked the question, she found herself scanning the driveway where Molly's car was parked and then the empty curb beyond the lawn and farther down to where the road curved. But there was no other car and no other familiar face from Chicago.

No Brody.

No Sean either, which struck her as even more strange.

"Freezing my butt off," Molly answered with a cheeky grin. Rubbing her hands together, she tried to pull the sides of her coat together, but that adorable big belly of hers wouldn't let it happen.

Gwen laughed, ushering her friend inside. Even without Brody, it was great to see Molly.

As much as Gwen was glad to be home when her parents needed her, she'd missed the city. She'd missed her friends and the crowds and the late nights. She'd missed the fun.

"Here, come back to the kitchen. I made some tea."

Molly started wrestling her way out of the coat. She was big for having over a month left before Baby

Wyse was due, and Gwen couldn't imagine it was comfortable spending that many hours in the car. So why had she?

She could only think of one reason, and suddenly, her stomach lurched.

"Molly, is everything okay? Did something happen to…" She couldn't even say his name, not when a hundred different horrible possibilities started slamming through her mind.

Why else would Molly be there?

"Geez, look at you. Don't freak out. Everybody's fine." Then rolling her eyes, she amended, "Mostly fine."

Mostly fine didn't sound good at all. *Mostly fine* meant that there was some part of something or someone—and it had to be Brody, because again, why else would Molly be there—that most definitely *wasn't fine*.

"No one's hurt. At least not physically." Molly stretched back, rubbing her lower back with one hand as she circled her belly with the other. "But I'll be honest with you. Brody hasn't really been himself since you guys decided to call things off."

Of all the things for Molly to suddenly get delicate about. "It's okay. You can say it. Since he broke up with me."

Molly tensed, her eyes going wide before a tiny stitch pulled between them.

"He didn't tell you what happened?" Gwen asked, unable to believe Brody would be able to keep anything from his friends, most of all Molly.

"Um… No, he did, though he was kind of spare on details. Not that I need to know. I totally don't. But like I said, he hasn't been himself, and I guess I was thinking since we got to be friends while you were together, that maybe you were having a tough time too. And with this stuff with your dad and you being stuck down here, I thought I'd drop in. Check on you."

Gwen had known Molly was a little different from the first time she met her, but this? Her eyes narrowed.

"Did Brody ask you to check on me?"

There was no way he would be that selfish, asking a pregnant woman to drive three hours alone...

"Are you kidding me?" Molly scoffed, gingerly lowering herself into her chair while Gwen poured them each a cup of tea. "He'd lose his shit if he knew I was down here. And that's nothing compared to Sean."

This really wasn't making sense.

"So what are you doing here? I mean, I'm glad to see you. Believe me, I am," she assured, stretching a hand across the table to give Molly's a squeeze. "But why make the drive down. Why not call?"

Gwen watched as Molly's face screwed up a little and she pushed back in the chair, trying to adjust to get comfortable. Every shift and wince adding to a sense of unease within Gwen. Something wasn't right.

"Stir-crazy, I think. Woke up this morning with a bee in my bonnet about getting down here. So, you seeing anyone?"

"What?" Gwen coughed, her eyes going wide at that not-so-subtle transition. "No."

Another wince, and this time, there was nothing insignificant about the furrow digging between Molly's brows or the way her eyes went saucer wide and dropped to her giant belly.

"Molly, are you okay?"

But already, the other woman was struggling to get out of her seat. Gwen jumped up, helping her to stand.

"Molly, look at me. Is it the baby?"

Molly was shaking her head, the movement slow, as if her thoughts were somewhere else. Then suddenly, she was a flurry of activity, waddling out of the kitchen and grabbing for her coat as she mumbled about needing to leave. Gwen was helping her, or trying to, but when Molly reached for the door, only one arm in her sleeve and a sort of shell-shocked look in her eyes, Gwen put her back against it, blocking the way.

"No way, lady. You're not leaving this house until you tell me what's going on."

"How's Ted?" Molly demanded.

What? Did they even know each other?

"Ted? Fine, I guess. I don't know…" she answered, her confusion and concern escalating together.

"You guess? So he hasn't, say, been some kind of *rock* for you during this rough time? Or, like, there for you in a way you hadn't expected? A comfort you don't know how you'd survive without?"

The only one who'd been those things for her in the past year had been Brody. At least that's how she'd felt. Ted was a friend, but once she'd taken a real look at what was between them, once she'd realized how she felt about Brody, she'd stopped thinking about Ted as anything else.

"Wait, don't try to distract me. I'm talking about you, Molly. You're acting weird, and I don't mean you driving down here by yourself. I'm talking about right this minute, the way you're breathing through your nose kind of long and slow… Oh my God, are you having a contraction?"

Molly swatted her out of the way. "What I'm doing is leaving. I need to get back to Chicago."

She muttered something about Sean killing her, but Gwen could barely hear it as she called back into the house, telling her mother she'd be right back. And then she was out the door after Molly, racing down the sidewalk in her slipper socks.

"Molly, wait. Come back inside a minute. I'll get my bag, and we can go get you checked out."

"Don't be ridiculous. I'm only thirty-five weeks, and when I was at the doctor's two days ago, they were pretty confident I was going to have a heck of a wait ahead of me. It's Braxton-Hicks or something like that. But all the same, I want to get home." She opened the driver side and winced again, trying to lower herself into the seat.

"Is that *another* one?"

Molly scowled at her. "That's me trying to get this big body into this little freaking car. Relax."

"No way. I'm not letting you drive anywhere by yourself."

The car started. "What are you going to do to stop me?"

Gwen looked down at her empty hands and then back to the house. If she went inside, Molly was going to leave.

Running around to the passenger side, she got in.

<center>~~~</center>

An hour later, Gwen was white-knuckling the dashboard with one hand, the back of Molly's seat with the other. "Molly, we're still an hour and a half away from

Chicago, minimum. *You're not going to make it*. Give me that phone right now."

"I can't reach it. It fell between the seat and the door." A bead of sweat trailed down Molly's brow, but she wouldn't release her death grip on the steering wheel to wipe it away. "And we can totally make it. This is a false alarm. First babies always take forever, so even if this is real labor, there's no way I'm having this baby until well after I get back to Chicago. Sean never has to know that I drove down to see you. We'll just call him from the hospital. In Chicago. When I get there."

"Believe me, Sean is not going to care that you drove down to see me. All he cares about is you and the baby being safe."

Molly let out a snort that turned into a gasp. Then after another strained breath, she hissed out, "He'll care."

"Yes, but only about you being safe. Molly, you're not thinking straight. This *isn't* safe for you, it's not safe for the baby, and it's not safe for me either. You have to pull over and let me drive."

And give her the phone and let her call Sean and an ambulance and Brody. No, scratch that, not Brody. But the ambulance...definitely.

"Molly!"

Molly hit the brakes and pulled over to the shoulder of the deserted highway.

There were tears in her eyes that broke Gwen's heart. "There's nothing wrong. It's too soon."

Gwen nodded. "It definitely is. But still, wouldn't you feel better having a doctor tell you that?"

Molly's chin quivered, and her face crumpled. "Y-yes."

Thank God. "Then why don't you let me get you to

one?" Tentatively, she opened the passenger-side door, just a crack in case Molly decided to change her mind. But something told her her friend had begun to see reason. At least to some degree.

"You'll drive me to Chicago?" Molly asked.

"Definitely." Not a chance. The only place Gwen was driving this car was to the closest hospital. But first she needed to get Molly's phone, because she hadn't been able to grab hers, or her purse, or her shoes, or even her jacket when she left with this little firecracker who'd been about to go around the bend.

Molly's face was red, her breath coming in short pants. Yeah, those were way too close.

"Can you help me out of the car?"

Gwen was out of her seat and rounding the front end in a flash. When the driver-side door opened, she heaved a sigh of relief. And then before Molly had a chance to grab it herself, Gwen pulled the phone from the driver's side door pocket. "I'll hang on to this for you. Here, let's get you out."

Slowly, she finessed Molly out of the driver seat, but seeing the lines of strain on her friend's face, she asked, "Hey, how about the back seat?"

Molly nodded. She took a step and then froze in place. "Molly?"

Eyes filling with terror, she whispered, "My water just broke."

Chapter 25

As a rule, Brody wasn't much of a fate-and-destiny guy. He didn't buy into the idea that the universe had a plan for him or everything was predestined. But after today, he'd be hard-pressed to deny that there was some greater power at work. Because before the incident with Gwen's dad and her lost phone, when phone numbers came through as unavailable, he didn't answer them. But for whatever reason, today, when it mattered most, he answered that unknown number even though he'd been meeting with one of Belfast's distributors.

And then he'd almost had a heart attack as a calm, controlled voice from the other end of the line relayed what was happening on a back road in the middle of Illinois.

Molly was having her baby.

On the highway.

With the closest ambulance still twenty minutes out.

And Gwen was delivering it.

He'd been out of his seat in a flash, his heart slamming as he knocked over his chair and then tripped against another table before rushing for his car. What he knew was this: Gwen had only been able to make the one call, and unwilling to get off the line with 911, she'd given them the only phone number she knew by heart, which was his. He'd given them Sean's number directly and then gotten in his car to go over and pick the guy up. No way was Sean going to be able to drive himself.

Hell, when Brody got behind the wheel, it took him a second to get his shit together enough to pull into traffic himself. But then he'd cut through the city and pulled into the Wyse Hotel loop as Sean burst out the front doors, his face a mask of agony, the phone pressed to his ear.

Every minute was grueling. The helplessness and uncertainty unbearable. Sean stayed on the phone the entire time, holding for each update as it came through. And in between, neither of them wanted to say what they'd both been thinking. Gwen had given them Brody's number, which meant Molly hadn't been able to give them Sean's. And more than that, Gwen hadn't even been able to go into the contacts on Molly's phone to look for Sean's number because there hadn't been time.

Then, after a silence that seemed to stretch forever, came the worst moment of them all. Sean buckled forward in his seat, his hand over his eyes, his mouth open as a sob ripped from his chest.

Brody nearly wrecked the car right there, but somehow, he managed to hold it together long enough for Sean to catch his breath and through the tears choke out, "It's a girl."

Brody blinked, felt the wetness on his cheeks, the burn behind his eyes. He nodded to one of his oldest friends, unable to find words beyond the simplest to convey his relief and joy. "That's good. That's really good."

Gwen had delivered the baby girl in the back seat of Molly's car as the paramedics pulled up. From first reports, their daughter was doing well, but Molly had lost a lot of blood. She was unconscious, and the paramedics were getting her back to the hospital. Sean was barely holding it together. More information was exchanged, more questions fired back, more demands made for information that wasn't available. But eventually, Sean had to let them go. When the phone rang again, it was Gwen. She was with them in the ambulance, and Molly was awake.

Brody broke more speed laws on the way to that hospital than he could count, but he got them both there by late afternoon, and when he pulled up to the main entrance, Sean was out of the car before it came to a complete stop. Less than five minutes later, Brody was being directed down the hall to where Gwen was seated alone in a small waiting area. Her hair was a mess, caught up in a lopsided bun with loose strands sticking out and falling around her face. She was wearing a tank top, jeans with mud stains around her knees, and a pair of slipper socks that had seen better days. She was so beautiful that it hurt to look at her.

Her head came up, and she blinked a few times, her lashes still tipped dark from tears.

She wasn't his anymore. But when she stepped into his arms and he felt her shoulders quake and her fists ball against his shirt as she finally gave in to the emotions of what had happened, it felt like she was.

"You never told me you knew how to catch babies," he whispered into the top of her hair, breathing in the scent of her.

Giving up a feeble laugh, she whispered, "They tell me I'm a natural." And then she was crying against his chest, breaking his heart with each quiet sob. "I was so scared. There was so much blood." She shook her head, pressing further in to him, as if she couldn't get close enough.

His hold tightened. "You saved her. You saved them both."

And then, because he couldn't stand not seeing her face for a second longer, he tipped her head back and met her eyes. "You're a hero, Gwen."

She stepped back, giving him a watery smile.

He didn't want to let her go, didn't want to lose the warm, soft feel of the woman he couldn't stop thinking about within his arms, but he knew he had to.

The chairs where she'd been sitting were empty. No bag, no coat, nothing.

"Jesus, Gwen, is this everything you have with you?"

"Molly was in kind of a hurry to leave." She picked at one thin strap of her tank and closed her eyes. "I had a hoodie, but Baby Wyse needed it more than I did."

He couldn't even begin to imagine what it had been like for her out there, for all of them.

He shrugged out of his jacket and held it open for Gwen to slide her arms into. Like everything of his, it was enormous on her, the sleeves hanging well past her fingertips, even when he cuffed them. It reminded him of Christmas Eve in the snow.

"If you're not warm enough, I can find a blanket or something."

Shaking her head, she pulled the jacket tighter around her. "No, this is perfect. Thank you."

She looked so tired. So small. And all he wanted to do was pull her in to him and hold her close again. But she was already moving back to the chair she'd been in when he arrived. Her gaze anywhere but on him.

He took the chair in the facing row and waited there with her until a nurse in pink scrubs walked over.

"You can come back with me if you'd like to see them now," she offered with a smile toward Gwen. Everyone loved her. She was a hero.

When they got back to the room, Molly was propped up in bed, a tiny pink bundle nestled against her chest and Sean leaning in close. His brow was pressed to hers as he spoke in quiet tones.

"We can come back," Brody suggested, not wanting to intrude on a private moment with this new family. But the nurse shook her head, ushering him in.

"They asked for you. It's okay."

Brody went to Molly's side, gently smoothing her corn-silk hair as he smiled down at the precious new life in her arms. And then Sean was wrapping Gwen in a hug so tight and long that Molly finally had to tell him to let the poor girl go.

When she and Sean had wiped their eyes, Gwen crossed to the bed and, running a gentle finger along the baby's cheek, murmured, "Well, you sure clean up nice, don't you?"

Molly sighed. "She really does, doesn't she?"

With five weeks left to their due date, Sean and Molly hadn't been able to agree on a name yet, so for the time being, the little bundle was going as *Princess* to Sean, and *Pushy* to Molly. To Brody, she was just a miracle.

Another nurse peeked in to check on everyone, and when she left, Molly shook her head. "They're in and out of here nonstop. If they're not poking or peeking at me, they're trying to get their hands on this beautiful girl."

"It will only be a couple days, babe," Sean assured. "And then we'll be back at home, just the three of us."

"Don't get me wrong. I'm not in any rush to leave."

She smiled weakly at Gwen. "Pretty sure I made some kind of promise about never dodging a hospital again. But it's all kind of a blur."

Gwen peered up at the ceiling before turning back to Molly. "Yeah, don't worry, *I remember* every second. And it was a blood oath, if we want to get technical."

Having earned auntie status the hard way, Gwen got to hold Baby Wyse first. And if she was a natural at anything, it was this. Everything about her was gentle and soft as she cooed down at the tiny bundle in her arms.

Brody took a picture with his phone before Gwen peered up at him with that gorgeous smile he'd been missing every minute for the past month. "You want to hold her, big guy?"

He looked to Sean and Molly first and then stepped in close to take her.

He'd held babies before, but never one this new or fresh. Never one this pink and small and perfect. Beneath her tiny knit cap, she had a shock of white-blond hair, ocean-blue eyes that only opened for him for a second, and the tiniest rosebud of a mouth. She weighed nothing in his arms, and after one whiff of her perfect head, he finally got the whole new-baby-smell thing.

Gwen wasn't surprised when the nurse came in and suggested they give the new family some quiet time to rest. Sean was going to stay in the hospital with Molly, and good luck to any nurse who tried to kick him out.

Brody was on the phone by the gift shop, a large shopping bag in hand, when Gwen stepped out of the ladies' room. She could only imagine him picking out baby things and wished she'd been there to see it. Or maybe not. She had it bad enough for him already, and she couldn't imagine the sight of those enormous hands fingering through tiny baby garments would make it any more manageable.

"I got a room at the hotel down the road. Figured I'd at least stay the night. Be around if they need anything tomorrow. But I can give you a lift back to Dobson tonight—or tomorrow morning, if you'd rather stay."

Stay? With him?

He cleared his throat, glancing away. "I mean, I could get you your own room."

Of course that's what he'd meant. And even if it hadn't been, it's what she should have wanted. But either way, it didn't matter because—

"Gwennie!"

Brody tensed at the sound of her name echoing down the hall. And then they both turned to where Ted was closing the distance between them at a slow jog.

He'd made it. The guy always came through, even when Gwen tried to talk him out of it.

"I'm so sorry you had to drive all the way out here. Thank you," she said.

He looked back and forth between her and Brody. "Anything for you, babe."

Babe?

"Damn, no idea how people managed to find each other before cell phones." Ted chuckled, coming up to her side. "Made it out here faster than I thought, but then spent the last twenty minutes scouring the hospital for you."

She raised her hands with a helpless laugh. "Sorry, I didn't think to set up a spot to meet."

"Don't worry about it. Neither did I." He pushed a hand through his neat hair. "O'Donnel, you come in with the new dad?"

Brody looked down at his shoes and took a deep breath before bringing his head up. "Yeah. Quite a day."

They all nodded as the silence grew uncomfortable. Then Ted was diving back in. "So do we still have a stray car out on the highway that needs picking up?"

Gwen's heart sank. The car. She'd completely forgotten about it. Swallowing past the knot in her throat, she nodded. "I know where it is, if you don't mind adding even more driving onto the day."

"Not at all. How about we grab a cup of coffee and something for the road, because I'm starving. We'll ride out together, and you can drive it back here. Yeah?"

Gwen shuddered. She felt like she could barely walk, let alone get behind the wheel of a car and drive. But she didn't want to leave it for Sean to deal with over the next couple of days either.

"Sure," she agreed at the same time as Brody said, "No."

He met her eyes and then turned back to Ted. "How about we give Gwen a break, and you and I go get the car? I booked a room down the road where she can take a shower and change into some clean clothes." He held up his shopping bag. "It's just some stuff from the gift shop. It probably won't fit great, but I figured at least they'd be clean."

At that moment, it didn't matter that he'd broken up with her. That he'd broken her heart. He could have broken the planet in half, and she still would have thrown herself into his arms. Hugging him with the little might she had left, she whispered, "Thank you."

The arms that were always so quick to pull her in closer remained at his sides, and his only response was a gruff "Welcome."

Chapter 26

TED DIDN'T LOOK ANY MORE EXCITED ABOUT THE PROSPECT of spending the next half hour together than Brody was. But honestly, it was the best solution. No way was Sean leaving Molly. It didn't make sense to have the car towed thirty miles. And Gwen looked like she could seriously benefit from a little privacy and quiet.

They went over to the hotel from the hospital, and Brody got checked in while Gwen waited in the lobby and Ted got a sandwich from the restaurant. He could tell Ted didn't like leaving him alone with Gwen, and if the tables were turned, Brody would have felt the same way. Hell, he *did* feel the same way. The idea of them together… It was tough.

And after a month, it wasn't getting any easier.

"Here are your key cards, Mr. O'Donnel," the clerk behind the counter said, handing them over with Brody's receipt.

He thanked him and turned. Gwen was sitting where he'd left her ten minutes before, tucked into an uncomfortable-looking sofa, a vacant look in her eyes.

Damn, it hurt to see her so worn out.

When he walked over, she looked up at him, offering a small smile. "Everything set?"

"I feel like maybe I should carry you, you look so beat." The words were out of his mouth before he'd thought better of them, and then he was kicking himself, because that bare hint of a smile was gone.

He didn't get to carry her anywhere anymore.

He didn't get to joke about it, or remind her of it, or do any of the other things he wanted to do.

"I think I've got it," she said, pushing up from her seat. But even that small effort left her wobbling on her feet.

He steadied her with a hand at her elbow, and then— because she needed the support and not because he needed to feel her against him—he pulled her in to his side and wrapped an arm around her as they walked toward the elevator. "Come on, Gwen."

The hotel was small, with only three floors, and his room was on the top. When they got there, he guided Gwen to sit at the edge of the bed. He dumped out his gift-shop purchases beside her.

"I didn't know what you might want, so I tried to cover the bases." When Gwen picked up the purple sweatshirt with the orange logo from the local high school, he added, "The selection was limited."

There were tears in her eyes when she blinked up at him. "I love it."

Yeah, well, he loved her. And the words were springing around on the tip of his tongue, begging for him to open his mouth. Instead, he headed into the bathroom and turned on the shower for her.

Meeting his reflection in the mirror, he was surprised to see how normal he looked.

Because he felt like he was dying.

One deep breath and a stern reminder to fucking man-up later, he walked back out. Gwen was still on the bed, all the gift-shop supplies he'd bought for her laid out in a neat row. "Shower's going. We'll be gone about an hour, so take your time. You've got a key card on the end table and some cash in case you decide you want to go downstairs and get something to eat. Or if they have room service, which I kind of doubt, knock yourself out."

"You got this for me?" she asked, that one last-second purchase cradled in her hands.

It was a stuffed teddy bear, a little smaller than Baby Wyse, with scruffy brown fur and a sign tucked between its arms that read, You DID IT!

Brody could feel the heat crawling into his cheeks, because seriously, what had he been thinking? Except that he was so proud of her. So grateful. So fucking in love. He'd just wanted her to have something that expressed the first two, since chances were, he wouldn't have much opportunity to do it in person.

"Thought you deserved a little cuddle from someone who appreciates what you did today. Silly. Impulse buy. Seemed funny at the time, but you don't need to—"

"It's perfect. Thank you."

"Try to get some rest."

Ted was pacing in front of the elevators when Brody got back downstairs.

"Everything okay up there?" Ted asked, looking like he might want to go and check for himself.

"Yeah. You ready?"

Shoving his hands in the pockets of his coat, Ted jutted his chin at him. "Coat?"

Shit. Gwen had still been wearing it when he left. Probably not something Ted wanted to hear. "Don't need it. Let's go."

It was already dark when they got on the road. Brody had directions from the paramedics who'd taken the call, and the GPS on his phone was lighting up the interior of Ted's sedan. It was a cramped fit for him, as with most cars, but the main source of discomfort was the forced proximity to the dead-last guy he wanted to be packed in with.

"Should be coming up in another five minutes or so."

A stiff nod was Brody's response. *Perfect.*

Surrounded by farmland, there was nothing for them to see but the swath of light on the road ahead of them. He rubbed his chest, thinking about how Gwen must have felt. How helpless and afraid.

"Pretty remote," Ted remarked as if reading his thoughts.

"Lucky they weren't farther out."

Another mile marker passed in silence and then, "I don't know why you did it. But it was the right thing."

Brody's muscles locked, and he pushed a long stream of breath out through his teeth. He didn't want to do this. Not with *fucking Ted.*

Not now. Not ever.

Staring out over the dash, he gave the only answer he could. "I wanted her to be happy."

Ted was nodding like he got it. Which Brody hoped to hell was true, but if he did, then why was he asking?

"She will be."

Brody's head snapped around. "She isn't *already*?"

"What?" Ted stiffened in his seat. "I mean, yes, she is. I'm only talking about this *today*. It's been a rough one for her, and she'll be happy to get home."

The muscles along Brody's spine were prickling. His eyes narrowed.

He didn't want to ask Ted or have to take his word for

anything. But Brody didn't have anything to go on. He'd been talking himself out of calling her or getting in his damn car and driving to go see her for weeks. And yeah, he knew she wasn't the type to go from Brody's bed to Ted's overnight, but this was the guy she'd been in love with forever, while Brody had been a fucking blip in her life. And it had been a month.

"You're together, then?"

The light from the GPS was enough so he could see Ted swallow and his eyes cut over to him. "Getting there. You know how Gwen is. I mean, it's definitely coming, but she doesn't…you know…from one guy to the next."

You know.

Brody was pretty sure he knew what *you know* meant. And while hearing that Gwen hadn't yet was like a freaking balm to his soul, surprisingly, it wasn't doing as much as he'd hoped to quell the need to drag Ted from the car and pound the snot out of him for even thinking about Gwen and *you know*.

Blowing out another steady breath, Brody made himself ask the only other question he had to have answered.

"But you told her, right? Everything. She knows how you feel."

Ted straightened and met his eyes dead-on. "She knows."

Brody rubbed a hand over his face. "That's good."

A minute later, Ted put on his signal. "There's a car up there."

Once he got back to the hotel, Brody texted Sean that he had the car and he'd bring the keys by when he saw him in the morning. He gave the plates and his room number to the woman at the front desk and then headed up to get Gwen.

He wanted her to be happy.

She will be.

Fuck. He was grasping at straws again, seeing what he wanted to see and hearing what he wanted to hear… because he wanted *her*, and he'd take any excuse he could find to justify that pursuit.

The lights were on in the room when he let himself in, and Gwen was asleep on the bed. She'd showered and changed into the clothes he'd gotten her, and he could smell the hotel shampoo in the air around her. She must have only gotten her hair half dry before she knocked off, because it was doing that rebellious, wavy thing that happened if she didn't get it all the way dry. He loved her hair like that. A little loose and wild. Soft like silk between his fingers. She had his coat clutched in her arms, and when he looked closer, the bear he'd given her too.

Ted had pulled into the Mobil station when they got back in town, which gave Brody a few minutes before he had to give her up all over again. He sat on the edge of the bed beside her. It was more than he ought to let himself have and less than he wanted, but his feet stayed on the floor, and that was as much of a compromise as he could make.

Thinking she might be cold, he started to ease the jacket from her grasp so he could lay it over her shoulders until Ted showed up. He'd barely moved it an inch when her brow furrowed and her body curled in on itself.

He chuffed a quiet laugh and let her have it, giving in to the idea that some small part of her might be holding it close because it was his.

A few strands of that honeyed blond fell across her face, and she wrinkled her nose. Telling himself it was to help her sleep, he brushed the strands back and tucked them behind her ear.

Her lashes fluttered, and he held his breath as her lids lifted. Sleep-hazed eyes met his, and the corner of her mouth curved as she let out a tiny purr of contentment that went straight to his groin.

"Mmm, Brody," she said breathlessly, reaching for him as she had that last morning they were together in Chicago.

Her fingers grazed his arm, and it was as if a current shot through him, jolting his half-dead heart back to life.

Only she must have felt it too, but not in any good way, because her hand snapped back, and when the sleep cleared from her eyes, she looked away.

"Sorry. I didn't mean to…shit… Sorry. We're back," he muttered, feeling like an ass for waking her. For touching her at all.

She was pushing up to sit, inching away as she did. "I didn't mean to fall asleep like that. I only wanted to close my eyes for a minute."

"You needed the rest." Fuck, why couldn't he have kept his hands to himself? "Wish I could have let you sleep the whole night."

"That would have been an awkward morning after. Waking up to your ex in your bed." Holding up the bear he'd given her, she tried to tease, sounding as uncomfortable as he felt. "Her favorite stuffed animal staring you down."

There were worse ways to wake up. But instead of telling her that, he took a deep breath and made himself put some distance between them. He went to the window and looked out over the parking lot below.

He could see Gwen in the reflection from the glass, there but not there. She was looking around as if she didn't quite know what to do with herself. What to say. Which probably hurt worse than anything else. The words had always been so easy between them. So right.

"I miss this."

Another jolt to his heart. He turned, not sure he'd heard her right.

"I miss having you as my friend." *Right, her friend.* He nodded, not trusting himself to speak. Because he missed that too. And more.

Her head came up, and she lifted her shoulder in one of those helpless shrugs. "I kept thinking I might hear from you."

"You were waiting for me to call?"

She wagged her head. "I mean, not because I thought you'd changed your mind or anything. But because you have this sort of crazy reputation for staying friends with everyone you date. So I thought…" Her smile turned bright, and she pulled a little face. "But you didn't. It's okay. It might have even been better. But I guess I wondered why you didn't want that with me. Because I'd kind of thought we'd been pretty good friends was all."

She was killing him. How was he supposed to answer her? How was he supposed to tell her that he couldn't be her friend because she was the first woman he'd ever looked at and known he would never, ever be able to leave it at that?

Look at him tonight. He'd sworn he wasn't going to do anything more than give her a place to clean up. But then he'd been sitting beside her on the bed while she slept. Touching her hair. And when she'd said his name and reached for his hand, fuck, he'd been a single breath from pulling her into his arms and begging her for one more night. For one more hour. One more minute when he could pretend she was his.

There was a knock at the door, and Gwen blinked a few times, clearing the vulnerability and questions from her eyes. "It doesn't matter."

"Gwen." Christ, it mattered.

She smiled brightly and walked over to hand him his jacket. "Thank you again for the room and the clothes. For everything. Gotta run." Pulling another one of those goofy faces, she went to the door. "I've probably kept Ted waiting long enough, right?"

The air rushed out of him in a punch.

"Bye, Brody."

Chapter 27

THE DOOR LATCHED SHUT BEHIND HER, AND TED GAVE HER A nervous laugh.

"Thought I was going to have to send a search party for you in there… Hey, Gwennie, you okay?"

Her hands were shaking, and the smile she'd forced into place crumbled.

No, she wasn't okay.

"Can we go?" She couldn't handle it if Brody opened the door and found her out in the hall about to ugly cry because her heart wouldn't stop breaking for him.

"Yeah, hey, that's fine."

Only it didn't feel fine. And with every step she took, the sense of dread and loss got worse.

He'd left her. Ended their relationship in no uncertain terms. And while he'd been generous and protective with her all day, it hadn't actually been about her as much as making sure the woman who had helped his best friend was taken care of. It was about Brody being decent and good and the kind of man who did the right thing, whether it made him uncomfortable or not. Right?

But then she was thinking about the way he'd touched her hair, smoothing it back from her face. That hadn't looked like some obligatory kindness, and it hadn't felt like it either. It had felt like Brody not being able to keep his hands to himself. It felt like tenderness and caring and connection.

Except he'd let her go. And he hadn't had a thing to say when she'd broached the subject of friendship.

"Gwen, are you coming?" Ted asked as the elevator doors rattled open.

"Sorry. Yeah, I am." Shaking her head to clear all her jumbled thoughts, she took one last look down the hall. He wasn't coming after her. She stepped into the car and pressed a hand over her belly.

Ted let out a long breath, giving her one of his reassuring smiles as he stepped closer and wrapped his arm around her shoulders, readjusted, and then pulled her in again. She knew he was being sweet, but the hold felt off, and all she wanted was to step back so she could breathe.

"I'm sorry you had to see him again. But maybe now you'll be able to put him behind you, once and for all."

That sick churn in her stomach started to rise, pushing higher. She thought she might be sick.

"Gwennie, it's time to let yourself move on."

God, everything felt wrong.

Like she was about to make a mistake she couldn't come back from.

The elevator doors opened, and Ted reached for her hand, brushing his thumb across the skin as he pulled her out into the lobby. "Come on. Let me take you home."

Her brows furrowed, and her feet dug in. "Wait, can we stop for a minute?"

Ted slowed. "Sure. You hungry or something?"

"I just want to talk. And not while we're in the car." She knew what she needed to do, and she knew how she was going to move on. But after that stroke of his thumb…despite all the times they had talked, all the times she'd told him not to wait for her, that she didn't feel the same way, he hadn't really listened. This time, Ted needed to hear her. Because he needed to move on too.

Ted nodded, his eyes shifting nervously away. "Yeah, you bet."

The seating area was empty, so she headed over to the couch where she'd waited for Brody earlier.

Ted didn't wait for her to start. "Look, I know what you're going to say. Your feelings aren't going to change, and I shouldn't be waiting on something that isn't going to happen. But, Gwennie, I *want* to wait." She opened her mouth, but he held up a staying hand. "I believe your feelings *will* change. They changed once, right? And now that O'Donnel's out of the picture—sorry, but I mean, he's let you go twice—maybe that's the closure you need. Maybe we can go back to being us. The way we were or, I don't know, the way we should have been. The way we can be."

She waited to make sure there wasn't something more he needed to say. When this conversation was over, she didn't want there to be anything left unsaid. No more questions, no more doubts.

Then she took a deep breath and thought back to all the times and all the ways this man had been a friend to her. The very best friend.

"Have you ever thought about how much time we had? About all the chances and all the years. About why, in all that time, we never took the next step?"

"I was waiting for you, Gwen. I knew you loved me, but I didn't think you were ready."

Not after that first kiss. Or her first time. Or the

handful of times in the handful of years after. How could he not see it?

"But just the fact that we were *willing* to wait, Ted. That we were *able* to wait. Doesn't it say something to you that both of us were so content with what we had that in all that time, we never pushed for more? That the idea of finally being together wasn't worth the risk of exposing our feelings or even broaching the subject of more?"

He'd been in her bed, in her body, and yet on those mornings after…they'd still carried on the facade.

"What are you saying, that we didn't really want it? Because that's not—"

"I'm saying that we didn't want it *enough*. I'm saying that deep down, I think maybe we knew *this wasn't the one*."

Ted's head bowed, and he rubbed his hands over his face and through his hair before looking back to her. "You're wrong."

"I can't tell you how you feel or what's real for you and what isn't. I can only tell you how *I* feel. What's in my heart. And, Ted, you were my *first* love. What I felt for you was sweet and safe and something I hung on to longer than I should have." She closed her eyes, realizing in that moment that Ted had been the blanket at the end of *her* bed. "Maybe it was because you were just too good of a guy that I held on to the fantasy. Or maybe it was because we've been such a big part of each other's lives since before we could even walk. But for me, that *first* love wasn't *real* love. Not the kind that could *last forever*."

"And you think that's what you had with O'Donnel?

Even though you were only together for a couple of months and he left you."

She nodded, blinking at the tears so quick to push past her lids. "Yes."

She knew it was.

"Why?" Ted demanded, pushing out of his chair and pacing the carpet in front of them. "What makes you think this love is real when what you felt for me wasn't?"

"It's different, Ted. It's like now that I've been with him, I finally know what it feels like to be whole. And when I'm not with him, it feels like something *vital* is missing inside me. It's different because it feels like I'm going to die if I walk out those doors and go back to Dobson with you instead of going back upstairs and laying everything on the line with him." Looking down at her hands, she sighed. "With Brody, I'd take *any risk* for even the smallest chance we could be together."

"But he was willing to give you up."

And that had hurt more than she could bear. "I still don't understand what happened. But when he looks at me, I don't feel like he's over this any more than I am him. Maybe he freaked out. Maybe there was some kind of a reason and—"

"It's because of me."

Her head jerked up. "What?"

"I'm the reason," he admitted without looking at her. Then after a deep sigh, he went on. "I was getting in his face that last night outside your house. And when he told me I'd already had my chance, I lost it. I said I loved you, and when he realized I'd been waiting for you? Hell, I could see something change in the way he was looking at me. Like all of the sudden, he saw me as a threat."

Because he'd never actually believed Ted was the good guy she'd seen him as. And then it turned out he was.

"And when he asked if you knew, I lied about it and said no."

Shocked, she coughed, "You what?"

"I'm sorry, Gwennie." Regret and shame filled his eyes. "I didn't want him to know you'd already chosen him."

You deserve the guy who's willing to wait… You deserve the guy who'll love you for his whole life…

Pressing the heels of her hands into her eyes, she turned away, sick over the choice Brody had made for her. Over the days and nights he'd wasted and the thousand tears she'd shed.

She'd been hurt before. Devastated. But this… Her heart couldn't break again. She wouldn't let it. Fortunately, she had another emotion at her disposal, and it was plentiful.

Fists balling at her sides, she turned back toward the elevators.

"Whoa, Gwen, what are you doing?"

Right… Ted. She straightened her spine and faced him head-on. "You should go back to Dobson."

He shook his head and took a step toward her, but then seeing her face, he stepped back and held up his hands. "But how are you going to get home?"

"On my own. I'll handle it."

Molly owed her a favor. Maybe she'd borrow Molly's car since they weren't going to need it for another day.

Drive home to get her wallet, and when she came back, she'd stop at the dealership she'd seen on the way into town. It was time she got her own car.

"I don't want to leave you like this. I know you're mad."

"'Mad' doesn't quite cover it."

He took a big breath, maybe gearing up for another argument, but just then, Brody barreled out of the stairwell, tearing through the lobby and out the front doors.

She looked at Ted, who was shaking his head. "In a hurry?"

A second later, Brody was back, those sea-green eyes storm-tossed and wild as they scoured the lobby and landed on her.

"Thank fuck," he growled, stalking toward them like a man possessed.

Gwen's breath caught as that deep pull started in the center of her chest. He was coming for her.

"Ted, I'm sorry, man," he said, his eyes still locked with hers. "I am. I tried to do the right thing. I really did. I know you love her. And I know you're the fucking good guy she always told me you were, and I'm the reason she stopped seeing you that way."

He stopped in front of her, his eyes caught somewhere between desperate and demanding. "But I can't fucking do it, Gwen. I can't let you go without a fight. I can't let you have the happily ever after you've been dreaming about since you were a girl, just because it turns out this guy might actually be good enough to give it to you."

Ted swore, pinching the bridge of his nose.

"Not unless you tell me you're happier with him than you ever were with me."

"Happy?" she asked shakily. The butterflies that

had been flitting around in her belly from the second he started toward her were chased away by a swarm of angry hornets.

Arms crossed, she drew a long breath in through her nose. Not a calming one either. "I haven't been *happy*," she bit out, taking a menacing step toward him, "since you broke up with me over a month ago."

From the corner of her eye, Ted pursed his lips and took another step toward the door. "Hey, I'm going to leave you two to it."

Brody's chin pulled back. Obviously, this wasn't the reaction he'd been expecting. But then the corner of his too-sexy mouth hitched up. "You haven't?"

"Don't you *dare* look glad about that, you big oaf."

His hands came up in front of him. "I'm not."

But when he ran his hand over his jaw, the smile underneath was even bigger. "You're so…*mad*." He looked *delighted*.

Finger out in front of her, she started toward him. "You better believe I'm mad. I was about to go up there and *beg* you for another chance."

His face blanked, all humor gone without a trace. "What?"

Oh, she was so pissed. "A month, Brody." She poked his chest. "Do you have any idea what that was like?"

"Yes," and God, the gravity of that one word was almost enough to stop the tirade she was just getting going. But not quite.

"To feel like one day, you've found the man you want *forever*"—another poke—"and the next, have him treat you like every other damned piece of asparagus that's come before."

"No."

"*I loved you* and you…left…me." *Poke, poke, poke*.

His face was tortured. "Baby, I was trying to do the right thing. But I'm not anymore."

She arched a brow at him, and he shook his head, realizing what he said.

It was almost funny, but enough of her mad had burned off that the hurt was back. And that she couldn't handle.

"Aww, baby, no. Please don't cry."

Grabbing hold of her anger with everything she had, she forced back the tears and poked him again.

It must have been what he was looking for, because he smiled, catching her finger and bringing it to his mouth for a kiss before pressing it to his chest. "Didn't anyone ever tell you not to poke the bear?" His voice was a low rumble, and she closed her eyes, absorbing the sound of it.

Apparently, that was a mistake. Next thing, she found herself folded over Brody's shoulder like she'd been that day walking back from Belfast. Too shocked to do more than grip his belt, she gaped as he strode toward the stairwell.

"What do you think you're doing?"

"You said you were headed up there anyway. Just helping you along."

Through the middle of the hotel lobby, caveman style?

"Let me go," she demanded, trying to hold on to at least a shred of indignation.

"Can't." God, the way he said that one word, it made her heart skip.

When they were in the stairwell, his hold shifted, bringing her forward. A bounce, and she was suspended princess-style in his big, strong arms.

"You have something against the elevator?"

"I didn't want to risk having to put you down if some little old lady got in with her walker."

"I'm really mad at you," she said quietly. "This show of brute strength isn't going to get you out of it."

Even if it was making her heart race to have him carrying her up all those stairs without so much as losing his breath.

"I'm *really* in love with you, Gwen."

"You left me," she whispered.

He looked tortured. "I'm so sorry, baby."

Once they were inside his room, the door closed behind and the security latch thrown, Brody set her down, keeping his back to the door like he was defending against her leaving.

"I was trying to do the right thing. When I found out *fucking Ted* wasn't some user asshole taking advantage of your feelings, that he was actually everything you'd thought he was, I felt like I'd stolen something from you. You'd wanted him all your life, and if I'd let you be… Fuck, I thought you'd be with him. That you'd have what you always wanted."

"You didn't think that might be a choice *I'd want to make for myself*? You didn't think it was even worth a conversation?" She wiped at her eyes with the back of her wrist. "You didn't think *we* were worth *a chance*?"

Pushing off the door, he walked the rest of the way into the room.

"I didn't want you to have to choose. I knew you

cared about me. I knew what we had was something good. Too good for you to be able to walk away without being all torn up over it."

"If it was so good, then why were you so sure I'd choose Ted?"

"Because you'd been choosing him for twenty years. Picking him over the chance to have a life with anyone else. Giving him all your firsts." He shoved his hands through his hair. "Because it turns out he's actually a fucking good guy."

"He is a good guy," she admitted, but then crossing her arms, she added the stern clarification, "But he's not *that* fucking good of a guy."

Brody's head came up, his eyes locking with hers. There was a dangerous glint there, and she stopped to do a few mental calculations before elaborating more.

Ted had cleared out of the hotel before Brody went all caveman on her. He'd probably been on the road for ten, maybe fifteen minutes by then. So he *should* be safe.

"He lied to you about telling me how he felt."

"You mean you only found out now?" he asked slowly, that gravel-and-glass scrape in his voice suggesting he knew that wasn't the case.

"I mean I'd already made my choice, Brody. I knew how he felt about me. I'd known since New Year's Day. And I'd chosen you without a second's hesitation. The only heartache it caused was the kind someone feels for a friend who's suffering. Because that's what Ted was to me. From before I even realized what was happening between you and me, I knew friendship was all I felt for Ted."

Brody wiped a hand over his face, his eyes roving

over the room before landing back on hers. "Gwen, I'm so fucking sorry. I didn't know."

That had been her mistake.

"At the time, I didn't think you needed to. In my mind, Ted's feelings were completely separate from you and me. I didn't think they had the power to impact our relationship at all. And because they weren't any threat to you, to us, I decided to respect his privacy. I wish I'd told you, Brody. Almost as much as I wish you'd trusted me enough to ask."

"I'm asking now." He stepped in close, searching her eyes. "Can you give me another chance?"

Her breath left her lungs in a rush. And with that, the butterflies were back.

But he wasn't getting off that easily. Not after this last month. "What if I say no?"

His normally ruddy complexion went pale. "I know I ought to respect that, but, Gwen, I won't be able to let you go without fighting for you."

"You won't?"

"No way. And I'm not talking about waiting in the wings for twenty years, hoping you'll have a change of heart. I'm talking about waiting outside your apartment with flowers, and making you laugh with all the silly stories about my friends, telling you how much I love you every single day. I'm talking about driving down to Dobson every night until I get your dad behind me and then—"

"You'd do whatever it took?" she asked, trembling with emotion.

"I'd do anything. Everything."

"*Everything*. That's quite a lot," she murmured,

stepping closer so she could run her fingers over the top button of his shirt. His head bowed as he studied that single point of contact between them. "Would you use your body?"

She saw the moment her quiet words registered. His breath punched out, and his eyes shut tight. And when he opened them again, his lids were heavy, his focus intense.

"I would." Reaching for his back, he grabbed a handful of his shirt and pulled it over his head.

This time, she was the one to lose her breath. His biceps bunched and lengthened, the mass of his shoulders rolled, and his chest expanded. He looked even bigger than she remembered, more perfectly cut.

She swallowed, dragging her eyes up until she met his.

"Would you use your strength?" she whispered, already breathless.

"Without a doubt," he promised, slowly leaning forward to wrap one massive arm high across the backs of her thighs. He lifted her up against him, groaning when her legs hooked around his waist. Holding her with one arm under her rear, he braced against the wall with the other, making the muscles across his chest, shoulders, and arms bulge and flex. He was beautiful.

"Would you use your kiss?" she whispered, aching for the contact. The connection.

"Relentlessly," he rumbled close to her ear.

His lips brushed the shell in a kiss so teasing and light that goose bumps cascaded down her arms. He gathered her hair back and cupped her cheek. The warm wash of his breath spilled against her neck, his mouth so close that her skin tingled with the need for contact. Then another barely there brush of his lips at the tender skin beneath her jaw.

She bit her lip, waiting for more. But then Brody was *tsk*ing quietly, shaking his head as he ran his thumb along her bottom lip.

"Gentle."

This was the man she'd fallen in love with.

Then slowly, he leaned closer, replacing his thumb with another soft, grazing kiss.

"*More*."

"Absolutely," he answered against her mouth.

"Please, Brody."

His hand slid around the nape of her neck, and he pulled back to look in her eyes. "Anything, baby."

And when their lips met again, there was nothing tentative or testing about it. They came together in a slow, sinking glide so sure and good and right that she felt it through every part of her being. It deepened by degrees until they were lost in each other, clutching and clinging. Holding tight.

And when they broke apart, she stroked his cheek with her thumb and tangled her fingers in the russet waves of his hair.

"I was going to fight for you too," she whispered breathlessly.

"You were?" he asked, carrying her to the bed. He laid her back and slid his arm beneath her hips to move her up the mattress before climbing over her to settle between her legs.

She nodded, pressing her palms to his bare chest. "I was ready to do anything."

"Anything? That's quite a lot," he said, giving her back her words. "Would you give me your heart?"

She smiled up at him. "I already have."

"What about forever?" he asked, his voice deep with yearning.

Her heart skipped, and she searched his eyes. "Is that what you want?"

"I want you, Gwen. Any way that I can have you. But if you let me choose? I want you forever."

She could barely breathe. "You're talking about…"

"The cake, the flowers, the best men and bridesmaids. I'm talking about making you laugh and smile for all the days of our lives. I'm talking about Baby O'Donnels and our own love story where we grow old together and have a happily ever after better than you ever dreamed possible."

Her throat was tight, her heart full. "You want all that?"

He touched his forehead to hers and closed his eyes. "I know it's fast. And I'll wait for as long as it takes until you're ready. But yeah, I want all that."

"What if I'm ready now?" she asked, sliding her knee up the outside of his leg.

His mouth curved, and then he pushed himself up above her, a sexy glint in his eyes. "Then maybe you'd be so kind as to reach into my right pocket for me."

She raised a brow. "You have a condom in your pocket?"

Turning his head, he laughed into his arm. "What? No. Baby, just…can you reach in there for a second?"

Heat pushed into her cheeks as she slipped her fingers into his pocket, feeling around until—

"What is this?" she gasped and, after wiggling some

more, pulled up the stunning platinum band with three brilliant diamonds.

Lowering himself over her again, he took the ring and held it between them. "It's the ring that belonged to my great-grandmother who, according to her daughter, was the only foolish romantic in the whole family. I asked my mom for it a month ago, before I made the biggest mistake of my life. And if you want to know why Molly showed up like she did this morning, it's because she was there yesterday when my mom came into Belfast to give this to me. I was going to put it in the safe. I wanted to put it out of my mind, but every time I tried, I started thinking about what it would be like to have you wear it, and it just kept going back in my pocket."

She blinked up at him, and the tears that leaked from the corners of her eyes were about joy and love.

"So, gorgeous, I guess what I'm talking about is how much I love you. And I'm asking, Gwendolyn Sidney Danes, if you'll give me forever."

Threading her fingers into the fall of russet waves surrounding his face, she nodded and pulled him in to her kiss. "It's a date."

Epilogue

"JESUS, BRODY. SARAH DOESN'T EVEN HANG ON THIS tight." Max snickered from where he was hunched over the throttle. The engine revved, and the gleaming black bike shot forward as they cut through the city traffic. "And would it be too much to ask for you to pry your junk out of my ass and sit back a fucking inch?"

"Laugh it up, man." If Brody sat back any farther, he'd be bouncing down the damn street.

Finally, they pulled up to the church where Sarah, Emily, and Molly stood in matching heather-gray dresses amid a crowd of friends and relatives.

Not exactly what Brody had in mind when he and Gwen talked about making an entrance for the big event. Crawling off the back of Max's bike, he slapped the guy on the shoulder. "Thanks for the bailout."

Max winked at Sarah, who'd been watching with a kind of screwed-up frown on her face. "I know. He ruined the sexy wedding-day motorcycle magic for you."

Brody groaned, his eyes coming up to meet Emily's. Her brow arched.

"I warned you, Brody. 'Just meet him at the church,' I said. But did you listen? No. What were you thinking letting Jase anywhere near the transportation *to your wedding*? You know what happens when he's a best man."

Brody pushed his hands back through his mane of

hair. "I thought being just one of three best men would dilute things down some. Hell, Sean's got enough luck in his pinky finger to counteract that black cloud that seems to follow your husband to weddings. Where are they anyway?"

Molly stepped up, all smiles as she pointed past his shoulder. "That's Janice's car now."

Thirty seconds later, Sean and Jase were crawling out of the backseat of her four-door sedan, their tuxes looking remarkably good for essentially having spent the last fifteen minutes wadded up and crammed into a space too small to contain them. Jase bumped his head getting out, then leaned back in to hand his assistant's son the toy robot caught in his jacket.

"Any word on the limo driver?" Jase asked, stepping up to his wife and wrapping an arm around her waist.

Emily pressed a kiss to his cheek. "Broken nose, but he'll be fine. And what did we learn today?"

Jase rubbed a hand down his face. "No pre-wedding lawnmower dance moves. I really didn't know he was behind me." Then turning to Brody, he shook his head. "I'm sorry, man. I didn't want to mess up your day."

Brody pulled the guy in for a hug. And then Emily too.

"Only thing I care about is the girl inside. The rest… Hell, it's just a party." Pulling back, he rubbed a hand over his chest. "How's Gwen doing?"

Molly beamed. "She's having the best time. Her mom and that Mrs. Normandy are both a little tipsy from mimosas this morning, and the three of them can't stop laughing."

Sarah waved to her husband, who'd already parked

and was crossing the street at a jog. "She wanted a few minutes alone with her parents, but honestly, she's one of the most relaxed brides I've ever seen."

That was what Brody wanted to hear.

The church doors opened, and one of Gwen's younger cousins popped her head out and called to the girls. One after the next, they hugged Brody and gave their husbands a quick kiss before starting up the stone steps to the church, while the guys cut around to the side where they would wait.

Sean had six-month-old Gigi, Gwendolyn May Wyse, tucked in the crook of his arm where she was happily gumming his knuckle. Max was unsuccessfully trying to get one impossibly tiny ruffled sock on her perpetually kicking foot. And Jase and Brody were just staring at the little miracle their friends had created.

"You guys thinking soon, or are you going to wait a while before getting yourself one of these?" Jase asked.

Brody and Gwen had talked about it. He loved the idea of her as a mother and making their own little family, but selfishly, he wanted her to himself for a while. "Couple years, probably." Turning to Jase, he raised a brow. "You getting any closer to convincing Emily?"

Jase stared at Gigi a few seconds more before moving in to take the sock from her uncle and put it on in one swift motion. He smiled like he'd just won the lottery, pulled out his phone, and immediately texted his wife. Then beaming at his friends, he grinned even wider.

"You might say that."

Next thing, they were all huddled around Jase's phone looking at the first ultrasound from Baby Foster. Brody stepped back and wiped his eyes, happiness overflowing inside him as he stood with the best men he knew, the guys who had become his family.

The music changed, and his heart started to pound. This was it.

After sharing in so many other happily ever afters...*his* was walking down the aisle, gorgeous in her white fitted gown, the kind of love in her eyes that promised forever.

Read on for a peek at where it all began

May the Best Man Win

Chapter 1

August

ON THE UPSIDE, THE PRELUDE HAD ALREADY BEGUN, AND chances were good that Mozart's Sonata in E-flat Major pumping through all those organ pipes would cover any sounds of distress emanating from St. A's sacristy.

Jase Foster crouched in front of Dean Skolnic, groom du jour, and cursed. This had to stop happening.

"You think she's gonna notice?" Dean asked, wincing as Jase pulled one strip of duct tape after another off the garbage bag of ice currently secured to Dean's shoulder.

"The arm?" Jase clarified, because while he wasn't an every-Sunday kind of guy, they were in a church so he couldn't flat-out lie. "No, man. I really don't."

Lena would take one look at her husband-to-be's swollen black eye, and she wouldn't see anything else.

Strike that.

She might notice the greenish-gray pallor of Dean's normally ruddy complexion, because coupled with the way he was gulping air like a goldfish, it didn't bode well for his stomach or anyone within splatter distance.

The door opened behind them, and Father John plowed in, five foot six inches of bristling irritation and grizzled holiness. Scowling at the scene in front of him, he snapped his fingers and pointed at the guilty-looking crew of lesser attendants—mostly Dean's cousins who'd driven in that morning—plastered to the back wall. "Crack the fucking window."

Jase steeled himself against the laugh clawing to get free. Because, yeah, Father John had a mouth on him. Something Jase had discovered when he, Max, Brody, and Sean were muscling Dean out of the limo, barely clearing the door before the driver peeled off. The priest had stopped dead in the mostly empty back parking lot, taken one look at Dean, and let loose with enough four-letter words that even the guys—seasoned professionals in the expletive arena—had been coughing into their fists, studying the thick canopy of trees above and the new asphalt beneath their feet, basically looking anywhere but at the pint-size priest with a bear's temper.

"How we doing, Father?" Jase asked, pulling the bag of ice free and stepping out of blast radius. "Need any help?"

More grumbling as the priest elbowed one of the groomsmen out of his way and opened the window himself. "Seems you've done enough already."

Probably. But Jase was chalking this morning up as a learning moment. No matter how bad the groom's nerves, a quick game of hoops on the way to the church was not the answer, especially when evening out the teams required bringing the limo driver into the mix.

Cutting a look over at Max, Jase pushed to his feet. "Let's get his jacket on."

Max Brandt was working his cop stance with his legs apart, his arms crossed over his chest, and a don't-fuck-with-me scowl firmly in place. He nodded down at Dean. "Get serious. He's gonna blow. We don't put it on him until he does."

Hell. Jase glanced around the tight confines of the sacristy to the cabinets stocked with candles, chalices, napkins, and the rest of the holy hardware, and he mentally amended *Fuck* with the requisite apologies applied.

Jase wanted to think Dean could pull it together, but when it came to hurling, Max could call it from a hundred yards away. Even before the Chicago police force honed his powers of observation to a sharpened critical edge, the guy had had a hinky instinct about when to clear a path. That, and about women too. Both handy skill sets to have.

Grabbing a plastic trash bin from next to the hanging rack of choir robes, Jase shoved it into Dean's good arm.

"You heard him, Dean. Make it happen, and we'll get you out there."

That was a promise, because unless one of his grooms had a definitive change of heart about marrying the woman waiting down the aisle, no-shows didn't happen on Jase's watch.

The door opened again, and Brody O'Donnel stepped inside. He wasn't as tall as Jase or as menacing as Max, but the guy had presence. He was solidly built with a broad chest and a wild head of russet waves that fell well past his ears, which he'd only half bothered to tame for the morning's nuptials.

Whistling out a long breath, he eyeballed Dean, who was doing his best to manage the task assigned to him. Then nodding around the room, Brody grinned. "Father. Guys."

Father John looked up and broke into a beaming smile.

"Brody," he boomed like the guy was his prodigal son returned, even though the two had only met the night before. Then shaking his head with a warm laugh, he declined when Brody pulled a flask from the inner pocket of his single-button tux jacket and, shameless grin going straight up, held it out in offering.

"Aw, come on, Father John. It's the good stuff," he ribbed before passing it to one of the braver cousins.

Brody could always be counted on for two things: his uncanny ability to make friends with just about anyone and his propensity for always having a flask of "the good stuff" on hand for emergencies. Which made sense, considering he owned Belfast, one of Lakeview's most popular bars. Booze was, in fact, his thing.

"Brod, so what're we looking at?" Jase asked, knowing they had to be running out of time.

"The girls are about ready to go. Sean's smooth-talking the Skolnics, and I've got the safety pins, but…uh…"

Jase knew that drawn-out qualifier. Whatever Brody had to say, Jase was sure he wasn't going to like it. "What?"

"Maid of honor had the pins and wouldn't give 'em up if I didn't tell her what was going on."

Emily Klein. Fucking fantastic. Because after managing to avoid her throughout the entire engagement, now, with everything else that morning, Jase was going to have to deal with her getting up in his grill?

"She's coming?"

"Nah, I talked her down pretty good, so—"

And that was as far as Brody got before the sacristy door swung open again and that old familiar tension knuckled down Jase's spine. He took her in with one sweeping glance and then—just to piss her off—went back for a second, slower pass. She should have looked like Natasha Fatale from those old Rocky and Bullwinkle cartoons. She had the height, all right, but instead of the severe black hair, wickedly arched brows, bombshell body, and calculating scowl, Emily was every kind of soft. Soft strawberry-blond hair spiraling in loose curls over her shoulders. Big, soft-brown eyes. And a soft, shy smile that hid her poison-dart tongue. Even her body, tall and athletically lean, had a softness to its modest curves—curves that had distracted the hell out of Jase in high school but that he'd become immune to in the passing years.

Since he'd finally seen through her *soft* snow job to the cold, hard ice queen beneath.

"Jackass," she greeted, with a soft smile just for him.

"Emily. What can I do for you?"

"Brody mentioned Dean had—"

Dean coughed into his trash can, and Emily's superior scowl shifted to the man of the hour.

She looked from Dean back to Jase, her mouth gaping open in soundless horror. "*Is that dislocated?*"

The shoulder looked bad, Jase knew. And with anyone but Emily, he would have been all about the explanations, apologies, and assurances. Dean was going to be waiting at the end of that aisle, ready for Lena, even if Jase had to hold him up there himself. But since it was Emily… "No."

He waited.

Emily's toe started to tap, a nervous habit she'd had forever. One he took unhealthy pleasure in exploiting.

But Brody, a perpetual fixer fortunate enough not to have any history with Femily Fatale, stepped in with a reassuring shrug and his signature lopsided smile. "A little roughed up is all. Don't worry about a thing. He's fine."

Which was when Dean retched up the contents of his stomach and a round of applause sounded from the attendants stationed around the room.

Go time.

"Nice job, man," Jase offered, taking the trash-bag liner out of the bin and shoving it in Emily's direction. To his utter delight, she was so startled that her hands came up before she'd had the chance to think. And then she was stuck quite literally holding the bag.

Hauling Dean up by his good arm, Jase and Max worked the guy into the jacket and started pinning his sleeve to his coat. It wasn't perfect, but if ever there was a pinch, this was it.

"Oh… Oh no… Oh… What am I supposed to do with this?" Emily asked shakily behind him.

Jase didn't look back. "See if one of the groomsmen can help you with it."

He'd love to leave her hanging, but this was Dean's wedding, and he wouldn't be doing his friend any favors by screwing over his bride with a missing attendant. Even Emily.

"Uh-uh, no way," Brody said, laughing. "That has 'best man' written all over it. You know the drill, dude. With great power comes great responsibility, or some shit like that."

Not a chance. "Power to *delegate* responsibility. Hey, you with the braces, take this to the Dumpster out back and meet us up front."

The skinny kid let out a groan but hopped to, taking the trash bag from Emily and scurrying out the door just as Sean Wyse strode in. Smoothing back his immaculate hair, he flashed a picture-perfect smile at Emily. "Looking breathtaking today, but I think you're mixing with the wrong crowd here. Can I walk you back to the girls?"

Emily was chugging Sean's BS like it was a Starbucks mocha latte, cocking her head appreciatively but declining all the same. Then she was out the door, and the too-small space around Jase opened up enough that he could breathe.

About time.

Sean reached into Brody's pocket and helped himself to a swig of what was probably Jameson. "You ladies ready yet?"

Brody started lining the guys up in order for their trip to the other end of the church, while Jase took care of the sweat beaded on Dean's forehead with a handkerchief he knew better than to attend a wedding without. Then grabbing Dean by the side of his face, he looked him straight in the eyes.

"You good, man?" he asked, hoping like hell Lena was in it for the duration. Dean was too good of a guy to get screwed over. "Ready to do this?"

Dean swallowed and nodded. "Yeah. I am."

The same thought that tore through Jase's mind every time he got one of his grooms ready echoed then—the thought Emily Klein had played no small part in reinforcing:

Better him than me.

Jase smiled his most confidence-inspiring smile, the one that closed deals, and jutted his chin toward the door. "Then let's get you married."

Chapter 2

STICKING TO THE FAR SIDE OF THE LEFT AISLE, A PINCH OF floor-length blush chiffon in hand and her smile straining at cheek-cramping proportions, Emily Klein skimmed past an usher seating the last of the late arrivals as she hustled toward the bridal room where Lena was waiting with the girls.

Best man her butt.

Seriously, how did Jase Foster keep getting this gig?

Obviously, the guys loved him. Couldn't get enough of the whole bromance business Jase had perfected back before it was even a thing. But the women? Come on, like they hadn't heard about the time Jase got Neil Wallace to the altar a mere two hours late—because the boat they took out that morning on a whim ran out of gas. Or when Jim Huang wore an eye patch to the altar because of some "epic" game of finger football gone wrong. Or when Trey Wazowski needed to start a suspicious course of antibiotics before leaving for the honeymoon.

Cripes, Emily had heard them all, and she hadn't even been at those weddings.

And now, because Lena had turned the same blind eye to Jase's questionable record as all those other brides, here *she* was, saddled with the task of preparing her friend for the fact that her husband-to-be looked like he'd been jumped in a dark alley on the way to the church.

Stopping in front of the paneled door not solid enough to muffle the twittering chatter within, Emily took a bracing breath.

A chuckle sounded from a few paces away, and she turned to find Paul Gonzalez shaking his salt-and-pepper head at her. "I thought the bride was supposed to be the nervous one."

Emily gave Lena's dad—who'd been her boss before his retirement—an affectionate smile. Like his daughter, the man was small in stature but big in heart, and Emily had always had a soft spot for him. "I don't know, Paul. Seems like someone ought to have a case of the nerves, and Lena's as cool as a cucumber."

Stepping over to her, Paul laid a reassuring hand on her shoulder. "Relax, Emily. Everything is going to be fine. Even if nothing goes according to plan—though something tells me since you had a hand in all this, it will—the day will still be perfect. Lena's marrying the man she loves. Nothing else matters."

He was such a sweet old guy. And so misguided.

But that's what she was for.

"You're right. Okay, I'll relax." And then flashing a wink as she slid into the bridal room, she quietly added, "Just as soon as the cake is cut and the bouquet is thrown."

"Yay! You're back," Lena sang out, delightedly rushing to Emily's side.

Dressed in formfitting raw silk with a mermaid flare that emphasized her curvy physique, the bride-to-be looked gorgeous, every lustrous mahogany coil pinned in place, her warm complexion flawless, lips glossed, and each lash curved in exacting detail.

Lena was ready to go.

"Is Dean nervous?" she asked in a hushed voice, leaning close like she was protecting the other bridesmaids from the truth. "Remember how he was before he got his car? With the pacing and all those lists—and that was just *leasing* a Bimmer. This is *forever*. He's got to be nervous. He is, isn't he?"

Emily stared into her friend's deep mocha eyes and shook her head. "Nervous? No way." Not anymore, she didn't think.

Lena bounced in her beaded pumps. "So tell! Is he completely devastating in his tux?"

Yes, completely. Only Lena probably wasn't talking about Jase, so no need to clarify the whole ugly-on-the-inside business.

And this was where it got dicey. Because while Emily knew Lena needed to be prepared for what Dean was going to look like—*before* she hiked up her skirt and started sprinting down the aisle barking out orders to call 911—she didn't want her friend freaking out before she'd even set foot down the aisle. So time to employ some of those well-honed public relations skills and put a little spin on the situation.

Emily took Lena's hands and pulled her friend over to sit on the floral love seat beneath the window.

"It's a gorgeous tux, Lena. We totally nailed it with the cut. The guys are all ready to go. But just so you're prepared, Dean took a little spill on the way to the church." When the limo driver got overeager for a rebound, started throwing elbows, and knocked him down. Yeah, she'd caught up with Braces, and he was a talker. "He has a bit of a black eye"—*a bit* because it was really way more red and blue and disgustingly swollen than actually black so far—"but he can't wait to marry you."

Lena looked past Emily to the door, like she was already considering that sprint. "He's okay?"

Okay would be stretching it. "He's waiting for you up front, hon. I guess his shoulder is banged up a smidge"—and his arm is safety-pinned to his jacket to hold it in place—"but it's nothing that would keep him from marrying you today." True story.

Satisfied, Lena smiled at Rachel, Marlene, Lorna, and the rest of the attendants hovering around the mirror, helping one another straighten straps and smooth hair. "Time to line up, ladies. I need one minute with Emily, and we'll be good to go."

The girls filed out the door, and then it was just the two of them.

"Today is because of you, Em," Lena said, squeezing Emily's hands. "If you hadn't been there three years ago...I don't think I would have been able to leave. I wouldn't have found Dean. None of this would be happening today."

Emily's heart gave a soft thud as she looked into her friend's sweet face. She was so happy, so confident: so different from those first months Emily had known her, when there'd barely been any light in her eyes at all. Emily had recognized in Lena the kind of quiet despair that had shaped her own life so significantly.

"No, Lena. You'd have gotten through it on your own." She had.

Lena shook her head. "You were with me through the worst days of my life. And nothing makes me happier than to have you here at my side through the very best one."

Blinking past her tears, Emily pulled Lena in for a tight hug. "You deserve this."

Lena pulled back and, with an arched brow, replied, "You deserve this too."

"Someday, maybe," Emily said with the smile she wanted Lena to believe. "But today's all yours. Are you ready?"

Her friend blinked back her own tears and nodded quickly.

"Then let's go."

Paul was standing at the door, his arm out, waiting to walk his only daughter down the aisle.

Emily adjusted Lena's skirt and handed her the bouquet before taking her spot in line ahead of them. The groomsmen who'd been waiting to the side paired up with bridesmaids.

A text alert vibrated the phone she'd managed to camouflage within her bouquet, in case of any wedding emergencies. Heart pounding, she checked and, seeing the message was from Jase, stifled a groan.

You got your end done?

Jackass.
She texted back what was bound to be the truth.

Better than you.

Then, with a tilt of her head, she flashed a winsome smile toward the front of the church, where Jase was waiting to walk up with Dean. He saw. The scowl said it all.

The music changed, and a hush fell over the church as the processional began.

Lena's words echoed through Emily's mind. *You deserve this too.*

She might, but that would mean inviting someone to get closer than she ever let people get. It would mean opening herself up to something she wasn't so sure she could handle again…whether she deserved it or not.

About the Author

Hard-core romantic, stress baker, and housekeeper non-extraordinaire, Mira Lyn Kelly is the *USA Today* bestselling write-at-home mom of more than a dozen sizzly love stories with over a million readers worldwide. Growing up in the Chicago area, she earned her degree in fine arts from Loyola University and met the love of her life while studying abroad in Rome, Italy…only to discover he'd been living right around the corner from her back home. Having spent her twenties working and playing in the Windy City, she's now settled with her husband in rural Minnesota, where their four amazing children and two ridiculous dogs provide an excess of action and entertainment. When she isn't reading, writing, or running the kids around, she loves watching action/adventure movies and the Chicago Blackhawks, blabbing with the girls, and cooking with her family and friends.

Also by Mira Lyn Kelly